HK9

A H FitzSimons

Published by Open Path Books 2022
ISBN 978-1-8383829-3-3

Part One previously published as the novella *Gatekeeper 17* 2016

Earlier versions: *The Hunter-Killer* published 2017, 2018
Hunter-Killer, Hunter-Killer Revised Edition published 2021

Extract from *Cianalas* adapted and used with kind permission of the author Michelle Gray

Gracemount Gym used with kind permission of the owner Robert Landells

hunter-killer.uk

For Anna

Acknowledgements

I thank my late friends, Robert McCall and my dear Aunt Georgina Cranston, whose guidance with Gatekeeper 17 and early versions of The Hunter-Killer was crucial. I would also like to thank Ann McCluskey for editing and proofreading part one, Rubén Manso for editing part two, Rory Hadley for proofreading part two and Ivan (Ozzy) Eyre, Roni Ferguson, James Lindsay, Dugald McCallum and Bernward Wenzel for their ongoing support and encouragement. Special thanks to Major (Retd) Ian Johnson for his invaluable assistance throughout the writing of this book, and to Michelle Gray for her keen observations on life in South Uist and her beautiful essay *Cianalas.*

Author's note

Although this book contains a warning about the future, it is first and foremost a work of fiction. However, I did attempt to bring some authenticity to the story through the asides and the characters within them. In most cases, real names have been used and the stories surrounding the respective individuals are true. When the asides touched on the main story I often had to make minor changes. These changes are detailed at the end of the book.

HK9

PROLOGUE

September 2001

Since rupturing his achilles, John Benaicha's life had spiraled out of control. With his left foot in plaster, hobbling around on crutches, his frustration had built to a dangerous level. Benaicha wasn't just used to training, it was his job, his future, and being inactive whilst he lost fitness and strength was nothing short of torture. It was the first time his body had failed him, and it had happened at the one time he needed it not to — when the NFL were taking an interest in him. Every athlete on the planet knew the kind of money that was in American football, and it was going to elude him. There wouldn't be another opportunity. He was already bordering on being too old: next year he would be.

As was often the case, Benaicha's frustration was vented at the people he loved. It seemed he could do nothing to stop it. A month remained before the cast was due to come off. He knew deep down he wouldn't make it; at least, not with his marriage intact. He had gone from not drinking to being on the brink of full-blown alcoholism in a few weeks. Benaicha didn't do things half-measure. He always put everything into it, and that was one reason he had become such a successful athlete. The other reason was genetics. From being a lightweight at the age of thirteen, within two years he stretched the tape measure as much in width as in length. It seemed as if all he had to do was walk into a gym and his shoulders grew an inch. At fifteen he had rugby coaches from all over the country watching him play in school games. At seventeen he was six foot three and his body was dressed in what was known, in bodybuilding terms, as a gorilla suit.

Everyone noticed him but they seldom stared. Usually, it was a sidelong glance, an awareness, then a shift in direction to avoid him. People saw him as a threat and if you asked them, they would say there was something dark and menacing about him, but few would make the connection to the film that would have terrified them as children. In the thirties and forties, the actors who played the role of Victor Frankenstein's creation wore a steel framework underneath their jacket to fill out its gigantic shoulders. Benaicha had the same monstrous shoulders wearing nothing more than a T-shirt. The fewer clothes he wore, the more threatening he became. He never really got used to the glances, the avoidance ... the fear. Always uncomfortable in his own skin, aware that whatever he did would be seen by someone.

Yes, a month is far too long, he thought to himself as he hobbled towards the drinks cupboard. His foul mood did not take kindly to what he found there; only one bottle of vodka, and only half full — which wouldn't get him through the night. But worse than that, after a long sleep in the afternoon he was almost sober, and that was a state he wanted to avoid at all costs.

For the first time in six weeks he left the flat. He hobbled around the mini-supermarket, searching for the spirits, finding it odd that people were brushing against him when they passed. Then realizing, as he stood in the queue at the checkout, that no one was paying the slightest attention to him. He was so confused that he left the queue, parked the trolley near the exit and hobbled out of the store. He stood a few yards back from the front of the building. On the street it was exactly the same, no one noticed him. Then, through the fast clearing fog of alcohol it dawned on him what had happened. When he stopped training he started losing muscle mass. This process gathered pace when he began substituting vodka for food. Now, huddled over a pair of crutches, there was no threat and no reason to notice him. In just over a month his gorilla suit had transformed itself into a cloak of invisibility. Suddenly, John Benaicha, the man, was seeing life for the first time.

And he revelled in it. He stopped drinking that very night. He began reading books on human behaviour. As with everything else, he threw himself into it. He simply could not stop people-watching. He would spend hours standing in one spot, trying to determine the men and women's backgrounds and what they would do next. He became a veritable expert on body language, clothing and hairstyles. One mild evening in October, a few days before the cast was due to come off, he stood at his favourite position about six yards across from the entrance of his local store. Leaning on his crutches, he watched the comings and goings.

A young couple, hugging and laughing, the woman holding tightly on to a bottle of wine. A man who'd bought cigarettes and could barely wait to get outside to light up. A procession of weary men and women, heavy shopping bags pulling them down on one side. A thirty-something woman with a bag probably weakened by age, to the point where the bottom of it gave way and it spilled its contents over the pavement. An old man and a five-year-old child. On seeing the woman trying to pull herself and her shopping together, he spoke to the child and motioned to a space on his left. The girl, who Benaicha assumed was his granddaughter, immediately obeyed, and waited, it appeared patiently ... for all of ten seconds. Then, for no apparent reason, she glanced to her left and started running in that direction. Benaicha immediately looked at the old man — he hadn't seen it. The young observer looked back at the child. Dressed in a light blue summer frock, she ran like any five-year old girl, arms held at shoulder level, hands waving in time with the bouncing of her ponytail. She ran full of joy and life, oblivious to what was going on. And that might be a problem. Her guardian thought she was still behind him.

Seconds passed. The young man looked at the girl, who was fast approaching a crossroads; to the old man, back to the girl ... back to the old man kneeling beside the young woman. It was still the same, nothing was changing. People were passing in the street, but no one was aware of what was unfolding. John's mind raced through the factors involved. The girl may know this stretch of pavement and would stop at the kerb, or she may have been taught about the dangers of the road and to never step on to it on her own; or her grandfather may turn any second and call out to her ... or he might not. Another second passed, as John's mind went into overdrive, listing the reasons against shouting at her to stop — with the volume he commanded, 'foghorn' being the word most used by others to describe it — he would frighten not just the girl but everyone else on the street, and he would be invading territory that belonged to close family. He had seen the violent reaction this could bring. Parents, grandparents or otherwise did not take kindly to anyone shouting instructions at their child. It was as if a stranger had forcibly broken into their home while they were sitting down to Sunday lunch.

The ponytail bounced; the old man continued to pick up spilt tins; a luxury car drove past, its left indicator flashing in slow motion, which in turn triggered the start of a siren in John's head, building in volume — the car wasn't just big, he knew the model, it had a huge engine. The power didn't enter his mind, just the weight, and that was what had set off the siren. The weight would turn a car like that into a child killer. One tap, that's all it would take. He could see it happening: the girl full of joy running out of pavement ... running out of time. He could hear the screech of brakes, the innocuous sound of the tap as the girl was hit, then the half-second of flight through the air; the ponytail swept forwards covering her face, the sickening crack that would never leave him as her head impacted against the hard tarmac.

From the old man back to the girl, the nerves in John's knees screamed at him to run even with the cast on ... the siren in his head screamed at him to act. It didn't matter if, in response to his shout, everyone in the street would freeze, aware that something shocking was taking place. It didn't matter if he terrified the girl, or her grandfather attacked him, or he ruptured, tore and ruined his vocal cords and never uttered another word in his life — the only thing that mattered now was that the girl stop. The signal to tense his stomach and throat muscles had been given. His mouth opened—.

'Mireille.' The word was called out with barely the slightest hint of urgency. The girl stopped on a dime, two feet away from the end of the pavement. Her arms dropped to her sides. The ponytail rested. Her head slowly turned to look behind her, tilted to the side, the smile replaced by a display of irritation that her run had been interrupted. The old man spoke again, 'Come back'. The girl turned around. The smile returned. The ponytail bounced. The arms waved. John didn't even see the car drive past. He was spellbound by what had, and was, taking place. He knew what was coming though, and his eyes narrowed in preparation for the stern, brutal words that would be shouted in the face of the child. The reprimand had to be given. It was life; the girl had to understand the terrible danger she had been in. He knew it was coming, but inwardly he cringed; aware of how hurt the child would be, the tears, the hot tears that would fall ... so many of them.

The girl ran, the old man knelt, she reached him but there were no harsh words shouted, or even spoken. The girl placed her hands on his shoulders, kissed him on the lips, and tender words were shared. John stood transfixed by this open display of affection between grandfather and granddaughter. He knew now it had to be that bond. He had been wrong about the warning, but of this he was certain. The scene was too touching, too beautiful to be anything other than that shared between close family.

Before the relieved observer had caught his breath, the girl twisted to the side and, in a movement she had clearly done a thousand times, swept her right leg over and across the old man's back. He stood tall with the girl secure, sitting astride his shoulders.

John watched them walk away until they were out of sight. He had already decided they had to be a military family for there to be that level of discipline, yet he wasn't certain. He was twenty-five and had never seen anything like it. The entire scene had left him in a state of confusion. Still rooted to the spot, he looked off into the distance at the point where he had lost sight of them.

'I'll never forget this,' he whispered.

He never did.

FIFTEEN YEARS LATER

Three days before the European Referendum

The digital clock sitting on the bedside table next to Amanda Jeffries turned to 03.29. The young woman opened her eyes, sat upright and hit a button on the clock cancelling the 08.00 alarm. She rose and moved purposefully about her partner's flat. After showering she dressed quickly — black trousers, dark-green cashmere jersey — then packed her small holdall.

At the kitchen table, she sipped a mug of coffee and ate wholegrain toast, finishing off with a bio yogurt. Ordinarily, she would have a long drive ahead — Inverness to the outskirts of Edinburgh could easily take four hours, but today was the start of a week's holiday. The work she'd completed was the reason for her not sleeping. She had never felt so good about herself and her future. She had finally, after years of research, achieved something. Today was going to be her day; she had no plans, other than to get in to her car and drive.

Before leaving she looked in on Callum, deciding whether or not to wake him. She dismissed the idea: it would most probably develop into one of his longer goodbyes; she would end up back in the sack and miss the best part of the day. After locking the front door behind her she walked the twenty or so metres to the car park. She looked upwards as she neared the driver's door of her red Astra. The sun was just visible on the horizon, the sky was bright blue, and it was going to be a great day.

Perhaps Amanda's near euphoria was the reason she didn't pay much attention to the sound of rapidly approaching footsteps. Whatever it was, her life was in the process of taking a sharp turn. Suddenly she felt an arm around her waist; before she could turn her head a hand had wrapped itself over her mouth pulling her head backwards. Adrenaline shot through her body. Questions shot through her mind, and with the questions, one overpowering emotion — terror.

*

Mireille Robertson cut through the same car park on her morning run. It was a little after four, and in the bright sunshine she could see something was happening at the far end. There were two cars parked alongside each other, a black Range Rover and a red Astra. It appeared as if two men were physically forcing a woman towards the rear of the Range Rover. Mireille, who had slowed to a jog on entering the car park, stepped up her pace.

Alan Conway saw the girl approaching. He nodded to his colleague, who took over the task of subduing their target. A former Royal Marine, and a hand-to-hand combat instructor, Conway didn't mind in the least beating women. He had always despised the increasing role played by them in the military. He eventually came to terms with it when he accepted that if they wanted equality, then they would get precisely that. It was unfortunate for the girl, but the decision had been made for him: no witnesses. He would simply beat her to death.

It was predictable stuff, always the same actions from the naive civvy. They would run straight up to him, thinking they possessed the ability to stop what was happening. Although he knew he was becoming complacent, he couldn't stop it. He wanted there to be at least some resistance, allowing him to employ more of his skills. It would keep him sharp.

As the girl approached, and he saw her properly, his attention wavered. He was unaware at first why he had shifted all his bodyweight on to the balls of his feet, why he was suddenly on edge. He knew it was something that takes place when you're highly trained. Your senses pick up the danger signals and take appropriate action. Conway's adrenal glands had been given a wake-up call and were dumping adrenaline into his bloodstream.

As she drew even closer his consciousness finally made the connection; there were a number of factors that didn't add up: the girl was wearing tight leggings and though her thighs were athletic, when her foot hit the ground the muscle didn't just balloon outwards, the definition between the giant muscles was glaring. This was the fast twitch muscle fibre; typical of someone involved in explosive sports. Then there was the style of running — the girl ran like a soldier — and her age. The combination of those simply did not fit together. His orders were clear: if there is doubt, eliminate the doubt.

He wanted the practice, he wanted to overpower her, but what he was seeing raised doubt as to his ability to do that. As the girl neared his doubt increased. With a nod of acknowledgement he moved his right hand to the holster in the small of his back. The Glock was firmly in his hand in an instant.

PART ONE

Boyle

JUNE 20

11.00 A.M.

Salisbury Crags. From the furthermost edge you get a good view of Scotland's capital – and a great sense of perspective. It was a hundred-and-fifty feet straight down. It was known as the death zone of Salisbury Crags – so many climbers had fallen that you now have to have a special permit to climb it. I stood a foot back from the edge. This was the point where in 1972 the Dutchman Ernest Dumoulin put the final touch of his plan into action. It was a simple plan: visit the country where there is a unique requirement for corroborating evidence in order to secure a conviction. Take a stroll along Salisbury Crags at night with the person you intend to kill, push them over the edge, and it would appear you have committed the perfect crime. Except Ernest had married the victim earlier that day, having just taken out a massive life insurance policy on her. As if that wasn't enough he tried to cash in the policy on the day after he killed her. Not exactly one of the world's greatest criminal minds, then.

A few years ago there was an online piece posted: a local newspaper recalling the murder. Ernest Dumoulin, having served his time and now a church minister in Germany, had left a comment on the piece: that the focus of attention should not be on what he did then, but that a small pretty flower can be raised from a mound of dung. If he thought his life now had purpose then all well and good, but his comment could be interpreted as suggesting there was some form of redemption. Which, of course, there wasn't — not when you've taken a life in the way he had. After that there is no way back; there can never be redemption.

I missed running up here, running at night around the city. It all ended ten years ago when my knees began to play up. There was no point in surgery; I had no problem walking and that would be enough. I hadn't given much thought to the implications of not running though. Not until an hour ago. 'Acute angina', with a bypass required 'as soon as possible.' The consultant said he'd put it down as urgent. The operation should be in a few weeks' time.

I hated hospitals; I hated the entire idea of it, the lack of control.

I drew my mobile from my pocket. I'd forgotten to switch it back on when I left the hospital. Three missed calls and a text. I listened to the first voicemail.

2

12.15 P.M.

Fettes, Police Scotland

The moment Wilson asked me to sit down I knew things were out of control. Fear: it's instantly recognisable. Carol Wilson had battled her way to the rank of superintendent in the time it takes a beat bobby to make sergeant, and this was the first time I'd seen fear in her dark-brown eyes.

We went through the routine where I told her what I knew and she filled in the details. It was heavy duty: two medical consultants had been found with their throats cut. Murders are rare in Scotland, but medical consultants? It was unheard of.

'Hulk masks,' Wilson said, looking down at her desk.

'Excuse me?'

She whispered the words this time, 'Hulk masks. Hulk masks, both victims were wearing one.'

It was the masks that seemed to be upsetting her the most. Murders she had experience of, but this was clearly something she didn't understand. She wasn't alone.

I watched her gather herself, her back straightening. She said, 'As soon as this breaks we'll have a media frenzy the like of which we've never seen before. Reporters, journalists, film crews; every move we make will be examined and re-examined on news programmes around the world. We have a small window, a few hours, in which we can operate off the radar — make the most of it. You will work independently of the main investigation and you will report to me. I want you covering the areas they might overlook. I've assigned Karen Dawes to be your eyes and ears in the incident room. She'll keep you updated. You want anything, let her know. The officer you used to work with, DS Morrice, is abroad on leave. Do you want anyone else?'

I shook my head.

'Didn't think you would. One last thing, don't lose your temper on this one, George. You know I won't be able to protect you again.'

Karen was waiting for me in the corridor. She led me towards the vehicle pool. 'Good to have you back, Boss.'

'What do you have?'

'Nothing from forensics yet. The first victim was found just off Princes Street. Rose Street Lane, at 7.20 this morning. John Richard Templeton, forty-eight, graduated in medicine from Aberdeen University in '91. Last two years he's been at the Royal, general vascular, wife, two children. Aside from a speeding offence two years ago, nothing; crystal clean. Second victim, found off Saxe-Coburg Street in Stockbridge at 8.30. Simon Antony Childs, fifty-one, haematology, also at the Royal, nothing remarkable about him either. Task Force is fully operational but CID and uniformed officers are still being seconded from every region. Fettes is being used as the city control room. We're cross-referencing the CCTV footage we have so far, but it's going to be coming in all day. Task Force officers are visiting all the hospitals and are either speaking to doctors directly, or issuing instructions to be passed on that they take precautions on their way to and from work. GP surgeries the same.'

'Anything on the Hulk masks?'

'Aside from someone venting rage, nothing.'

We arrived at the vehicle pool. Karen said, 'An unmarked traffic car came in this morning with a blown radio.'

The indicators flashed on a white Audi. She handed me the key then drew her mobile from her pocket. Almost immediately my own mobile began to ring.

She said, 'That's my new number. It'll be clear for you to get through to me directly. I'll be here until ... who knows? Anything I think you should be aware of, I'll text or call.'

'Karen, you'll probably be seconded to someone else. When you can, keep me updated, and don't worry if you can't get through to me. I'll have the phone off for a while, but I will keep checking for messages.'

'Sure, Boss. Now, about Gavin.'

'Wilson said he was abroad.'

'Tenerife, but his leave finishes day after tomorrow. I spoke to one of his team; the flight he's scheduled to be on is due in Edinburgh at 22.30. I could probably have security contact him in Arrivals.'

'Okay, let's see how the day unfolds.'

I stopped walking and turned to look as two marked vans pulled in and parked. The backs opened and officers in uniform poured out.

Karen said, 'Looks like Glasgow's first team has arrived.'

It would be the beginning of a steady stream today; officers from all over the country. In the old days when gang violence was rife in Glasgow, Gavin would have been transferred through there. The City of Glasgow Police used to have bright-red vans drive around the city with a bunch of officers —

mostly ex-servicemen — in the back. The red vans, and the beatings meted out by their occupants, were so feared that even petty criminals would piss their pants every time a Royal Mail van pulled up alongside them.

The City of Glasgow Police became part of Strathclyde Police in '75, but there was no Strathclyde, or Lothian and Borders Police anymore. We were now all members of Police Scotland, and a degree was almost a prerequisite for admission.

I opened the door of the Audi and threw my jacket on to the passenger seat. I looked over the roof at Karen, and held up two fingers to my lips. 'You stopped yet?'

'Two years.' She smiled.

'Good for you.'

The Audi smelled of leather. I drove it out on to Fettes Avenue, and bright sunshine.

3

1.20 P.M.

I parked near the south entrance to Waverley and walked the twenty yards or so to the Fruitmarket Gallery.

Rebecca was sitting by the window, wearing black leggings and a Black Watch tartan shirt. I felt a dull ache in my solar plexus. I felt that same ache every time I saw her. We hugged briefly.

'Thanks for meeting me,' I said.

'Are you okay?' she asked.

'Yes, but there's a problem at work. I didn't want to talk on the phone.'

'That's okay, it's good to see you.'

I said, 'I don't have much time.'

'What do you need to know?'

'Simon Childs, haematology, John Templeton, vascular. Do you know them?'

'Childs, yes. I've not heard of Templeton, but I can ask around. What's happened?'

'Know if Childs had any enemies; upset anyone?'

'Had?'

'Had. I can't tell you much other than that.'

She sat back in her chair. In two sentences I had told her two doctors had been murdered. I could see her trying to take in the implications. She was used to death: she saw it almost every day, but not this way.

'Do the media know? They can't,' she said.

'Not yet, but they'll know soon enough.'

She sighed, then remembered my question. 'Childs: well, he was very protective of his time so he could be curt, and often unnecessarily so, but I wouldn't have thought he had any enemies as such.'

'Curt with nursing staff or patients?'

'Both, but more with patients.'

I stood. I had to keep moving, 'We've contacted all the medical organizations, trying to see if they can find a motive, a link between the doctors, but so far they've come up with nothing. Can you think of anything?'

She pulled her jacket from the back of her seat, and pointed to the ribbon on the lapel. I would have noticed if she'd been wearing it because, unlike the usual awareness ribbons, this was gilt edged, navy with red tips.

'Last week, a visitor came in wearing it. I'd never seen one like it before. It turned out she worked for the organization, and she gave me her ribbon. They are relatively new, based in Marchmont. I think they are planning some kind of national database, but I know they are also compiling a record of complaints made against doctors.'

I kissed her on the cheek and left, aware that the dull ache in my stomach would remain for the rest of the day.

Rebecca: I always felt emotional turmoil after seeing her, and each time always worse than the time before. Though we both grew up in Paisley, the first time I met her was in Edinburgh when I was a DS. Even amidst a melee in Accident and Emergency I couldn't help but notice her. She had an intense femininity and the attraction between us had been obvious from the beginning. However, my desire for her was only part of it. I hadn't been in Paisley for decades, but recently I was driving through the town on a Saturday night. It was a bustle of activity, yet there were no flashbacks to my own childhood. Everywhere I looked I saw Rebecca as a teenager – going out with her friends, running down the street, laughing; her vibrant energy and love of life, dazzling. The past I imagined her living was haunting me. I lay awake all that night thinking about her, wondering about what could have been.

I called Karen. Five minutes later she called me back with an address in Lauder Road. 'Difficult place to find, Boss. It seems they are keeping a low profile at the moment. The Director, Mrs Audrey Hall, is expecting you. And an update. Are you ready for it?'

'Go on,' I said.

'Two doctors have been reported missing; they left for work early this morning, but never arrived.'

'Left where?'

'Ann Street to Astley Ainslie, the other from Westgate in North Berwick to the Royal. Hold on, something's just come in—.'

I drove up The Mound and over George IV Bridge. I'd be at Lauder Road in minutes. Sitting in the driving seat of the Audi, I could detach myself – it was good to feel my hands on the steering wheel, feet on the pedals; it was good to feel in control of something today, because in Scotland's capital city, things were in freefall.

I was passing the herbalist on Bristo Place when Karen came back on.

'Another body has been found,' she said.

It wasn't the traditional blue light on the unmarked traffic car, more a collection of little flashing blue lights – I hit the switch for them and for the siren. In three minutes I was parked up alongside the rear entrance of the Astley Ainslie hospital. Two uniformed units had already arrived and had established the perimeter for the crime scene.

I was shown round to a group of bushes near the Charles Bell Pavilion. The way the officers were reacting it was clear they were all relatively junior; this would probably be their first murder.

A patient, out for a smoke, had discovered the body. No one had touched it, and I got a strange feeling looking at it. The Hulk mask with the throat cut beneath it. An odd paradox: the child-like innocence of a Marvel comic against the brutality of a murder victim. Two worlds colliding. It held you, kept you mesmerized, giving your mind time to make the adjustment.

'We have an ID yet?' I asked.

There were three officers nearby, they looked at each other then back to me.

One of them said, 'We've been ordered to secure the scene, not to touch anything until the main investigation team arrives.'

I stepped forward and said quietly, 'Well I am here, so stop stalling and ID this guy.'

The officer put on a pair of surgical gloves, bent down and carefully pulled open the victim's jacket, even more carefully extracting a wallet, dropping it into an evidence bag then passed it over to me.

I used the sides of the bag to open the wallet. Dr Raymond Whiteson.

I said, 'Where's the patient?'

The same officer pointed at the marked Fiesta, 'In the patrol car, he's giving a statement to Susan, I mean, Officer McLean.'

'Good, keep him there until a senior officer arrives. You know it's crucial the media don't get hold of the details, so extend the perimeter, and seal off this entrance completely.'

'You're not staying?' he asked.

'You've got it covered,' I said.

*

Lauder Road. Ordinarily, this was one road that it was almost impossible to drive up without slowing down. On a day like this, if you listened you could almost hear the horses and carriages from over a hundred years ago echoing through time. The upper floors of the town houses were bathed in sunlight and stood proud, separated by gardens and green and yellow hedges, on what had to be one of the widest roads in the city.

I stood at the address Karen had given me. There was a brass plaque beside the door — UPREC. I pressed the bell and waited. I could hear the sounds of summer — the birdsong, the branches of the trees in the garden swaying in the light breeze — and it carried me back to an evening from summers past.

I was in the beer garden of The Peartree following the retirement party for one of the chief inspectors. These gatherings were always the same: heavy drinking and back-slapping. As more alcohol was consumed, onlookers would begin to think that the safety of the entire population of Scotland was dependent on the thirty or so men in the garden, but if you were sober, as I was, everyone seemed to be temporarily insane. I had had enough and was on my way out when several women came in through the gateway. I don't know how many, as really all I saw was Rebecca. It was the first time I'd seen her since the incident at A and E, and the first time I'd seen her out of uniform. She wore a body-hugging green scooped neck top, her skin was deeply tanned and her black hair shimmered in the sunlight.

In the past I'd told a lot of women they looked stunning, but that evening I realized that whenever I had, I'd been lying, for when you're truly stunned by a woman's beauty you don't say anything. So I just stood there making small talk, spellbound. We saw each other several times over the next few months but as much as I wanted to, I could never make the first move, and if she showed a sign that she might, I backed away. She must have thought I wasn't interested, when in fact, no man wanted her more.

The door opened, a slim woman in her late twenties in a grey trouser suit stood behind it. She led me towards the main reception room and motioned for me to wait as she knocked on the door and stepped into the room.

'Mrs Hall, Detective Inspector Boyle to see you.'

I entered and was greeted warmly by Hall. She was tall and thin, her high cheekbones dominating her face. We went through the greeting ritual. She placed her hand on the back of one of the armchairs.

'It's Audrey, Inspector; please take a seat.'

'George. Audrey, thank you very much for meeting me at such short notice.'

'Well, George, how can I be of help?'

Audrey looked younger, but I could tell her age the moment I felt the skin on her hand. She was from my parents' generation ... and they had died over twenty years ago.

I said, 'There's a situation, and I would be very grateful for some information.'

'I'll help in any way I can.'

'First, could you tell me what you do here?'

'We uphold and protect the rights of every citizen in this country; hence our acronym UPREC. We all know there's a flaw in the reporting system, and it's not simple — human error, lack of communication between different reporting centres. The list is long and the whole thing becomes very complicated. The answer, however, is very simple. We are not bound by government restrictions. We are the public watching out for each other: a database of all complaints and concerns raised. The concerns are then processed by a computer program which generates reports uncontaminated by human error or bias.'

'So, what do you do when you have a number of concerns about the same person? I take it we're talking about individuals here and not organizations?'

'We're talking about everything: people, departments within organizations or the organizations themselves. The action we take will be appropriate, and that could mean involving the police or the press or we may deal with it through our own legal department. If our program highlights something, it is because the offence, abuse, misconduct or inappropriate behaviour is being repeated.'

'Audrey, you are talking about a huge undertaking; a massive operation.'

'UPREC is in its infancy, and we are the first office to become operational. Currently, we have seven more at the planning stage throughout the UK. We are funded by the public and we work from home.' She opened out her arms. '*This*, is my home. The Savile debacle showed the extent of the problem. If an organization like ours had been fully operational he would have been brought down within a few months of his abuse starting.'

Hall went on to tell me more about the positive impact this kind of organization could have. My mind wanted to explore the implications of what might happen if the public got behind her organization, but it would have to wait. It was time to get what I came for.

'I was led to believe you have been compiling complaints specifically against doctors,' I said.

'Yes, we are, each branch office will collate information for the database but at the same time will specialize in one field. The speciality of this office is those suffering from illness. In general terms our goal is to empower patients. One of the ways we can do this is by changing the culture that has existed for too long in the National Health Service — that those suffering from illness are helpless. They aren't; the research is there, it's just been ignored. Belief, confidence, self-worth: they are all hugely important factors.

She leaned towards me. 'Then there are the cover-ups. Doctors are human; they make mistakes like the rest of us, but many of them won't admit to it. There are systemic failures throughout the entire reporting and complaint process.'

Hall stood up and walked over to the window. I checked my mobile for messages from Karen. 'The entire process is flawed, George, and it is typical of institutions. There is a conflict of interest at every stage. The hospitals fear lawsuits so they will protect their staff and in so doing protect the institution. Doctors are a tight-knit group; they will protect each other. I am afraid it's just human nature — you can't override it. You protect those close to you.'

Hall returned to her desk, sat down facing me and said, 'At the moment, no one knows about the reputation of any specific doctor; they can go undetected with scores of complaints and even more concerns raised against them. We might not go as far as publishing a list, but for any member of the public who wants to check on a doctor who will be involved in their family's care, then we can advise them.'

'Advise?'

'If we felt it appropriate, we would advise caution about having that specific doctor involved in their care.'

'You may run in to some lawsuits there. You're talking about blacklisting,' I said.

'Call it what you will, but I somehow doubt that the doctors in question would want details of their inappropriate actions publicized in a lawsuit.'

'Complaints and concerns. Audrey, what's the distinction?'

'Complaints often suggest legal action, where the party making the complaint seeks some form of redress. A note of concern is a warning being given about behaviour to help others in the future. The database will hold both, the idea being that once we become established, people will no longer have to go through the stressful journey of placing a complaint when their only interest is to protect others.'

'The database: you've been recording both complaints and concerns raised against doctors.'

'For several months now, and on a local basis we have already recorded a large number.'

'Then perhaps you could help in respect of any information you have on these doctors—?'

She wrote down the details. 'If the system was fully operational that information would be accessible immediately, but at the moment we have to do it manually, so it's going to take some time. If there are concerns about these doctors, I expect you'll want to know who made the submissions. We really would have to contact those people and ask them for permission to give their details.'

I stared at her, letting seconds pass in silence. 'There isn't time. This stays between us. Today, three of the doctors whose names I gave you have been found murdered; the fourth has been reported missing. The most recent murder took place less than two hours ago, barely a stone's throw from here. Anyone who has been involved in any kind of complaint, or has raised any kind of concern against any of those four men, is a suspect. There is someone, or a group, going around Edinburgh killing doctors. Help us find them, Audrey, before we find their next victim.'

*

Karen had called to tell me that the first post-mortem was finished. I drove down town to the City Mortuary in the Cowgate.

Audrey Hall could provide key information, but I couldn't help but want to understand what was going on in her head. I thought the last thing someone her age would want would be to take on such an ambitious, high-pressure project. Then there was the emphasis on cover-ups by doctors. But really it was more than emphasis; it smarted of obsession. On the surface it appeared that the purpose of Hall's organization was to provide a deterrent against the abuse of power, but there was something else going on. Although I didn't think Hall could be involved in any way in the murders, I wasn't taking anything for granted today. I did like the idea of the database though; I had always had a fondness for deterrents.

The concept of deterrent seems to have been lost over recent years, eclipsed by other factors such as human rights and overcrowding in prisons, but mainly by what is deemed as 'appropriate' punishment. Deterrent and punishment are so closely related that it is difficult to determine where the emphasis lies, but there have been a few exceptions.

In an interview, Norman Mailer described how Mobutu, the dictator of Zaire, had ensured that his country was a safe place for foreigners during the time around the Ali-Foreman fight in '74. He had a thousand of the leading criminals, irrespective of who they knew, or if they paid for police protection, rounded up beneath the stadium where the fight would take place. One hundred were taken out and summarily executed. As Mailer explained, the key to it being an effective deterrent was in the selection of the hundred — they were picked at random. There was a parallel to the Roman Army's use of decimation, which was employed as a punishment for, but also a deterrent against, cowardice. Decimation, in those days was used in the literal sense — the removal of a tenth. Lots were drawn and one in every ten men were executed.

The judicial and legal system always fell short of creating an effective deterrent. Research has shown that increasing the severity of a punishment does not have much effect on crime, while increasing the certainty of punishment does have a deterrent effect. Increasing the severity of punishment would only have impact if people believed there was a likelihood they would be apprehended for their actions. Here was the key to the success of the executions of one in every ten in Zaire. It was nothing to do with punishment: it was pure deterrent. Mobutu was making it clear to the criminal population that the connections that would usually protect them meant nothing, and if anything went wrong during the time around the fight he would wipe them all out. The threat couldn't have been more real — there would be no escape, no wrangling, no legal loopholes, no excuses.

In many ways Hall's database aspired to this. It made its intention clear from the outset in the way it collected data. The note of concern was the key; it was more than semantics. If a sufficient number of genuine notes of concern were made then Hall's organization had a moral duty to make the public aware and warn them of the potential threat from that person, department or organization. Any subsequent actions by the police, legal action or damage to reputation were merely a by-product of what was effectively a high-tech word-of-mouth warning system. But the by-product would be the greatest part of the deterrent. People who abused power would realize that the protection offered to them by the instinctive acts of friends, colleagues, institutions and a wall of red-tape could now be bypassed. If the database gained the publicity it needed, and notes of concern were submitted, it wouldn't be long before the worst offenders were flagged up. The more examples that were made, the more publicity there would be and the more people would recognize the power of the database — they would stop filing complaints through the established formal channels, and would instead file with UPREC. The whole thing would snowball. No one would be too high to fall.

No one too high to fall. What would my namesake, Great-Uncle George, have made of that ... and of UPREC? George Middleton, raised in a tenement flat in Glasgow, had gone from obscurity to become the man who was widely remembered in the history of the Scottish Trades Union Congress as its greatest General Secretary. UPREC, the collective power of the general public united in creating a deterrent, facilitating criminal proceedings ... and, or, destroying reputations — there would be redress in the balance of power. Great-Uncle George was a man of the people, and for the people, and he would have loved that aspect of it. But in practice how would it hold up? He didn't stay long as a member of the Communist Party. Perhaps he saw when he was in Russia that ideals don't work that well in practice; they are dependent on those running them. The bigger an organization becomes, the more things can go wrong. Although an idealist, George Middleton was known for being very realistic about his goals, focusing on what was attainable as opposed to distant objectives. I think he would have gone for one institution at a time, rather than all of them at once. UPREC aspired to great things, but the size it would have to become was mind-blowing.

*

I parked alongside the morgue. I was walking towards the building when I met the pathologist on his way out.

I greeted him first, 'Dr Jenkins.'

'Detective Inspector, I haven't seen you for a few years.'

'I've been working out of town.'

'Well, I am afraid you've wasted your time coming here, the initial report has been sent over to the Ops Room.' He stopped walking and looked at his watch, 'As you're here; I'm sure you're aware Dr Childs' throat was cut. His body was discovered just after seven this morning. He bled to death in the hour before that. I would say around six-thirty. The only thing that was odd was the way his throat had been cut: it had been sliced open from the inside out.'

'Inside out?'

I wondered if he knew the man he'd just cut open.

He said, 'I've not seen anything like it. A razor sharp object, almost certainly a knife, penetrated the side of the neck and then was pulled outwards.'

'Any sign of a struggle?'

'None at all, and the other thing that I don't fully understand is the reason to cut the throat that way: it obviously produces a lot of blood. The knife that was used, one side had a jagged edge. It made even more of a mess as it was pulled out. A pagan ritual perhaps. Blood-letting. Today is the Summer Solstice after all.'

'It seems unlikely,' I said.

'Perhaps you are right, but I know that it is one theory that's being pursued. Personally, I can't think of any other reason why you would cut the throat that way.'

I could think of two.

A mobile ringtone sounded. 'Excuse me, I have to take this,' Jenkins said, as he turned away.

I stepped out of earshot. It was unlikely I would get anything more out of him, but I would wait around just to make sure. I reminded myself that it was often the seemingly insignificant details that provided the best leads.

I hated all mortuaries, this one in particular; from the outside it was an eyesore. The bricks themselves were a deep blue-red, like blood had seeped into them over years. You certainly wouldn't want to spend time here. My natural instinct was to arch my neck backwards, look directly upwards, and escape into the blueness of the sky.

I'd always loved the sky, and when I was a child I used to think I would be a shepherd or a forester when I grew up, so I could be out in the open, under the sky all day. But events transpired to take me elsewhere. Civilians know it as The Parachute Regiment, but for those who've served it's known simply as The Regiment, or The Regt. Whenever I thought about it, I usually thought of one action in particular, but now, as I looked at the sky, I thought of a sunny day in Aldershot in '86 ...

It was the start of my fourth year in the Army Physical Training Corps and I had been posted back to The Regiment. I had started out in 3 PARA but now I was to be posted to the Second Battalion — 2 PARA. The day after I arrived they had the Battalion seventeen-mile march. As the senior PTI, I took them out.

One of the sergeants, Taffinder, wasn't handling it well, as he — like a few others — had desk jobs, but there was an ambulance following at the rear, so I wasn't unduly concerned.

Back at camp, I was informed by the company sergeant major that Taffinder had died an hour earlier, and I was to report to the commanding officer.

I didn't reach his office. He was standing outside and when he saw me, called out. 'Sergeant Boyle, you've just arrived here, and, for the moment, no action is being taken against you; but my training directive clearly states that the seventeen-mile march is to be done tactically in five hours, and you were going too fast.'

Then I was told to report to the regimental sergeant major — in the sergeants' mess.

I put it off as long as possible, walking into the mess an hour later. It was full, maybe with eighty men, all at the bar and drinking hard. Cigarette smoke and alcohol fumes polluted the room; the noise was deafening. That is until I walked in, still in my PTI blues, to their Para greens. The group nearest me stopped talking and then a wave of silence slowly swept to the back of the bar. All eyes focused on me. Seconds stretched into eternity. Then the first shout came from the centre of the bar.

'There he is!'

'Yeah, that's him!'

'He did it ... he killed Taff!'

From the back, a scream.

'MURDERER!'

Then the whole room erupted in unison. 'MUR-DER-ER, MUR-DER-ER, MUR-DER-ER ...'

There are few secrets in The Regt., though it seemed from the expressions on the faces around me that I still held on to mine. But there were two men in the room who were noticeably silent, and when I looked at them, they looked away.

I walked to the bar and ordered a pint. The man next to me spoke loud enough to be heard above the chanting.

'How long you here for, Boyle, how long's your posting?'

'Two years,' I said.

His eyes widened, 'Two fucking years; you'll have wiped out the entire Battalion by then.'

4

4.30 P.M.

I drove towards Holyrood Palace. As I suspected, Jenkins had nothing else to add other than to tell me to read his report.

He was right, cutting the throat from the inside out with a hunting knife would produce one hell of a lot of blood, but the jagged edge would also tear the flesh and conceal any marks on the neck. Like marks made from a stun gun. That could explain why there were no signs of a struggle.

Stun guns; who would supply them? Last time I checked, possession alone of a stun gun carried an automatic penalty of five years. I called Karen and gave her the name of someone who might know a supplier. She called back a minute later: no known address, she wasn't even sure he was still alive.

I took a left towards Leith Walk via Easter Road. As I drove through Abbeyhill I passed the spot where The Cat's Pyjamas used to sit. It wasn't the greatest nightclub in Edinburgh, but it certainly had its moments. One of those being closing time on a Sunday in '89 when a group of sixteen men decided to round off their night by ambushing the four doormen — Alan McDonald, Davie Rice, Jake Kenny and Jimmy Pace.

Many of the sixteen were seen at Accident and Emergency. The difference between a good night out and having your face permanently rearranged came down to one error in judgement. If that group had scoured Scotland for doormen to ambush, the worst choice they could have made was to pick the four at The Cat's Pyjamas.

I knew Jimmy Pace from way back. Jimmy was a third-Dan black belt and former European lightweight Shukokai Karate champion. He had a strong moral code and a hatred of bullies. Jimmy weighed less than 160 pounds, so was often seen as a soft target to those not from Edinburgh. A giant German sailor and his mate made the mistake of picking on the quiet, slightly built doorman. The German's ship was docked at Leith and the following evening the entire crew, minus two, turned up to buy Jimmy a drink. He wasn't around that evening so instead the ship's crew had a party with the bar staff, buying them drinks all night. The giant had been terrorising everyone on the ship, but that ended after Jimmy had broken his jaw and knocked out all his front teeth. Every five minutes one of the crew would stand up on a chair, raise his glass and toast Jimmy in German. The bar staff, by now half cut, were joining in standing up on the bar doing the same. When I heard the story I pictured the scene on the boat — the giant lying in his bunk, his jaw and mouth on fire. He would never be the same after that kind of beating, especially from a man half his size. He would fear everyone now.

It happened to so many men whose vastly superior strength gave them a sense that they were indestructible. Sonny Liston had such a physical presence that he intimidated his opponents by merely looking at them, but after Ali took him apart he was a broken man. The same thing happened with George Foreman. You ask someone about Foreman now and you think of this big affable man who sells grilling machines, but before Ali knocked him out in Zaire he was a monster: the biggest hitter ever — his punches lifting the mighty Joe Frazier up in the air before crashing him to the canvas. Zaire changed the entire history of the heavyweight division. In taking away Foreman's indestructibility, Ali almost certainly saved a number of lives. Max Baer killed Frankie Campbell in the ring, his brain having been knocked completely loose from his skull. Ernie Schaaf's death is believed by many to have resulted from the punishment he took from his fight with Baer. Yet Baer's punching power fell far short of Foreman's.

It made me think about Jimmy, and the ripple effect of his stone fists on the water that was street life in Edinburgh. In breaking the confidence of so many bullies he had probably saved scores of men from savage, life-changing beatings.

We all have a ripple effect; few as brutally positive as that of Jimmy Pace. My effect was quite the opposite and it was the reason I had avoided him since our last meeting in February '82. He was working on the door of Pipers in Lothian Road and had a thick, one-inch line of tightly packed stiches on his throat next to his windpipe. The week before things had kicked off with a team through from Glasgow; the deep cut was from a Stanley knife. Jimmy was indifferent to it; such was his familiarity with acts of violence.

I heard so many stories about him but hadn't seen him since that night in '82. Nightclub security was different in Edinburgh now; there were few real doormen left. Even Jimmy had gone: pushing sixty he finished his last shift in 2011. Door stewards took the place of doormen, who had become a dying breed with the introduction of CCTV cameras. The change in gym culture had accelerated their demise: where men used to train to fight, now they trained to look good. The so-called alphas and their steroid-enhanced delts and ripped abs spent most of their gym time strutting in front of mirrored walls. In the seventies and early eighties you'd be hard pushed to find a mirror in the changing rooms, let alone the gym floor. In those days it was inconceivable that in four decades the hardest trainers in the gym would be women.

*

I parked near the foot of Leith Walk. I left my jacket and tie in the Audi, rolled up my shirt sleeves and walked into the Central Bar. I looked for, and found, my target at the corner table. Old Gordie was reading a newspaper whilst sipping away at a rum and black. I ordered a double at the bar, sat down beside him and slid the drink over.

'Inspector!' He jumped up in his seat. 'Ah've no seen ye fir years. Where ye bin hidin?'

'Not too far away, Gordie. Tell me, where can I find Raul Cassano?'

'Nae time fir small talk, Inspector, eh? Straight in there, muss be important?'

'It is important, and as I recall, Gordie, you owe me a favour.'

He looked at me as if I was a stranger for a second. 'Aye! Aye o' course, Ah remember, Ah do, Ah do. Well, Ah'll tell ye what; ah've nae idea where Raul is, but ma boy might ken.' He took a BlackBerry Classic from his pocket and very deliberately began pressing its keyboard.

'Good to see you keeping up with technology, Gordie.'

'Hate the wee thing,' he said, turning his attention to me, 'but we've just goat tae stay in touch,' he added, mimicking the voice from the TV advert. 'It's ringin. Ah'll juss be a minute, Inspector.'

It transpired to be ten minutes and two more calls before I had something to go on. I knew Cassano had a son, who had moved north and had nothing to do with the family business. What I didn't know was that Cassano had a grandson, who was studying at Napier University.

Traffic was getting heavy now. I put the blue lights on along with the headlights but left the siren off and headed for Fountainbridge. Birthplace of Sean Connery, Fountainbridge was an area going through massive redevelopment. The first McEwan's brewery, the Fountain Brewery, was built here over 150 years ago. The new Fountain Brewery opened in '73 and had dominated the area's skyline for almost 40 years. But like so many landmarks of Scotland's industrial history it was gone — clear ground now as it awaited the building of an arts centre. Even the smell of hops, which lingered long after the brewery closed, had faded into the past.

I had a choice; the block of students' flats opposite Fountainpark or the Brazilian café restaurant — Fabi's Kitchen — where Gordie's contact had said he'd most likely be.

The restaurant was nearest so I checked in there. A deeply tanned young woman behind the counter — presumably Fabi — told me that the regular students were due in any time. I decided to wait and get a bite to eat. It had been a while, and I might not get another chance today.

As I waited for Fabi's recommendation I sat with a coffee and went over all the information I had so far. I was waiting for a call from Audrey Hall. Her organization might come through for me and pick up a link between the victims that the official, established organizations might miss. It was a long shot, though. While the vast majority of doctors worked tirelessly to help others, Hall's focus of attention was on the misconduct of the minority and it was something that continued to trouble me. Yet, if the database was run correctly it had a lot of positives going for it, especially in relation to cases of abuse. Submitting a formal complaint is often an impossible process for those who have been subjected to abuse — the Savile investigation gave an indication of how much abuse was going on, and how victims would speak out when they realized they were not alone. Patterns in the abusers' behaviour then appeared which would have otherwise remained uncovered. But it raised a debate about whether the accused should remain anonymous whilst the investigation is going on. In the aftermath of the Savile investigation a lot of high-profile celebrities were investigated in full public view and their reputations tarnished, even those who were not actually charged, let alone found guilty. But that wouldn't happen with Hall's organization, which is effectively saying to the public, 'If you've suffered, or witnessed, abuse, misconduct or any kind of offence, let us know — we'll identify the patterns.' This would also protect the identity of whistle-blowers; they wouldn't be acting alone any longer. One of the fundamental differences to all other complaints systems, and criminal or legal processes, was that the initial 'investigation' was being done behind closed doors in the silent workings of a computer program. No one knew it was even going on.

My only concern with it was Hall, herself, and I suspected the whole thing may be the product of a personal vendetta against the organization that ran the show — the General Medical Council. Her passion was undeniable in what she said, and the way she said it ... 'The moment you initiate a formal complaint with the hospital against a senior doctor is the moment you fail to bring about change. The doctor's colleagues will back up his version of events, and as soon as a number of senior doctors are involved in a cover-up, then that cover-up becomes unstoppable. A fundamental principle of the GMC is the protection of its associates because a scandal involving a group of senior doctors would damage the most precious aspect of duty-of-care and the system itself — the trust that the patient has in those treating them. Without this, the system falls apart. The GMC justifies its actions as necessary to avoid damaging that trust. For the GMC it is, and always will be, about the greater good.' Hall paused momentarily; her voice lower when she continued. 'It's not only the GMC and doctors that see it. All too often the patient sees it, and they realize that the people who are going to suffer most from their complaint being upheld, and the resulting scandal, are other patients, so they drop it. In extreme cases they'll even sabotage their complaint.'

She thought she was telling me something I didn't know. Every institution had the same problem — abuse of power by senior staff whose concern was more about their reputation and that of their friends than anything else. The only difference was the GMC were answerable to no one, and that's what Hall was trying to bring to an end.

I knew I had to shut it all out, though. I had to focus on the job in hand and, for now at least, ignore how devastating it could be if my past history was made public.

So I waited for Ryan Cassano, who would hopefully know where his grandfather was — assuming he was still alive. And, assuming I can get him to speak to me, he might know who was supplying stun guns. Assuming one was actually used.

Three doctors found so far, all with their throats cut open from the inside out. As yet no link between the victims. Aside from the Hulk masks, nothing found at the scenes. Nothing from door-to-door enquiries or CCTV footage. No witnesses, no evidence, no motive.

Then there was the knife wound. The way sentries are killed in films, someone generally sneaks up behind them, puts their hand over their mouth and pulls them backwards, whilst cutting their throat.

There would be noise though — and probably a lot of it. There was only one way to make sure it was silent. Two movements performed as one: stab into the side of the neck whilst ripping the knife outwards, severing the windpipe and jugular. It was not part of military training; it was a technique used in the old days.

The masks: that was a ruse; a distraction. I was sure of it. I wasn't buying the pagan ritual thing either. Specifically targeted or random killings? Most likely targeted, but it wasn't a certainty.

The other doctor reported missing?

Dead. Drug-dealers go missing, rebellious teenagers go missing, frustrated housewives and 59-year-old men having mid-life crises. But doctors don't go missing.

I had almost finished eating when Karen called. A group of students came in at the same time. I stepped outside and took the call.

Karen's update was startling. A senior doctor had been found murdered at his home in South Queensferry, along with three other men. Details were just coming in, but when Karen gave me the name of one of the CID officers on site I hung up and dialled his mobile.

He answered at the first ring. 'George, so they brought you in. Not sure what to tell you. We've got four dead here. But it appears as if three were killed out of necessity. There is only one with the same MO as the others: throat cut from the inside out. Another haematology consultant — Dr Andrew Thompson. He was the only medical doctor; the other three were specialists in psychology and associated departments. They were killed by knife wounds, one to the heart, multiple wounds to the mid-section of the other two. Hunting knife; safe to assume it's the same as the one used on Thompson. Won't be certain until the post-mortem, but it looks as if Thompson was killed, then the others happened on the scene before the intruder could escape, which resulted in their deaths.'

'You're sure this is the work of one person, Ian?'

'It's my feeling. Maybe there was backup, but if there was then they stayed outside. One professional could do this, and I think that's what's taken place here.'

'A hit on Thompson?'

'I reckon.'

'Same mask as before?' I asked.

'No, Thompson was wearing an Iron Man mask. Somebody's playing games with us.'

'Anything else different?'

'No, but we'll know more when forensics are done.'

'Appreciate it, Ian.'

'It's good that you're in on this, George. I don't like it. Not the magnitude of it, something else. Be careful.'

I closed the phone off.

'Excuse me.'

I turned around, one of the male students stood facing me. 'Yes?'

He said, 'You're looking for someone?'

'Ryan Cassano.'

'I thought it might be me. I take it you're with the police?'

'Ryan, I need to speak to your grandfather – and no, he's not involved in an investigation, but he might be able to help.'

'May I see your warrant card?'

I held it out to him. He looked at it closely.

He said, 'I need to make a call first.'

He walked off a few metres and phoned either his father or grandfather, no doubt giving them my name.

I wanted to settle up the bill, but I wasn't letting Cassano's grandson out of my sight.

He walked back over. 'My Dad says if he knows you, or of you, he'll probably talk to you. He likes visitors from the old days. He's in a private hospital near the Royal. It's unlikely he'll get over this, so if he is going to speak to you, you won't have long; he tires easily.'

I phoned Audrey Hall and gave her the name of the medical doctor murdered in South Queensferry.

As I drove through traffic it occurred to me that this was how it was going to be all day, one lead to another, criss-crossing Edinburgh, probably ending in nothing.

Was I certain it was a stun gun, and not a taser? Tasers are generally fired from a distance of up to fifteen feet. They don't have the voltage or the pinpoint accuracy of stun guns, where you have to make direct physical contact. I felt sure a high-voltage stun gun had been used directly to the neck, and any tissue trauma from it was removed with the knife wound. It was a reason to use a hunting knife. The jagged edge is normally used to cut through wire and nylon rope – to cut animals out of traps. But in this case I was certain it had been used to tear flesh away.

Perhaps this was revenge. Maybe there were a number of people who had a grudge against each of the doctors; perhaps they'd all met at the support meetings held by Audrey's organization. Whoever was involved, the amount of planning had been huge. This wasn't something you think up in a few days; this would have taken weeks.

5

8.00 P.M.

Raul Cassano was in a single room in a newly built, private hospital in Little France. After waiting to find out if he would see me, I then had to put on a blue apron, wash my hands and wait while the nurses finished their tasks. I wondered if he was toying with me: keep me waiting for as long as possible before telling the nurses he was too tired to see anyone today. I checked my mobile, no messages. I watched the television, still no announcement. How long could they keep something like this quiet?

I sat and stared at the screen. Time passed, and the film that was playing, *Jack Reacher,* was nearing its end. Reacher, armed with an assault rifle, had just got the drop on, and disarmed, the chief assassin. They stood facing each other: it's lashing it down and you wait for Reacher's one-liner before he shoots the assassin. He has to, as he still has at least one more man to kill in order to save the District Attorney's daughter. But there's no one-liner. Instead, Reacher tosses the assault rifle to the ground and engages the assassin in a fight to the death. This was the point where the film departed completely from reality. Aside from knowing next to nothing about the assassin, on ground as wet as this the loser is often the man who slips first. Would Reacher throw away a weapon and unnecessarily gamble with another's life? No, except this was a film, so it's okay, but in real life it would never happen.

Well, if Audrey Hall was accurate about the NHS then it

did happen. Empowered patients, who believed in themselves, would fare far better than those who didn't. Nothing new there. It was a fundamental rule in winning any fight — self-belief was crucial.

A nurse appeared and told me I could go in to Cassano's room, but she warned me not to upset him, or tire him. She added that half an hour was the longest I could spend with him, which suited me fine. I wanted to be out of there in less than five minutes.

No such luck, Cassano was in a nostalgic mood. 'Detective Inspector Boyle!' He held up a withered, shaky hand as if he was welcoming an old friend. I had never been anything but a thorn in his side. Impending death can change you.

'Have you come to arrest me, or give me a beating?' He started to laugh and then cough, his frail chest heaving. He took a minute to collect himself, then added, 'Whatever it is, I did it, just take me away from these nurses.'

Cassano was five when his family moved from Italy to Scotland. His voice retained a soft Italian lilt but as was often the case, sounded odd when mixed with nuances and sayings from the streets of Glasgow and Edinburgh.

'I'm not here in relation to your activities,' I said, 'I am hoping you can help with some information.'

'Boyle, you disappoint me, you could have pretended, for a while at least.'

There wasn't time, really, but here was a man in the last weeks of his life. A man who, although an adversary, I had always admired. He had honour, a rarity amongst the criminal fraternity. No drugs, no murders, no prostitution — well, that wasn't entirely true — he had a number of high-class escorts. You wouldn't find any of his girls on the street though, let alone within a mile of Leith docks. I liked the man, and this would be my one chance to really talk to him.

'I was speaking to your grandson earlier. Looks a fine boy.'

'Unlike my son.'

'They say that the good points in someone tend to miss a generation.'

He smiled, 'So this is your good cop routine? I thought you left that to your partner, that bull of a man. He outside, trying to seduce my nurses?'

'Summer leave. He's been seducing Spanish nurses.'

'The two of you ... you made things difficult for me.'

'We made it difficult for everyone.'

'Ah come on now, Boyle, anything big went down and you were all over me like a cheap suit.'

I smiled, 'Of course we were, you were number one in the city, The Man. If you weren't in on it, you knew who was. But trying to get info from you, or your boys, was like trying to get blood from a—.' I stopped and looked directly at him. 'You do know, it was standard protocol?'

He nodded, smiling. 'The day we heard you'd been taken off the streets and sent to Tulliallan was like Hogmanay. A few weeks later, when we learnt that Morrice had been put behind a desk, it wasn't quite as good, but still enough to re-start the celebrations. Why though? What brought it about?'

'You know why.'

'I don't know the full story. What I did hear involved several flights of stairs, and a psycho-rapist bastard.'

'That's about all there was to it.'

'And that's what I like about you, Boyle, you don't give a shit about anything. That warrant card is a front. You wanted to put the hurt on men, you could of come work for me.

Could've been my right arm, my enforcer. Money would have been a lot better, and then there were the perks.'

I shrugged my shoulders.

'It's a surprise to see you back on the streets after so long away. No wonder they banished you though, you were linked to so many ... now I remember ... one of my team, young arrogant lad, bit of a handful. You kidnapped him; no arrest, just broke open his flat, dragged him out of bed, took him to a block of flats in Sighthill ... knocked down now ... like everything else.'

He looked through the window into the distance.

'Took him to the roof,' I prompted.

'That's right. Four in the morning, twelve storeys up, out on the roof. The two of you held him by his ankles over the edge. When you'd finished scaring the shit out of him, you left him up there. He was a real mess when we found him. He was covered in shit and piss but he was more of a mess mentally. He was never the same, all his confidence gone, forever. He was useless to me – I would have had no choice but to let him go, but he disappeared. Last seen at Waverley boarding a train for London. I knew you wouldn't have put him through that without a reason, so what did he do? What crime did he commit that was so bad?'

'You ever see the girl he went out with before that?'

Cassano shook his head 'I heard about her, but never met her.'

'She had class, too much for him and she ended it. He didn't like that, so he started terrorizing her. Her father didn't come into the station, somehow got my mobile number and arranged to meet me in private. Turned out this prick had broken into her flat, trashed the place, mutilated her dog, smeared its shit over the walls before drowning it in the bath.

That's where she found it. Father wanted her left alone: no charges, no court, no questions. He wanted it to be finished. His little girl had had enough. Asked us if we knew of anyone who could get this guy off her back.'

Cassano seemed lost in thought. Then smiled and said, 'Her Da wasn't asking you if you knew of someone, was he? He managed to get your number; he would have known you would do the job yourself.'

I nodded.

'I knew it had to be something. I could go on all night, listing the number of my boys that were frightened of you. The biggest one of the lot hadn't even seen you, and he was terrified of you. Strange though, how it came about. He heard you trained at that gym out near the ski slope. Mike was almost as big as your partner. Big lifter at his gym. The boys called him Iron Mike after Tyson. Heard he was a big user when it came to steroids and testosterone.

'He kept saying that he was going to train there, and that he would wipe the floor with you when he did. Way I heard it, he got a key and went in the middle of the night. And that was it. He went, he saw, he lost his bottle. His entire attitude changed. From being all bravado, he began merging into the background. He was there, he was still part of the team, but you had to look for him. No one knows what happened. He never spoke about you or any gym after that. How do you figure that? Something must have happened when he was there. Would someone else have been training at four in the morning?'

'No one would have been there, but they wouldn't have to be. I can tell you what most likely happened when he went.'

'Stuff that made him not go back?'

'Stuff that gave him nightmares, stuff that scared him shitless.'

Cassano smiled. 'I want to hear all about it, every detail. But first, let's deal with that information you're after.'

He'd been showing signs of fatigue, and I was glad he'd asked this now.

'Who's supplying stun guns?' I said.

'You want to know about Tasers as well?'

'No, just stun guns.'

He thought for a moment. 'Connie Shokner. No one else'll handle them. I've never liked that man.'

'Know where I can find him?'

'Reiss McGillivray. I take it you know where he'll be.'

I nodded. 'Thanks, Raul.'

'George,'

'Yes?'

'Be careful with McGillivray. He won't be on his own. He'd never take you on, not one to one. Not in a million years. Now', he announced, 'the story about this gym.'

He settled himself.

A nurse came in, checked his pulse, temperature, and blood pressure, while I considered how to find a way to turn Mike's visit to Rab's Gym into a bedtime story. It wasn't so easy when you consider that the one word used to sum up the high street gym was 'image', and the word for Rab's Gym was 'pain'. Rab's Gym was more a horror story, but Raul would want me to tell it the way it was, and there would be story enough in that.

Raul was engaged in a conversation with the nurse.

'Did you know, Amy, that the greatest compliment a woman will ever be given about her beauty is the one she never hears?'

'No, I didn't know that, but I somehow think you're going to tell me.'

'I am,' Raul announced. 'And you should pay attention because you, of all women, should know this.'

'I'm listening,' Amy said, as she scribbled away on her patient's chart.

'You see, the woman's beauty is so devastating the man knows that, no matter what he says, no matter how good a line, how great a compliment it is, it will still be an understatement of such magnitude that, to him, it could only be seen as an insult ... so he says nothing.'

The nurse replaced the chart and looked at Raul. 'And I should know that, should I?'

'Yes, you should,' I said firmly.

'What?' The nurse turned to look at me.

'Because it's true,' I added.

'I told you,' Raul said. 'You don't listen to me, do you?'

The nurse looked from me to Raul. The smile was there but she did a good job of keeping it hidden. 'I give up,' she said in faux dismay, shaking her head as she left the room.

Raul and I looked at each other and smiled. He commented again on Amy's beauty. I thought of Rebecca. Raul settled himself again.

'The Gym,' I began. The patient smiled, and closed his eyes to better picture it. 'If there was snowfall in winter the Gym appeared isolated, alone in the middle of a giant field; an apparition, a mirage, a mystical building which stood fixed in time while the rest of the world zoomed past. Rab's Gym was a place that almost every gym user had heard of but, for those who knew no better, viewed as an ancient relic, something that they thought they'd seen as a child in a black-

and-white movie, like a painting of Dorian Gray covered in cobwebs in the attic of an old house.

'But many knew that it was still very much a working gym, and they wanted to visit, to see inside, satisfy their curiosity. Though that wasn't the only reason,' I whispered. 'They wanted to be able to say they'd trained there and add "well, it was okay, nothing special." They wanted to be cool, and there was nothing cooler in training circles, than to be able to say you'd trained at Rab's Gym.

'Of course, the need to be cool was almost exclusively reserved to the would-be Alphas, the posers, like Mike; the guys who went to bars with rolled up T-shirts and flashed their bi's — or guns, as they call them. And the women would swoon, but only in the Alphas' minds. Yet, those minds craved a taste of the real thing — they wanted to be able to say it, they wanted that level of authenticity, and one session at Rab's Gym would give them that. Just one. The temptation was too great for Mike, and he got hold of a key, turned up at four in the morning, when he knew it would be empty, strutted through the door, and planted himself in the middle of the gym floor. "This is okay," he said out loud. "Bit basic, but I can train here." Then he really looked around, and saw the true size of the weights that were lined up on the racks like battleship shells. Mike's brain floundering, as he tried to convert the poundage of one of them to kilos. He knew, that no matter how much gear or growth he took, he would never manage to budge that dumbbell, let alone lift it off the rack. Then, he scanned the gym itself and saw the Spartan side to it: a gym that had no fridges to chill drinks, no widescreen TV's, or electrical points. There was no sign of civilization, no sign of humanity. Nothing, except a standard UFC cage, a bloodstained heavy punchbag, benches, weight racks, squat racks and ... what the hell? His gaze focused on the giant steel cylinder lying beside a squat rack that looked like a torpedo ... what was that? It wasn't until he saw the mask that lay alongside it that it suddenly hit him ... they had oxygen available for squatting, which meant one thing. The hairs on the back of his neck rose with the realization that Death Sets were performed here. And, like a hill walker who takes shelter from a downpour in a cave, then suddenly realizes that it is not a cave, it's a lair — the home of a beast that has woken and is now directly behind him — he can hear its low growl, feel its hot breath on the back of his neck. And the Alpha that was Iron Mike bolted, sprinting through the door, down the steps and across to his car.

'As the rev counter red-lined, the accelerator pedal floored in first, the truth dawned on him: it wasn't a beast's lair, it was a place where animals from a lost age roamed. He'd heard of dinosaur training, he'd read about it, but he had never thought he would see a gym that was based around it. Dinosaur training was compound negatives — forced reps and Death Sets. It was a type of training the sheer brutality of which, made him realize one essential truth. One word — one label. A word that was a whisper at first, but would wake him during the night, and trouble his days, until finally, with the passage of time, he began to convince himself that the visit hadn't taken place. He had imagined it. The day he succeeded, the word and label 'fraud' would be banished from his mind, and he would be back to being the real deal — the Alpha — and Rab's Gym would be nothing more than a bad dream. That day was far away though.

'Back in the present, for those who were driven, and could handle the pain and the blood and guts of it, Rab's Gym was a place where "Alphas", designer clothing, posing, and anything resembling iPhones or fitness trackers would never be seen. You didn't need to know your blood oxygen or stress levels, you knew you'd trained when you threw up or blacked out, or the next day couldn't walk or raise your arms.'

I was standing looking out of the window as I recounted the end of the story. I turned and saw that Raul was sound asleep. I looked out of the window again, as I tried to work out why I felt something was very wrong. Then, suddenly I remembered. It had been right there the whole time. I should have known, it had started with the last conversation between Rab, Gavin and myself after a training session. We were sitting outside as the sun was setting, and Rab—.

Amy tapped my shoulder. She led me outside into the corridor. 'Thank you,' her voice was warm, as was her smile. 'He doesn't sleep easily, but he was totally relaxed with you. He was so happy when he heard you were coming to see him. Should we expect to see you again?'

'I'll try to get in, in a couple of days.'

'Can I tell him that?'

'My job. It's not good to make promises.'

'I understand. But can I say you'll try?' Her eyebrows raised in anticipation. I sighed, acknowledging the reason she would have for pushing so hard.

'In two days. You tell him.'

As I walked towards the Audi I stopped, turned, and looked over towards where Raul's room was. I stood there for about a minute trying to get back to that conversation outside the gym, but my mind was already thinking of McGillivray. I turned and pressed the button on the key, the sound of the locks opening and the flashing of indicators announcing that I was back on the hunt ... and the clock was ticking.

*

There was a queue outside the new nightclub next to the Liquid Rooms. A band was playing; the excitement in the young men and women standing outside, palpable. I walked to the front of the queue and spoke to the man who appeared to be in charge of security. He led the way down the stairs to the manager's office. The energy on the street was magnified several times inside. Music boomed from the speakers. Inside the office it was relatively quiet.

Reiss McGillivray would be regarded as a high-flyer in certain circles. As a teenager his size and reputation brought him employment in the toughest kind of debt collecting. The money was dirty; he was collecting from criminals. The collectors generally worked in two-man teams; both men would have the capacity for violence but one of them would have no morals whatsoever. Even as a seventeen-year-old McGillivray was in charge, and when they made their home visits, he had to keep his colleague on a tight leash. One afternoon, they were collecting from a drug dealer who didn't have the money he owed. But, he explained, pointing towards a fourteen-year-old girl lying on the settee, 'My daughter's just there.'

When I heard the story, I wasn't sure if the dealer was saying that you can't get violent because my daughter's here. But McGillivray knew that the drugged-up dealer was offering his daughter in payment: McGillivray went berserk. He battered the dealer senseless, kicking him across the room, before lifting the television overhead and throwing it on to him. But it didn't sate his rage. He effectively destroyed the living room and kitchen, ripping doors off hinges, throwing the fridge and oven through windows. All this time the big man with him stood immobile, looking on in silence, wondering why his job was being done for him. McGillivray had morals all right, too many for that job, and he quit not long afterwards and found his way into nightclubs; but he still kept his contacts. I hadn't seen him in years, but events have a way of reopening old conflicts.

McGillivray had been sitting behind a large desk, but the moment he saw me, he stood up and walked over. 'What are you doing here, Boyle?'

'I am here for one piece of information. That's all.'

'Fuck off.'

'If I don't get it, I'll have you closed down inside ten minutes.'

'Aye, right.'

'I doubt the increase in police activity today has escaped you. We've had officers from all over the country arriving since early this morning. If you think closing you down is a big deal, you're making a mistake.'

McGillivray laughed. I stepped in towards him, my fists clenched. 'I don't have time to fuck around. You withhold this information, you'll never get another licence to operate. You'll be back to debt-collecting, and that won't be your real problem. If anyone else dies because you've withheld information I'll personally make sure you serve time.'

He stayed silent and stared at me. After a few seconds he said quietly, 'What information?'

'Shokner. I need to know where he is right now.'

Another long pause.

McGillivray stepped back to his desk. 'I'll have to make some calls. Give me your number and I'll call you inside the hour. And that's it between us. I give you an address and you stay the fuck away from me, permanently.'

'Fine.'

'Now get out of my face, Boyle. You don't intimidate me.'

I smiled and left. The head doorman, and one of his team had been waiting outside the office. I let the two of them lead the way up the stairs.

*

I drove to the top of Victoria Street, across the Royal Mile and parked where Mound Place meets Ramsay Lane, when a call came through on my mobile. It was Rebecca.

'I checked on Templeton. He was well respected by nurses and patients. I don't think that helps, does it?'

'It helps. Thanks, Rebecca.'

'There have been police everywhere today. Are you okay?'

'I'm fine; I'll call you when this is over.'

'Take care, George.'

It was after eleven but the sky was still alive with light; pale yellow on the horizon and streaks of blue resisting the black of the night. Somewhere up there, hidden behind thick, dark-grey clouds, was a full moon. I was at the railings looking down on to Princes Street. This was one of my favourite spots in Edinburgh. William Goldman had described it in *Marathon Man*: Scylla had stood on a spot close to here, looking at Princes Street. Goldman's assassin caught the enchantment of it all perfectly ... the most magnificent street in the world, and that if there ever was a street to die on, it would be this one.

The landscape hadn't changed that much since the setting in the early seventies, but the flavour and character that had been in the stores like Lillywhites and Forsyth's had all but disappeared, replaced by chain stores and phone shops. Only Jenners department store remained. But you still couldn't get away from the sheer beauty of the place itself. The gardens at the foot of the castle, the Scott Monument, the two hotels which used to be owned by rival railways, the red sandstone of the Caledonian at the west end and the light sandstone of the North British — now The Balmoral — at the east end; its prominent tower clock still running traditionally two minutes fast.

Yet I missed the Edinburgh of my childhood. The Valvona and Crolla that sold spaghetti that was almost four-feet long; the Dominion Cinema where the owner would stand on the steps outside, resplendent in his dinner suit, welcoming each guest personally to the evening showings. The shop and cinema were still there, but without the things that I loved the most about them, they weren't the same.

The sound of traffic flowing between the two hotels faded into the distance.

Take care. How many times had Rebecca said that to me? But with the stress in her voice; it wasn't just a banal phrase to sign off on. She meant what she said. She always meant what she said.

A year ago almost to the day she was sitting across from me outside Montpeliers in Bruntsfield. She was wearing black jeans and a black off-shoulder gypsy top. The sun was glinting off her hair, a gentle breeze brushing strands of it against her cheekbones. The sound of Chris Young's rendition of 'Rainy Night in Georgia' drifted out from the bar. People were walking close by but I was oblivious to them. It was one of those brief moments of peace in my life. If there was ever a time to tell her how I felt, a time to explain things, then it was now. But the conversation flowed naturally and I held back. As the sun dipped behind the houses I noticed she was getting cold. I took my jacket from the back of my chair and placed it over her bare shoulders. It was enormous on her, yet somehow it made her look even more beautiful. And as I sat looking at her, I realized that I could never tell her. In my jacket she was like a delicate rose wrapped in newspaper. On the surface, the rough paper enhanced her beauty, but she had no idea of the words that were written on it. When she found out, I would lose all contact with her. I didn't think I could handle that, or the knowledge that I would be betraying her if I slept with her. I would be an imposter. As much as I wanted her, a part of me needed things to stay as they were: she would continue to see me as the nice policeman, rough around the edges, but still an okay guy, and whatever had happened in my past wouldn't matter. But it did matter; no matter how much I wanted to, I couldn't change who I was ... or what I'd done.

My mobile was ringing. It was McGillivray.

As I walked back to the car I called Karen. 'Anything from The Bear?'

'Not yet, Boss. His plane should have landed by now. I have one of the security officers waiting to meet him in Arrivals. He's not someone you'd miss.'

No, there was no chance of that. Most of our crew were either too young or had no interest in rugby, so they never made the connection when I called Gavin that. But in the eighties, almost everyone in Scotland knew who The Bear actually was. Iain Milne, was, as the late and great Bill

McLaren put it, 'built like a tank'. The best tight-head-prop Scotland had, or will ever have. The Bear was never once pushed back in the scrum, and probably was the only prop ever to be penalised for pushing too hard. He was a nightmare for the opposing front row, and many resorted to underhand methods in an attempt to subdue his dominance, but their punches only resulted in broken knuckles. I saw him take a punch whilst playing for the Barbarians; it was a huge right hook which would have flattened anyone else on the pitch. The Bear didn't even blink and I wondered if he was even aware he'd been hit until I saw a wry smile play across his lips.

In '71, eight years before The Bear began to play for Scotland, the British Lions swept all before them on their tour of New Zealand. It was becoming a national embarrassment for the Kiwis. After nine consecutive defeats, Canterbury stepped forward on June 19, in a match that resulted in Scottish prop Sandy Carmichael, Irish prop Ray McLoughlin and Irish No 8 Mick Hipwell being invalided off the tour. Whilst the Lions had prepared themselves for a game of rugby, Canterbury were prepared for a street fight. I have often wondered how what is seen as one of the most vicious premeditated assaults in rugby history would have fared, or if it would have even taken place, if The Bear had been born a few years earlier and had played for the Lions that day. Perhaps it's as well, because if he had ever lost control in a game, the consequences might have been tragic.

There was a cost though to all that bone and muscle: The Bear could not run fast, but he was fit, he could keep going. One day, after witnessing a minor robbery, he lumbered off in pursuit. The robber, built for speed, sprinted away, but The Bear kept running and eventually caught up with him. Whilst being charged at the station the confused young man's

71

reply to caution was, 'I never thought that big bastard would catch me.'

That was Gav, he was a big bastard, and unlike Milne, who never once lost his temper and always played to the rules of the game, Gavin could be ruthless to the extreme. He had been solely responsible for changing the role-playing exercises at Tulliallan. Up until he went through as a recruit the instructions were to make it as realistic as possible. Gavin had played the angry husband who'd just come home to find his wife in bed with the next-door neighbour. He was supposed to resist arrest, which he did, very effectively. They had to abandon the exercise, and treat one of the arresting officers for ligament damage and the other for concussion.

I gave Karen the address with instructions for Gavin to meet me outside at midnight.

JUNE 21

It was in '67 that work began on building the Wester Hailes council scheme on the south-west side of the city. It was eight years later that most of the housing was complete. Although the facilities were improved, the area had always been, like other large council estates, plagued by anti-social behaviour. However, in Wester Hailes, the term 'anti-social behaviour' covered a multitude of sins.

I looked up at the block of flats. The sky was almost black now; perhaps a sign I should leave this well alone. The chances of getting positive information from here were slim. I doubted McGillivray would set me up, but it was always a possibility.

Connie Shokner, aka Craig Mason, had made his money in the eighties in scaffolding in Glasgow before a two-year stint in Barlinnie for serious assault. After his release he settled in Edinburgh and began dealing. On the street he was known simply as Shokner. It was no secret he had adopted the name after seeing the prison sports film *The Longest Yard*. Robert Tessier had played the muscle-bound inmate with the shaved head who had killed seven men with his bare hands. Mason bore an uncanny resemblance to Tessier: right down to the falsetto voice and long narrow nose which, despite his upbringing in the rough end of Glasgow, had remained unbroken.

I looked at my watch: ten after midnight. According to McGillivray, Shokner would be at this address for only a few hours. I was running out of time. I had worn my jacket and tie when I went to the Royal; now I left both in the car and walked over to the flats. The entrance was dimly lit, though the out-of-service sign was clear enough on the lift. Brown paper wrappings from the nearby chippie, squares of tin foil with tell-tale brown burn marks of heroin and empty cans of lager and cider littered the floor. The close stank of urine and vomit, and a voice inside my head told me to turn around, get back in the car and drive.

I managed the first couple of flights easily enough. Thereafter, my breathing became strained. By the sixth flight I was moving in slow motion as my legs struggled to bear my weight. I could feel beads of sweat trickling down my back. The walls were beginning to move on their own. I had to keep going, I reached the foot of the last flight but my breathing was coming in rasps now.

'No' lookin in great shape therr,' a voice called to me.

A look-out, there's a deal going down inside. Turn back.

I looked up at the man leaning casually over the balustrade. He was big-shouldered with the smile of confidence that comes with youth and strength.

Turn back.

I started the ascent to the top floor. 'Whoar d'ye think you're goan, auld yin?'

I looked up at him waiting until I caught my breath. Last chance to turn back, do it now.

I focused on each step and continued upwards. 'I'm here to see Shokner,' I said.

''E's busy.'

'He'll want to see me.'

'Aye? An whit makes ye think that?'

I stood stationary, three steps from the top landing. 'Ask him, I'll wait here.'

'Aye, yir right, ye wull wait, right therr.' He pointed aggressively to the step I was standing on. He turned and banged on the flat door twice.

A few seconds later the door slowly opened. A man's head with short, red hair peered out. 'Whit?'

''E says Shokner wants tae see 'im.'

Red hair stared at me for a few seconds.

'Keepim therr.' The head disappeared.

Alarm bells were going off in my mind. A minute later red hair opened the door wide and stood to one side. A slim man in a black tracksuit bolted past me, leaping down the stairs four at a time. He'd be going to check outside to see if I was alone. Two minutes' later red hair's mobile rang. He answered, listened, looked towards me and nodded. 'This wie,' he said as he opened his arm out, showing me inside. We walked along the narrow entrance hall to the main room.

There's always a time in your life when you go into a room and find that it's the last place on earth you want to be. As I watched red hair walk to the window and draw the curtains, I realized that time had arrived.

Shokner, instantly recognizable, stood in the centre of the room with his hands on his hips. The man on his right was short and wiry and had a big grin on his face. That's when I felt an enormous arm around my neck pulling me backwards. He'd been behind the door and in focusing on red hair I had missed him. It was the kind of mistake an amateur makes. I'd been off the streets too long. I lifted my right foot and slammed it down on where his ankle should be, at the same time I wrenched my head forwards and whipped it back. I heard a laugh from above me. I was five-eleven and I'd butted his chest. Shokner stepped forwards and slammed his right fist into my exposed stomach. My lungs emptied of air; I wanted to double over, but the huge arm wasn't allowing me to move. Shokner hit me again, this time lower. I wanted to sink to the floor and curl up in a ball. I wanted it to be morning again, to be back on Salisbury Crags and to have left my mobile at the flat.

Shokner said, 'Lettim go.' The arm lifted. Against the demands of my body I managed to stay upright. I turned to look at the man who'd been behind me who now stood in silence on my right, blocking the door. If he was under seven foot it would only be by a fraction, and he was built proportionally.

A bare bulb dangling from the ceiling was the only light in the room. It was a bright light, and it cast our individual shadows on to bare walls — the giant's shadow towering ominously over mine.

Shokner held the floor. 'George Boyle. Ah've way-id a long time tae meet you. But Deek therr, well, he's way-id even longer. See, you pit Deek's brither away for a ten stretch an that's bad news fir you, cause Deek, well, Deek's jist vindictive ba nature.'

Deek had worked his way around to my left side. The grin had disappeared replaced by a look of concentration. He was clearly concealing something in his right hand. It could have been a Stanley knife with the blade retracted, or a razor, except I'd seen someone else hold their hand in exactly the same way. It would be a switchblade.

Shokner continued, 'Ah've always wondered 'bout somethin, and you can tell me if this story is true. Eight or nine years ago, a blood crazed rapist and you were involved in a fight, where he ended up wi almost ev'ry bone in 'is body broken and brain damage. The man's no walked a step or spoken a word since. Now, the way Ah heard it, 'is injuries werr the same as fae fallin doon six flights o' sterrs. But the building the fight took place only had two flights o' sterrs, so ma question is, did you carry 'im up the sterrs in order to throw 'im doon them repeatedly? Cos' I heard he was a big fat fucker.'

I wondered where Shokner had obtained his information. He *was* a huge man, and he had come at me with the same open razor he'd held to a twelve-year old's throat while he raped her.

Three years later that poor girl took her own life.

There was, and still is, no real deterrent against rape, even today after all the campaigns only a small percentage of rapes are actually reported, and of those rapists who are convicted, the sentences are insignificant when compared to the permanent psychological damage inflicted on the victims. As far as I was concerned, the fat bastard who would spend the rest of his life in silence, sitting in a wheelchair, had got off easy.

Deek continued to edge forward. He seemed intent on plunging that switchblade into my left kidney. He was the immediate danger and I would have to deal with him first. Then, the absurdity of my train of thought hit me. It wasn't so much that I'd been weakened by Shokner's punch to my groin or that there were four of them in this room, or that I was slow, and overweight, and had a heart condition. I had been in a time warp at Tulliallan for the last seven years, and only now, in this room, did I realize I had bypassed middle-age.

I was an old man.

I should have waited outside. I should have waited for The Bear.

I had thrown the rapist down the stairs initially, but it was Gav who suggested throwing him down them again, and it was Gav who repeatedly carried him back up them.

Right now I needed that power, that ruthlessness, because I didn't want to die in this room, in this flat, in Wester Hailes. I wanted to die quietly lying in the sun in Princes Street Gardens.

Shokner was shouting at me, inches away from my face. 'Boyle, did you carry him up the sterrs!' I stared at him in silence. Shokner smiled. 'Ah knew the storries aboot you couldnae bi true.'

I should have been trying to work out what option they were going to go for, either throw me over the rail outside, or hold me and let Deek repeatedly stick that blade into my kidneys. But my mind had gone back to the conversation that had started outside Rab's Gym.

We were all sitting on the grass, chatting, unwinding, enjoying the heat of the summer evening. Something wasn't right though; I could tell there was something on Rab's mind, he wasn't his usual self. An hour later, when I was having a drink with Gav in The Steading, I asked him.

Gav answered with a question of his own, 'Did you not notice the heavy bag had been re-sited?'

'Of course, it makes more sense to have it where it is now.'

'That wasn't the reason. It was re-sited because you damaged the beam.'

'There are a lot of big hitters there. You talk as if I was solely responsible.'

'*Probably because you were. You don't know the half of it. Shit, you don't even know what I'm talking about, you're in another world when you work that bag. It's not the bag that's the problem, it's you. Rab's not concerned about the cost of re-siting the bag or having the beam reinforced. He doesn't want you to work the bag again because of the effect it has on the members.*'

I shook my head, '*They're a tough bunch that train there ... all of them. You know it as well as I do. Hell, everyone knows there's no such thing as a normal training session at Rab's. It's a trial by fire. Always has been and always will be. Every single time they walk through the door in to that gym they know what they're in for. There's nothing we do that they haven't seen before.*'

'*They are a tough bunch, yet every one of them stops what they're doing when you go on that bag and they watch transfixed ... and they all have the exact same look on their face. Fear. You don't train old-school, you don't train, period. You go on the bag bare-knuckled, and when you go into that zone, you're in a fight, and it's not a bag you see in front of you, it's a human being, and he's alive and you are dead set on destroying him. And we both know who he is.*'

We sat in silence for a few minutes.

'*As tough as they are, the gym members are frightened that your temper is going to spill over and they'll be in the firing line. I know that won't happen. You know how to channel your anger, but I worry about what it's doing to you.*' Gavin added softly.

I looked at him.

He looked back, then turned to stare at the bottle of lager he was holding. Another minute passed in silence, before

Gavin, still staring at the bottle, said quietly, 'Sometimes things just happen, there's no reason, they just do.'

A muffled noise came from the front door, followed by what sounded like a body hitting the ground. Red hair was first to investigate with Shokner and the giant not far behind.

Deek's mask of concentration had gone, the grin back on his face. I realized his concentration had been focused on keeping himself restrained. Now that Shokner had left the room, the true Deek could resurface.

Deek, as many small men do, had learnt to use a knife, but he had made a mistake in allowing me to see he had one. If someone is really competent with a knife, then their victim doesn't see it until it is too late. They also tend not to use switchblades. Deek had correctly assumed I was right-handed, and continued to edge round on my left side, with that goddamn smile on his face. I hated that smile. It comes from those who feel they have control, from those who enjoy making people afraid.

A crashing noise from the hall corridor, the entire building seemed to shake. It *was* Gavin, I knew the certainty of it. I knew the sound that went with him throwing a man against a wall with such force it rendered his victim unconscious. Now was totally different to what had happened a few minutes ago. The memory of the conversation in the Steading was not a good one. Yet right now it was what I needed to hear. It may have been a while, but I still had it, the power was still there. I felt the adrenaline course through my veins. Whenever it did that just prior to extreme violence I could feel the muscles on my shoulders expand, as if my body knew where I would need to exert the greatest power. Then things started to move in slow motion. They say a fighter's

80

world is measured in milliseconds, and it's because their focus reaches an apex. I guess this always happens when death is close.

The left jab is a punch you won't see in a street fight. It's the fastest punch, but it's not a powerful punch, and in a fight against a man with a knife, it's not effective enough to even slow him down. In a street fight, everything you learn in the gym goes out of the window, especially if you're fighting for your life — when you're doing that you instinctively want to inflict the maximum amount of damage, your body wants to release all the power it possesses. The left jab won't do the job. It's a work of art that scores points in boxing but simply has no place in a street fight. So no one would expect it to be used against them; and that was partly why I was going to use it. The other reason was that my left jab was no work of art.

It's rare that you find out the damage you inflict in a fight; even rarer that you find out the damage each blow inflicts.

Nowadays, when troops finish a tour of active duty they have a stop-off on the beaches of Cyprus. They sit in the sun, relax, have a few beers, adjust and unwind before going home. But decompression is a relatively new aspect of war. On the boat back from the Falklands it was mayhem. You'd have thought we'd have got all our aggression out in the fighting and killing, but we were on a knife edge. Old scores were being settled. You bumped into someone; it exploded into an all-out fight. Men were literally having the shit kicked out of them, and all the time this was going on the officers laid low in their quarters. I was out on deck at night when my rage boiled over. I knocked another Para unconscious with my first punch, and I followed through, dropping to my knees, raining in short rights to his face. It was pitch black and I would have kept punching, but it didn't feel like I was hitting a face; it was too soft to be a face.

He was in sick bay for two days, his jaw broken in three places, and he'd lost five teeth. I'd hit him six times. Wolff's law: bone density increases with the gradual increase of stress. Even before I'd joined up I'd worked the heavy bag bare knuckled. After the conversation with Gavin, I stopped working the heavy bag at Rab's, but I did something else to compensate. I began by gently punching walls. Over time the punches had steadily increased in power, to the point where I had to change the place I hit every few months. The walls in my flat looked okay, but they shudder when I hit them now.

I was focused on two things: Deek's right hand and the shifting of his bodyweight. I'd made the decision to step in and strike the moment he flicked the blade open. The way he was edging round to my left side, the smile on his face, it was all about the appliance of fear. The flicking open of the blade would be the best part for him; he would want to see my reaction.

I had gone through the punch in my mind; it was seared on to the blueprint on my subconscious. Perhaps it was knowing Gavin was a few feet away, but I didn't wait for the blade to open, the punch flew from my shoulder on its own.

I was vaguely aware of the blood spraying out as Deek fell backwards. I followed him down to the carpet, driving punches into his exposed face and neck. It eventually sank in that he was no longer conscious. My mind shifted gear. I turned and looked around wildly — the room was empty. I ran towards the hall where I saw the giant in a clinch with Gavin. No, not Gavin — someone else.

I leapt over a body. As soon as I reached them I realized it was a woman who had the giant's arms caught in a lock against his chest. They were facing each other each with their backs against opposite sides of the hall. The giant was on my left which meant his ribs were more exposed to my right hook. So I unleashed it, wielding every ounce of my bodyweight into each punch. He tried to bring his huge hands around to grab me, but the woman held his arms with such force they barely moved. He stared directly at me, his eyes wide open, a clear sign he was in shock. He simply couldn't comprehend what was happening. He was trapped — and I'd found my rhythm. I'd never used an axe to cut down a tree before, but this would probably be as close as I would get to it. After the first half dozen punches his shattered ribs were no longer protecting his internal organs.

There's usually some sound made when under excruciating pain or in a state of mental terror. The loudest I knew of was the high-pitched scream of a rabbit; a death scream that can be heard over a mile away. But from this man there was nothing; the only sound was the rhythmic beating of my fist against his side. I kept wielding, swinging in, again and again; each punch harder than the one before.

His bladder was spilling when the woman let him fall to the ground. She stared at me. 'It's over,' she said.

I glared at her, my fists still clenched.

It wasn't over.

It would never be over.

She spoke again, this time a look of concern on her face. 'Are you okay?'

I wasn't okay. The corridor, my world, started spinning. My feet lost their grip.

*

I opened my eyes, and stared at a smoke-stained ceiling. My mouth was dry, and at first I had no idea where I was. I looked down — I was lying on the settee in the main room. The woman was sitting on her knees next to me. Seeing her up close I realized she was only a girl, nineteen, twenty at most.

'You okay?' she asked.

'How long was I out?'

She smiled, 'Two or three minutes.'

I turned my head and looked around, 'Where's Gavin?'

She looked around the room then back to me, 'Who's Gavin?'

'Who's with you?' I said.

'No one. I'm on my own.'

I ran the fingers of my right hand through my hair as I tried to make sense of this. 'Who are you?'

'A friend.'

She stood and lowered her hand. I took hold of it and I was lifted to a sitting position. My chest felt tight.

In the bathroom I rinsed my face in cold water. My shirt had blood all over the front and right sleeve. I went out and stood between the door of the main room and the hall corridor and surveyed the carnage. The girl was checking for pulse rates. She held her fingers to Deek's neck.

'Who's alive?' I asked.

She took her fingers away and looked around for something to wipe them on. 'He isn't. The man with the shaved head isn't, and the big man isn't.'

Shokner dead? Then the lead to the purchaser of the stun gun, and my only suspect, was also dead. 'This was all for nothing,' I said.

'Was it?' she said as she walked towards the front door. She then busied herself putting red hair and the look-out in the recovery position. She turned towards me. 'You're still alive.'

'Yes, I am, and thank you for that. But who *are* you?'

'I've told you, a friend.'

I called Karen and requested that an ambulance and the nearest unit attend as soon as possible. Hopefully, the unit would arrive before the ambulance. I wanted to hand this over and be long gone before any medics set foot in here.

With no movement from anyone we worked our way downstairs. I wasn't interested in crime-scene protocol; I wanted to find out who this girl was. At the bottom of the stairwell, almost hidden by discarded rubbish, lay the man in the black tracksuit. I noticed his right arm was bent at an odd angle.

We stood outside. We were partly lit by street lights; the sky having clouded over was dark now. It was warmer and I was surprised no one was around. The entire block of flats seemed deserted. I leaned against the wall of the building and ran my right hand across my forehead.

'Who sent you?'

The girl was looking off into the distance. 'Major Robertson,' she said.

It was the last name I expected. 'Major Andrew Robertson?'

'The same.'

That made no sense. 'Major Robertson is dead. He died in a car accident fifteen years ago.'

'Along with my mother and grandmother.'

My mind launched itself back to a rainy day in Inverness and the funeral of my former OC. Robertson's father standing straight with a little girl at his side.

'Mireille,' I said softly.

She smiled.

That the girl who saved me was Major Robertson's daughter would normally have left me stunned, but the day had acquired a surreal quality to the point where I had become emotionally detached from everything.

'How did you find me?' I asked.

'I went to Fettes; no luck getting in the front, so I went around the back and there was a WPC having a smoke, I asked her; I didn't even have to go inside.'

Karen: if there was a day to break a two-year stint without a cigarette, then this was the day. I said, 'She wouldn't have just told you where I was.'

'Not straight off. I must have been blocking the entrance; I didn't realize until a couple of male officers tried to push past me. There was, how should I put it, a confrontation. She had been reluctant to talk to me at all before that.'

I could imagine the scene: Karen would be worried she couldn't get hold of Gavin, and then after seeing the power and potential for violence in Mireille decided she was the next best thing.

'Are you police or military?' I asked.

'I'm a literature student at UHI.'

'How did you get here?'

She pointed to a red Astra. I said, 'It would be better if you're not seen here, so let's move the car.'

'I need a change of clothes.'

She was wearing a black sweatshirt and black leggings; they looked fine but they were probably soaked in blood.

'Do you know the city?' I asked.

'Only the airport.'

'There's a twenty-four hour Tesco a mile or so in that direction,' I said, pointing north. There was time for shopping. With Shokner dead I had nowhere to go.

'I'll find it.'

I said, 'I won't be here long. I'll see you in the car park.'

I took a mental note of the registration number as I watched her walk to the Astra. She had the thighs of a champion speed skater and powerful sloping shoulders. Yet I still couldn't understand how she could have subdued the giant; and that was after beating three men unconscious and killing a fourth.

I had been there, I had seen part of it and the aftermath, but I still couldn't believe it.

I watched a flashing blue light in the distance draw closer. I found two high-viz jackets in the back of the Audi and put one on. Not a good fit, but it would do for now. The patrol car pulled up beside me. I gave the briefest of reports to the arriving uniformed officers and drove to Tesco.

When I pulled in to the car park I could see Mireille coming out of the store entrance. She was wearing her new clothes: black combat trousers and a grey tank top. After jumping into the passenger seat she pulled a black shirt out of a bag and said, 'I figure this is about the right size, but they were limited for colour.'

I stood at the side of the car and stripped off the blood-stained shirt. Two girls, arm-in-arm, swaying as they walked across the car park, shouted that I continue with the trousers. They staggered off with a mild display of mock disappointment, clearly too drunk to notice the blood on my body.

Mireille parked the Astra at the far end of the car park. I waited for her to get back in — I wanted to ask her why she had chosen today to come and see me, but before I could my mobile rang. Audrey Hall; her tone anxious. 'I may have something for you, Inspector, but I need to speak to you in person. How soon can you be here?'

'Ten minutes.'

It wasn't quite one side of the city to the other, but ten minutes to Lauder Road would require going through a number of red lights.

Mireille sat in silence. I focused on the road and getting as much acceleration out of the Audi as I could. The streets were quiet and we made good time. I slowed as we drove into Bruntsfield. We passed Montpeliers, where I'd sat outside with Rebecca. I had walked back to my flat that evening, carrying the jacket she'd worn over my arm. The song that had been playing in the bar still echoing in my mind. The moment I closed the door behind me I buried my face in the jacket. I wasn't just trying to breathe her in; I was trying to hold on to something that I now knew was out of reach. I don't know how long I stood there, my back leaning against the door, my face wrapped up like a child's in a dream world.

I hadn't worn the jacket since. It hangs on its own at the back of my wardrobe as a reminder, on the many occasions when I need one, that there is something pure in my world; something I haven't ruined ... or destroyed.

7

1.15 A.M.

Lauder Road was lit in a soft shade of pink by its streetlights. Two warm, yellow lights were visible through the windows of Audrey's house.

With Mireille waiting in the car I walked to the front door, which opened before I reached it. I was shown directly into Audrey Hall's office. She stood tall behind her desk, but her face showed deep concern. This was a different lady from the one I'd spoken to a few hours ago. What was she afraid of? She asked me to sit down.

Audrey said, 'I have had visits from two teams of detectives. I informed both teams that I was in constant contact with you; and acting on information given by you I was looking into our records. That was all I told them; other than they would have to contact you for further information.'

'How hard did they push?' I asked.

'They weren't happy with it. A uniformed Inspector made a thinly veiled threat that it was an act of obstruction on my part; but I can be quite stubborn when I want to be. As I see it I am co-operating fully with a senior detective, and I would pass any information I obtained on to him, but as I had no information to give him, or them, at that time, the whole issue was irrelevant. Things have moved forward since then, however.'

She paused and walked to the window. I waited for it; this would be where her fear lay. 'In relation to the information you gave me, one name kept coming up. I have to say before I give you his name that I am convinced he would take no part in physical violence, whether directly or indirectly.' She turned towards me. 'What does not make sense is that all the doctors you listed, every single one, was implicated in covering up the inappropriate treatment which led to his wife's death.'

I recognized the name as soon as she said it – Stephen Dowas was a former major in the SAS. When he retired from the army he worked as a consultant, but also made a very lucrative income by training, and supplying, ex-servicemen as mercenaries. Audrey Hall may have been convinced that he had never been involved in physical violence, but the opposite was true. This man had killed on numerous occasions.

'How is it that the main organizations don't know about Dowas? Didn't he make a formal complaint?'

'He knows how the system works, Inspector – the conflict of interests. Rather than become caught up in a mire of hypocrisy, he wrote to each of the doctors involved. It's one of the reasons why he was so involved in our organization. He is well aware that institutions will often controversialize the complainant: they will find a way to switch the focus from the complaint to the person making the complaint. It's a tried, trusted and frequently used tactic to divert blame; the complainant is labelled as over-emotional and suffering from post-traumatic stress. The doctors named in the complaint act outraged that, in having such a high code of ethics, there would even be a suggestion that they'd done anything wrong. Many doctors believe they are above reproach, and the fact is they are, because the existing system, overseen by the GMC, protects them.'

Doubtless, here was Audrey's story, and her reason for developing the database. It was written all over her face –

someone she loved, probably her husband, had suffered unnecessarily. At some point during the complaint process she'd been branded as suffering from post-traumatic stress disorder. PTSD is real and destructive, but was Audrey Hall suffering from it? Were her efforts to bring down the GMC misguided? In some respects maybe, but after seeing the film Spotlight, and the sheer extent of child abuse that was covered up, it was clear that no institution should police itself.

I said, 'I appreciate the time you've given to this, Audrey. You say Dowas was involved in your organization. In what way?'

'He was one of our biggest contributors. If it hadn't been for him we wouldn't be in operation today.'

'His wife would have had private care then?'

'Yes, she had both private and NHS care, and often it's the same doctors that are involved. In the end his wife wanted to die at home, so he took her there and brought in care, but I think most of the time he nursed her himself.'

*

After giving me Dowas's address in Gullane, Audrey said she and her staff would continue to work and she would call if they came up with further information.

Gullane was only twenty miles away; it was a village on the coast where I'd spent many childhood summers staying with my aunt and uncle. I walked towards the car; things were moving forwards. Despite what Audrey Hall said about his character, Dowas was, to all intents and purposes, the prime suspect. He would still have his contacts in the military and enough money to have any number of people killed.

As I drove, I explained to Mireille where we were going

and why. It wasn't long before we had turned off the A1. I knew this road well. My uncle, the sales manager of Ford's in Semple Street in the late sixties, had his pick of demonstrators. I remembered rolling around the back seat of a Capri like I was on a rollercoaster as the tyres squealed around every corner. My aunt would voice her anger at the speed we were travelling; my uncle replying that the new tyres were at fault. He loved driving fast and the police couldn't stop him. After he thundered past they would set off in pursuit, but it was always a pointless and dispiriting exercise. Traffic cars in those days were two-litre Rovers; my uncle would be driving three-litre GTs. It was the Bonnie and Clyde scenario: that duo repeatedly avoided capture partly because they used thirty-calibre BARs, outgunning the police, and because the vehicles they used — Ford V8s — were far faster than any available to the police.

With the Audi's headlights illuminating the road east, I was retracing his tyre tracks from fifty years ago. I revved hard through the gears as the Audi careered around corners; its engine and tyres screaming out into the night.

A voice in my head also screamed out. Why the rush? If Audrey was going to contact Dowas she would have done so before phoning me. I took my foot off the accelerator and let the car slow down to fifty.

I looked over at Mireille and said, 'Why are you here, why today?'

She had her window down, the incoming breeze sweeping her shoulder-length blonde hair across her face. 'My grandfather told me that if I was ever in trouble I was to see you, and you alone. He said my father trusted you above all other men and that you would protect me.'

'So far, you've been protecting me,' I said.

'The night is young,' she said smiling, as she swept her hair back.

'The night is young,' I repeated and smiled. It was the first time I really saw her father in her. It was a phrase he said often, especially during the days of combat in the Falklands. Doubtless, it originated with her grandfather.

She began her story. How, whilst out running this morning in Inverness, she came across what appeared to be an attempted kidnapping.

As she approached, a man drew a handgun on her. She was only alive because the weapon jammed. She knocked him down, took the gun off him, cleared the round and shot both him and his partner — who had already fired on her.

Then came the bad news: both men were dead, and when she checked, both were carrying police warrant cards.

I slowed down even more for the last stage of the journey, allowing Mireille to tell me in her own time what took place after this. She had driven south on the A9 whilst the woman, Amanda Jeffries, tried to call several people at her work in South Queensferry, but all her calls had gone on to answer phone. She was at the start of a week's holiday, but she was desperate to get there as fast as possible. When they crossed the Forth Road Bridge detour signs were in place around where she worked. Jeffries, who had been reasonably calm for the last hour of the journey effectively broke down, certain that something terrible had happened.

'I told her I knew someone who could help,' Mireille said, 'but she went back to trying her phone again. She kept running through the four names of her team members leaving a message for each one. She then asked me to drive her to a friend's house in Trinity in Edinburgh. I waited there with her for a few hours until I was certain she was okay. She let me take her car to find you. I drove from Trinity to the individual stations before eventually ending up at Fettes.'

The moment Mireille said South Queensferry I knew the whole thing: all the murders today were connected. When I asked her to list off the names of Jeffries' team members, Dr Andrew Thompson was the first name she gave me. Of the five-man team, Amanda Jeffries was the only one left alive, and she would hold a key piece to the puzzle. But how big a piece did Dowas hold?

I parked up a hundred yards from Dowas's home. I would have felt better if I had had a search warrant, but it was too risky. The men Mireille had killed were probably carrying fake warrant cards, but if police officers were involved ...

*

Dowas's house was a two-storey villa surrounded by a large garden. The lights were on, but there was no answer at the front door. We tried round the back; surprisingly, the back door was unlocked.

Mireille waited at the door while I went inside. I walked along the hallway, and went quickly into the sitting room. The walls of this main room were wood panelled and on them were a number of military photographs of Dowas with members of his regiment. Off the hall was a large room that had been converted into a bedroom. It was obvious from the way the room was laid out that Dowas had nursed his wife here. I could see it; the long days and long nights spent sitting at her side, holding her hand, trying to take the pain away. This was a room of pain, and with that pain being unnecessary, it was, then, the Torture Room. Pain combated with caring, compassion and love, although in the end Dowas was always going to lose that battle. On the bedside table stood a thick glass vase, and in it were flowers — roses. They still stood upright, but the water had run out and they were dry and brittle. They were almost sepia; the stalks and leaves a grey green, the stiff rose petals brown. I looked closer. They had probably been yellow, but now, without water, they had turned into camouflage: brown and green, colours of war.

There was too much pain here. I backed out of the room, closing the door behind me as I learned to do, and had done, throughout my life. I would never stay in those rooms, those memories. I had learned how to sever them, by severing all emotions — severing all that was human.

After looking around the rest of the ground floor I climbed the main staircase. At the end of the hall was a door that led into Dowas's office. It was a big room with large windows and was dominated by a mahogany desk which sat by the window facing north. The desk was fashioned with a green leather worktop. A writer's desk, and Dowas had been writing. One word, 'Enough', on one page of A4. It lay in the centre of the desk, alongside it a hunting knife. A framed photograph also sat on the desk. The photo was of a good-looking woman in her forties, presumably his wife, dressed in a pink jersey and a loose, flowing lavender skirt. Going by her hair and skirt there had been a strong breeze at the time the photograph had been taken, but I was more interested in what lay in the background. A steep slope of sand around 25-feet wide.

I quickly looked in the other rooms; then left through the back door and, along with Mireille, returned to the car.

8

2.25 A.M.

Gullane Bents was to the west of Gullane Bay. Prior to his stint as coach and then manager of Rangers in the early seventies, Jock Wallace, whilst on a picnic with his family, discovered a steep slope in the sand dunes. He took his players there for pre-season training. Wallace's training methods reflected his own military training. Remembered as one of the hardest football managers ever, he forced his players repeatedly up and down that slope until most either threw up or collapsed. The players named the slope Murder Hill, and many believe it gave the Rangers players superior fitness and was the reason for them winning the league title in 1975, bringing to an end Celtic's nine-year reign as league champions.

Although it was after two, the beach was well lit by the full moon which had finally surfaced from behind the clouds. It was like the half-light of dusk in the old Hammer horror movies: you could see clearly, but there was a spectral quality to everything. My feet sank into the soft sand. I could smell the sea and the salt in the air. I loved the sea, the vastness and the purity of it. It was calm and the waves gently lapped up the beach. Off to the east, something lay in the sand. At first sight it looked like a big clump of seaweed. As we walked closer, we saw it was a body.

From the condition of his skin Dowas hadn't been in the water long; maybe as little as two hours. With the soft sand and the tide coming in there would be no actual footprints, no signs that two or three men had taken him into the water and held him under. They might not have done it that way; they may have dumped his body from an airboat.

I turned to see Mireille looking at Murder Hill. The expression on her face almost predatory. With her legs she could run up and down that hill all day and not even break sweat.

'Let's go,' I said.

Mireille turned and motioned to Dowas. 'You're just going to leave him?'

I looked at Dowas and then back in the direction of the car and said, 'I'll call it in, but we need to get to Jeffries.'

On the way back to the car I told Mireille what I'd found in Dowas's house and that I didn't believe his one-word suicide note had been written of his own accord. I wasn't buying any of it. I'd known men like Dowas. They didn't quit until the job was done, and Dowas would know that when a cover-up is involved, you don't go after the individuals to prevent it from happening again; you go after the system that allowed it to happen in the first place. He would have wanted an effective deterrent so no one else went through the same unnecessary suffering as his wife, and would have ploughed all his energy and money into Hall's organization. It was still in its infancy; he would have known he could make a difference.

I made a quick stop at Dowas's house. On my way out I switched my mobile on and called Karen. I was walking back to the car when she answered. I said, 'Karen, go outside for a smoke and phone me.'

'I *am* outside having a smoke. Are you okay, Boss? What happened at Wester Hailes? A report has come in about five men killed and—.'

I stopped walking. 'Five?'

'Three were found dead at the scene, two declared DOA at the Royal, and a sixth is critical in intensive care – he's not expected to last the night.'

I looked over at Mireille waiting patiently in the passenger seat. She looked like a young Catherine Deneuve.

'You still there, Boss?'

'Yeah ... Karen, I need to know what else has been happening. Any other murders?'

'Not doctors, not Edinburgh, but two off-duty officers were found shot dead this morning in Inverness.'

'Anything else?' I started walking again.

'There's a lot of people want to speak to you about Wester Hailes and that organization based in Lauder Road, UPREC, including the Superintendent. We've all left–' her voice trailed off; I could hear snippets of conversations as people passed in the background.

She came back on, her voice almost a whisper. 'There's a score of voicemails and texts left for you. I think Gavin must have missed his flight. Did that girl turn up?'

An image of Gavin surrounded by women in a nightclub in Las Americas flashed through my mind. I reached the car and opened the driver's door. 'Karen, I don't have time to explain, but the body of a former army major, Stephen Dowas, is lying on Gullane Bents just down from Murder Hill. His throat wasn't cut but I think the group that killed him is responsible for all the murders. Get a team down there now.'

I switched off the phone. I had wanted to tell Karen that I thought the murders might be an attempt to destroy UPREC, but it seemed too far-fetched. Or was it? People were more knowledgeable than they were in the past. The Internet had brought a new-found level of awareness to the general public.

The power of the doctor was slowly being eroded, patients were beginning to find their voice — they wanted to have a say in their care, in their future. They were challenging things now that in the old days they wouldn't have thought of doing. Although change was slow, UPREC was a giant step forwards in empowering patients that many in power in the NHS would want to avoid. Audrey Hall was right; hospitals want sheep that are easy to manage. Yet the chances of her organization surviving weren't great. Why risk going to such lengths to bury it?

*

As soon as we had cleared Gullane and were on the main road back to Edinburgh I turned to Mireille, 'What else did Jeffries say?'

'When we were driving, she was a wreck, really upset, but when we arrived at her friend's house, and she felt secure, she began to calm down and what she said made more sense.'

'Who's the friend?'

'I don't know, she was away on holiday. Amanda had her own set of keys.'

'What did she talk about?'

'The program she'd been working on. The advanced program designed for a virtual reality headset. Do you think it could be related to what's going on?'

'It is related, but I don't know how yet,' I said.

'She did explain it to me, though I didn't understand everything. According to Amanda there is a gate between the conscious and unconscious minds. This gate is controlled by the gatekeeper, who won't let any information coming from the conscious through the gate to the unconscious unless he accepts it as true. The gatekeeper works on logic and he protects the framework of logic and our belief system. He exists to maintain order, to effectively keep us sane. Amanda said there were two ways to bypass the gatekeeper.'

I said, 'I think I know one way. A long time ago I went to see a hypnotist at the Festival. It was stage hypnosis, a comedy show, exhibitionists getting up on stage, maybe a few of them went into a light trance, the rest just played along. The real action, however, was on the seat next to me. The girl I was with passed out until the hypnotist broke the trance of the volunteers on stage. We went to see him after the show, turned out Jane was a somnambulist, one of the two percent of the population who go into such a deep hypnotic trance they have absolutely no recollection of what happened during it. Well, this guy was desperate for her to come to his future shows so he could hypnotise her. She was, apparently, the perfect subject. The gate that Jeffries is talking about can be bypassed with deep hypnosis. Messages get through to the unconscious without the subject being aware, so they are not challenged by the conscious mind.'

Mireille said, 'That's right; she spoke of that kind of hypnosis. The other way is in life-or-death situations: people do things, feats of superhuman strength, because they don't have time to think. The primordial survival instinct takes over completely; actions are directed by the unconscious. The conscious mind, and along with it, the gatekeeper, aren't engaged in the mental process.'

I said, 'Yes, in immediate survival situations the conscious mind, logic, will slow us down. It's pure flight or fight, the unconscious will act where the conscious will calculate — as soon as we start to think about it we place limits on ourselves.'

100

Mireille nodded and said, 'Amanda was using hypnosis and life-or-death situations purely as examples to show me that the gate could be bypassed. She said I had to be open to the idea before I could accept it might work.'

'What might work?'

'The Gatekeeper program. A program specifically designed to access the unconscious and tap its power. Something that will affect everyone, something that doesn't require hypnosis or life-or-death situations. They used a virtual reality headset because the part of the brain responsible for processing images can't tell the difference between what is vividly imagined and reality. With the headset they found they could not only deceive the gatekeeper but temporarily bypass him and tap the power of the unconscious. They started to increase its effectiveness by adding a series of subliminal images into the program, but although the results improved, the changes remained short-lived. Then they began work on a program which would in theory allow them to re-program the gatekeeper.'

'How far did they get?'

'She said they'd identified a code that allowed total control of the gatekeeper.'

'If they'd found a code ... are you aware of the implications?'

'On the positive side, I know it has an impact on physical performance — increasing speed and strength. Aside from sports, I imagine there would be a demand for slimming applications. Instead of forced diets, someone would spend brief periods on the headset. I guess it could regulate appetite, speed up metabolism, that sort of thing.'

I braked suddenly as we approached a bend.

I said, 'You *know* it has an impact?'

'She had a headset with one of the early programs — Gatekeeper 9 — with her. Advances were so quick that most of the programs were superseded by newer programs before they could be fully tested. Gatekeeper 9 underwent no testing whatsoever. Technically, I should only have been programmed with it if I was being kept under observation, but after what happened in the car park ... besides Gatekeeper 9 was primarily to boost confidence, but she said it would have an effect on my physical performance. It did. I felt the increase almost immediately; it felt like I was twice as strong. But Amanda felt the confidence factor might have inflated the actual increases in strength and speed, which she estimated would be around 30 percent.'

'How long did you have the headset on for?'

'Less than a minute.'

'Why didn't she use it on herself?'

'She said it would conflict with her personality. Gatekeeper 9 was specifically designed for athletes. She said it was one of the reasons why the code was such a breakthrough. It got so deep, personalities could be altered by it. It overrode all past conditioning and set a new blueprint for the unconscious. That was a step too far for me; I couldn't relate to what she was telling me.'

'How long does the effect last?'

'With the master code she said the programming would be permanent, unless there was re-programming. As Gatekeeper 9 didn't have the coding Amanda felt the effects would start fading after a week, with a gradual decline over a few months. But she wasn't certain; it was more supposition on her part than anything else.'

'The master program, the one that took control of the gatekeeper, what is it called?'

'Gatekeeper 17.'

We had to get hold of Jeffries. In spending so much of her life training, Mireille's view of the Gatekeeper project was blinkered. She had missed something. I started to speak, thinking out loud as I processed this new information. 'If they've developed a program to gain direct access to the unconscious then they have access to the body's inner pharmacy, which could affect everything – potentially every disease. The body can produce its own killer cells which attack cancerous cells. Theoretically, if this program can do what Jeffries is saying then it could not only control the production of killer cells but direct them to attack specific tumours.

'Four men were found murdered in South Queensferry. We thought the target had been the medical doctor, Thompson, and that the others had just got in the way. We were meant to think that Thompson and a number of doctors murdered today in Edinburgh were the targets. But they weren't. They were the cover; they were the misdirection. We followed a trail of cut-open throats and Avenger masks.

'The target was the entire team at South Queensferry. Gatekeeper 17 was the target, destroy it and everyone associated with it, and set a grief stricken ex-SAS Major up for it. The one problem they had was Amanda Jeffries. When they found out she was on holiday, they had to either make her disappear, or take her by force to South Queensferry and kill her in the house with Thompson and the rest of his team. The latter was the obvious choice. Your intervention upset everything.'

Mireille shook her head and said, 'But why destroy something that could theoretically end cancer and other serious illnesses? Who would want to do that?'

'Every hour 12 million quid is spent on the National Health Service in the UK. Can you imagine how much of that 12 million is spent on medication? And that's not even taking into account private healthcare. Try and imagine the amount of money spent on drugs around the world in an hour. We can't, it's too much; you could go mad thinking about it. Wars are started for a fraction of the cost.'

'Are you saying pharmaceutical companies are behind this?'

'Companies within the pharmaceutical industry and private healthcare would have the most to lose, but that doesn't mean they are involved.'

We were back on the A1, a long straight road in front of us. I turned to look at Mireille, 'I've seen this kind of work before. We won't find out who's behind it. On the ground it will be teams of specialists, mercenaries, ex-military, maybe ex-Special Forces: two, three and five-man teams, who will have no idea who they are working for. They are paid to not ask questions.'

I stopped talking at that point, but I couldn't stop thinking: the team at South Queensferry made a mistake; they should have stopped around the time they developed Gatekeeper 9. Having the ability to build patients' confidence would have a massive positive effect as far as boosting immune function and triggering healing processes within the body. They would have probably got away with that, but where Hall's database was a step towards empowering patients, Gatekeeper 17 was a cataclysmic leap. The change was too shocking, too sudden, and would decimate private healthcare and effectively destroy the vast pharmaceutical industry. Had the team at South Queensferry been so focused on killing cancer and other illnesses that they had missed the bigger picture, or were they simply naive when it came to what people will do to protect their own interests? As Audrey had said, you just can't override human nature.

Yet it appeared Gatekeeper 17 had the potential to do precisely that. Amanda Jeffries had been talking about a program that in less than a minute could permanently change deep-set beliefs in the mind. It was effectively brainwashing. I didn't doubt the positive intentions of Dr Thompson's team but they were creating something that could be exploited. Was there anything the criminal underworld or the military would not do to get their hands on the program?

I took some comfort in acknowledging that criminals would not go to such lengths to cover up their actions. As for the military, the likelihood is that they would have gone in and seized all data relating to the project for reasons of national security. They would not need to kill anyone in the process, unless they were concerned that members of the research team could be compromised, and key information extracted.

What about the involvement of the two police officers in Inverness? Why hadn't they been identified as firearms officers? If they were off-duty, why were they carrying handguns? Were they working to the same end as the killers in Edinburgh by delivering Amanda Jeffries to South Queensferry alive? If so, who was giving the orders?

'They won't have tracked her, will they?' Mireille asked.

'What?'

'Amanda, will they have tracked her?'

I looked at Mireille. 'I think they might have. And if they have, and are still there, we'll be dealing with trained professionals, not the amateurs from earlier. I don't suppose there's any point in asking you to get out and let me handle this.'

She smiled. 'You're not going to call for backup, are you?'

I couldn't risk it, even though I was all too aware of the vast gulf between hardened violent criminals and elite soldiers. The Peterhead prison riot in '87 had gone on for five days when the SAS were dispatched to bring it to an end and secure the release of the sole hostage. Armed with four-foot wooden batons the SAS team wrapped the whole thing up in six minutes.

'We can't trust anyone now,' I said quietly.

9

3.20 A.M.

Trinity was in the north side of the city. The house Mireille
directed me to, however, was not in Trinity as such. It was
almost in Granton and it sat in its own grounds. I must have
driven past it a hundred times and never even realized it was
there. The house stood alone and was hidden by a large group
of trees. It had an enormous circular drive which curled
through the front garden. No cars around, which meant
nothing. If they were waiting for Mireille to return they would
not park here. We drove around the outlying area for a few
minutes and noticed nothing out of the ordinary other than a
white Range Rover parked about three hundred yards away.
It stood out because it was parked on the road alongside a
house that had an empty driveway. There could have been a
hundred reasons for not parking in the drive, but, as Mireille
pointed out, it was the same year and model as the one used
in Inverness that morning. It also had darkened, not tinted,
windows: you couldn't see what was inside. We parked on the
street down from it and walked back to Jeffries' friend's house,
taking up a position at the side of a hedge where we could
observe the windows.

I asked Mireille if she still had the handgun from this
morning. Combat trousers have deep pockets covering the
side of the thigh. From one she produced a Glock 19
Compact. She'd taken guns from both men but left the other
gun with Jeffries. She offered to hand over the Glock; I shook

my head. I had been a marksman with an SLR but I had always been a poor shot with a handgun.

'Where did you learn to use that?' I asked, motioning towards the Glock.

'In and around Rabun County, Georgia. You know, where they filmed *Deliverance*. My grandfather sent me over there for a year when I turned eighteen.'

'You learn to fight there as well?'

'A little, but most of it Grandpapa taught me.'

A light went on in a room on the ground floor. I said, 'Was he 3 PARA?'

'Originally Queen's Own Cameron Highlanders, then the Fifth Parachute Battalion, then 2 PARA.'

'He still alive?'

'I lost him in April.'

I found myself going back to Major Robertson's funeral again. I had spoken to Mireille's grandfather briefly but I hadn't known he had been in The Regiment. 2 PARA was originally formed from volunteers from Scottish Regiments, primarily the Cameron Highlanders, during the Second World War.

There were now two lights on in the house but there was no sign of movement. We decided to go in through the back and made our way around to the eight-foot stone wall; Mireille scaling the wall with ease. Sitting astride the top she reached down and pulled me up. Although I'd seen her strength in Wester Hailes, feeling it was quite a different matter. I was propelled upwards. From the top we both swung our legs around and jumped down on to the edge of the lawn and then ran low across the garden.

When we reached the porch entrance I was gasping for breath.

Mireille looked at me and whispered, 'You okay?'

I nodded initially but then shook my head. Eventually my breathing slowed, I tried the handle. Locked.

The door had a sturdy wooden frame, but the panels were glass and through them I could see the stronger inner door to the house was open. There was a light on in the room the porch led into — presumably the kitchen. If we broke through the glass door, it would be heard inside and we still had to cover around twelve feet before making it through the inner door. Without knowing the number of men inside the risk was high. I looked around to see Mireille standing a few feet back looking up at the sloping roof.

I moved back to her viewpoint and, in the early light just before dawn, looked at an open skylight in the middle of the slated roof. I whispered, 'You think you can get in there?'

Her eyes studied the back wall. The house had three floors; then there was the sloping roof to contend with. She looked at me and nodded.

We decided that I would break through the back porch door exactly two minutes after she had gained access through the skylight.

Using the drain pipe and window ledges she quickly scaled the back wall. The roof wasn't quite as simple, but she made it. I began counting the moment she disappeared out of sight.

I stood by the porch door and considered what would happen if things didn't go according to plan. Everything was dependent upon Mireille navigating three floors to be outside the kitchen door in less than two minutes — at which point I would kick the porch door in — providing the diversion, allowing her to enter the room and get the drop on the occupants.

When I reached 35 seconds the gunfire started. It was too late to look for a weapon, I had to move. I put everything into a front kick; the lock gave way, along with about five panes of glass. Throwing the door wide open I ran the twelve feet to the main back door and was going through it when I heard two shots, felt a tug on my left side, then ran straight into someone. We both hit the floor at the same time; I heard what sounded like a handgun skidding across the floor. The man I'd run into was big. He was also young, and he was on me in a second, hitting me with two short hooks on the left side of my jaw. I tasted metal as my teeth, and numerous fillings, took the jarring impact. Instinctively I grabbed his wrists and we rolled on the floor. He tried to use his weight advantage, I brought my right elbow across hitting him on the cheekbone — a glancing blow. I was breathing heavily. As much as I tried to prevent it he rolled me on to my back. What little strength I had left was used holding on to his wrists. I needed to use my fists but with him on top I had no leverage. He was pressing down on me. My left side felt numb. I struggled to breathe. His face was right next to mine. I could feel his fingers fold around my throat. He was smiling. My deltoids cried out in pain.

Suddenly he was off me. I watched as he was lifted up in the air, like he had been jettisoned out of an airlock into deep space, the expression on his face going through a range of emotions in a second: dominance, to incredulity, to fear. He was so big I couldn't see who was behind him, but I recognized Mireille's tanned forearm folded across his windpipe. His face draining of blood. As he lost consciousness she let him fall to the ground, then taking a step forward extended her right hand to me. I reached up, took hold of it and was hauled to my feet.

'In here,' Mireille said. She leant down, grabbed the big man's collar and dragged him through into the kitchen. It was one of those kitchens where the family would congregate at meal times; a big square room with an Aga cooker, a giant oak table and chairs dominating the centre. To the side lay an unmoving man in his early forties. She pointed at him as she dumped the big man alongside him, and said, 'He's unconscious. I'm going to look for Amanda.'

As she went through the rooms I found a roll of thick parcel tape in a drawer. Pulling their arms behind them, I taped each man's wrists together, then did the same with their ankles. As an afterthought I taped over their mouths. I went over to the sink and filled the basin with cold water. She had left two men lying unconscious in the kitchen; I wondered how many she had killed upstairs.

I stood above the big man and poured the entire basin of water over his face. I returned to the sink and filled the basin for the second, older man. Within two minutes both of them had regained consciousness.

Mireille half-ran into the kitchen and went straight over to them. She lifted the big man into a sitting position, then ripped off the tape covering his mouth.

'WHERE IS SHE?' she yelled.

He tried to suppress a smile but he couldn't stop himself.

My legs had been shaky up to this point, but I suddenly felt a surge of anger. I stepped in and repeated the question, this time whipping the barrel of the handgun I'd found in the porch, a Browning Hi-Power, across his face. His cheek opened up like a burst orange, blood spraying from the wound.

He looked up at me and smiled. I put the safety on, and lifting my jacket, slotted the gun between the waist of my trousers and the small of my back. I had decided I could do more damage with my fists — this had become personal. But I was too slow. Mireille was already on him, pulling him face down on the floor. After breaking the tape binding his ankles, she moved to his side, slammed her right foot down on the back of his left knee, raised his lower leg towards her, and with either end of his left foot in each hand, swivelled at the waist, employing her entire body weight she wrenched his foot against the joint. I winced, not certain if the sound of shattering bones and snapping tendons was coming from his ankle, knee, or both. His scream was terrible. I had heard the sound too often. It is the sound a victim makes: a cry of agonising pain and despair and it sent an electric shock up my spine. Mireille didn't seem to hear it. With barely a pause she repeated the move with his right leg. With the crunching of bones his scream this time was even worse.

The girl was capable of anything now, and I wasn't going to be able to stop her even if I wanted to. She moved on to the other man, ripping the tape off his mouth and ankles, but before she could pick him up, he shouted, 'WHITE RANGE ROVER! KEYS ARE ON THE TABLE!'

Mireille spun around, grabbed the keys, stopped to look at me for a second, then headed towards the front door. I couldn't think with the big man screaming. There was no point in trying to tape his mouth so I leant down and threw a hard, straight right to the side of his jaw. The screaming stopped as he slumped onto his side. As I straightened up, the other man spoke, this time his words were calm and measured.

'You'll be Boyle, then. I heard about you when I was at Hereford. Last of the boy soldiers, you went on to become the youngest sergeant ever in 3 PARA, Butcher Boy Boyle of

Mount Longdon. I heard you're a big man with the bayonet. You never gave those lads a chance—.'

'Like you gave the girl?'

'I had nothing to do with that,' he said.

'Of course not.'

'You're over your head in this one, Boyle. You're too late; the whole thing is tied up. You've got nothing on us except a body in the back of a car.'

I pulled out an evidence bag from my inside jacket pocket and from it the hunting knife.

His eyes widened.

I said, 'I destroyed the fake suicide note.'

He said, 'So? What are you going to do? No one will believe you.'

'I know, and they would believe you if you told them Dowas paid you to commit the murders. You think I'm going to let you ruin that man's reputation and destroy the organization he's been financing.'

'You can't do anything else. There is no other motive, you have no evidence. It's all gone.'

'I don't need you to have a motive.' I drew the Browning, switching the safety off as I did so. 'You served in the Middle East, you're suffering from post-traumatic stress.'

I heard the front door slam shut. Mireille.

I said, 'You should thank me. She'd break every bone in your body before killing you.'

I took a step forward and shot him three times in the chest. As Mireille burst into the room I shot the other man in the head.

Mireille screamed, 'WHY! Why did you do that? I wanted ... they'd tortured her before killing her!'

'You're too young for this kind of killing,' I said quietly.

113

She stared at me, then began pacing around the room. Eventually she sat on one of the chairs at the table. I sat on the chair across from her. A minute passed in silence.

She said, 'The Range Rover was empty except for Amanda. I searched the house; there's no sign of the headset. That's it then, isn't it?'

I nodded. Another minute passed. She was looking down at the table when she said quietly, 'After the funerals I started having nightmares. I became afraid of the dark. Then one night Grandpapa told me a story that my father told him. It was not long after my father arrived at The Regiment. He'd set the whole thing up beforehand. The platoon was woken in the middle of the night to go on a run. They dressed in combats and then were driven forty miles from camp. When the run started no one but my father had any idea where they were.'

As I listened to her, the events of the last few hours were forgotten and I saw the little girl who had been at her parents' funeral, sitting up in bed listening intently to her grandfather.

'My father was at the front and he led the platoon to an old disused swimming pool. He took them up the ladders to the high board and asked for a volunteer to jump off. It was December, pitch black and minus two degrees. No one could see whether there was water in the pool, and if there was, whether it was covered by a thick layer of ice. My father was standing at the front and not one of the platoon would look him in the eye. They all stood unmoving, then there was a surge from the back of the board, soldiers were being pushed to the side, someone was moving to the front and he thought it would be a senior soldier, a corporal or sergeant. But it was a seventeen-year-old that bulldozed his way forwards, running the last few steps and launching himself off the edge into darkness.

'That was the first time he saw you, and he said you were always like that, always fearless, always taking the initiative. After Grandpapa told me that story he showed me pictures of you and my father and the other men in The Regiment. I was never afraid of the dark after that.'

She raised her head and looked directly at me. 'I grew up listening to my father's stories, retold by my grandfather. I grew up listening to stories about you.'

'Those stories were from around forty years ago.'

'My father said you were the best soldier he ever saw.'

'I was the worst.'

'No. I know all about that. You had been blown clean off your feet by a mortar shell. When the medics finally got to you after the battle, you had five shrapnel wounds and concussion. It was three days before you could hear anything. Anyone else would have stayed down, but not you, you got up and charged with the rest of them. You had no idea your SLR had been damaged by shrapnel. When it jammed, you reacted to the situation.'

'There's no excuse for what I did,' I said.

She shook her head slowly and said, 'You've forgotten; training was different in those days. It's changed so much since then.'

I looked into her grey-blue eyes for a few seconds, and nodded slowly, acknowledging what had to be done. I said, 'You need to get out of here, Mireille; you need to change your appearance and disappear.'

'Why?'

'We don't know if the police are involved. The headset's gone and with it Gatekeeper 9. It will be delivered to whoever paid these men, along with all the information they got out of Jeffries. She will have told them everything she knows about you. How many women are there like you in Scotland, let alone the Inverness area? It may take them a day or two to identify who you are, but they will. It's a certainty they will have cleaned out all the files and research info at South Queensferry. You're probably the only real evidence the Gatekeeper project ever existed.' I glanced at the ceiling, 'How many men upstairs?'

'Three, they're dead. I checked.'

'Go through their pockets. It's unlikely they'll have ID, but they'll be carrying some cash. I'll check these two.'

Five minutes later we stood and looked at the small piles of euros, US dollars and twenty pound notes sitting on the kitchen table.

'You'll need this as well.' I handed her a black baseball cap I'd found in one of the pockets.

Mireille said, 'I don't understand, they can't stop this from being developed: the use of virtual reality programs to build confidence and combat illness—.'

'Right now the interest and money is in virtual reality games. In time they will look at other areas to make money, but the development in regard to combating illness will meet with strong resistance at a number of levels. Accidents will happen, people will be threatened, pay-offs made. Whoever, whatever, is behind this won't stop until you have been tracked down. You have to disappear.'

I took out my wallet and from it a card, on which I wrote a name and address in Glasgow. I passed the card to Mireille, 'Go there and hand over the card. He'll know I sent you. He'll give you a new identity; passport, driving licence, he'll tell you everything you need to know, and he won't charge you a penny.'

'Is it that simple?' Mireille asked.

'It is if you know the right people. From now on use cash only until your new identity is established.' I added all the notes I had in my wallet to the pile on the table.

She looked at me with concern, 'What about you? They'll know you are involved.'

I said, 'I am going to disappear as well. I have plenty of ready cash stashed away. The whole thing is too big, don't trust anyone ... and your old life, forget it: it's over.'

I saw a flicker of uncertainty in her eyes. I guess it takes time to adjust to the idea of letting go of all you know. But for Mireille that time was barely a moment. She folded the banknotes and placed them in one of the many button down pockets of her trousers and pulled on the baseball cap.

I said, 'I'll need the Glock, and the keys to the Range Rover.'

She carefully placed the Glock on the table, then laid the car keys alongside it. I said, 'Now go, we need to separate and I have to clear up here. Try and avoid CCTV cameras and get to that address in Glasgow as soon as you can. Uniformed officers are out in force all over Edinburgh; if you're stopped, tell them you're heading to Calton Hill to watch the sunrise. The bus depot is in the same area, first one to Glasgow leaves around five. When you go out the front you're heading south east.' I motioned the direction with my right arm. 'Take care of yourself, Mireille.'

She stood at the door for a few seconds. I busied myself wiping down the Glock, then the hunting knife. When I looked over again, she'd gone.

I peeled the tape off both men's wrists, then managed to get the older man's prints on the knife and let it fall to the floor. I did what I could to make it look as if I'd been alone. I picked up the Glock and fired two shots into the wall behind them, one with my right hand then one with my left. I could feel my legs beginning to shake. I drew the Browning with my right, backed up to the wall and slid to the ground, the Glock in one hand, the Browning in the other.

My left side was on fire. I knew I'd been hit running in the porch, but the black shirt and my black trousers had concealed the blood. I loosened my belt and pulled back the waistband to see the blood pumping out of the wound; a red puddle forming then slowly spreading outwards across the wooden floor. The belt, tighter with the Browning tucked in the small of my back, must have been acting as a form of tourniquet up until now.

I looked over at the door where Mireille had stood a few minutes ago. Was she right; had training changed that much over the years?

I was in my first week of basic training. Every recruit in the platoon was herded into a small room. It was the first time we'd come into contact with an officer and we saw it as being respite from the Platoon Sergeant screaming at us on the parade ground. The Captain smiled and asked us to sit, introduced himself, and then asked us what we thought our primary task was as soldiers. His voice was gentle, and one of us spoke about parachuting behind enemy lines. Another began to describe peacekeeping duties in Northern Ireland.

The officer savagely interrupted the recruit. 'KILL THE ENEMY! Not peacekeeping, but to KILL the enemy, whoever that is, THAT is your job, the one that comes before all others.'

To the others the shock impact of his words was greater because he'd deliberately put them at ease; he'd lulled them into a false sense of security that the world was a safe place, that they would never have to fire the powerful SLRs — the self-loading rifles that would become our personal weapons — at men, only at black and orange paper targets of men.

A lot of recruits dropped out of training that week. Not on that day; they left it a couple of days. When asked they would say, 'I miss my family' or 'I'm worried my girlfriend will leave me.' But that speech was the reason. They had suddenly realized that there was a cost to the life of adventure promised in the Army TV adverts. They wanted the security of life in Civvy Street, the security of a warm bed at night; not having to think about how many men they had killed that day.

I didn't though; I never gave it a second thought.

Of the land battles that took place in the Falklands War in '82 the one that most people will think of is Goose Green, where 2 PARA lost their CO. However the battle that had the fiercest fighting, and where more Paras lost their lives, took place two weeks later. Mount Longdon was a barren hill fully exposed to fierce winds. The Argentinians that defended it were conscripts, teenagers mostly, but fifty of them had been through a commando course and were highly motivated. They were well armed with heavy machine guns and snipers. The three in the trench that I leapt into near the end of the engagement, however, were not of this group of fifty. These were boys that were half starved. Frightened boys, all crouching together at one end of the trench, their arms reaching upward. Their weapons had been thrown down. There was no danger from them. Why didn't I see it?

The ripple effect; I didn't really think much about that: the friends, the brothers, the sisters, the girlfriends. I thought about the three mothers looking at the picture of their son on the fireplace, or bedside table, just before they turn off the light. The mothers who stood in the cold wind waiting for the boats to dock. Their eyes straining as they looked for their sons on the decks of the ship. The ache in their hearts increasing as more and more troops disembark, until, finally, someone — perhaps an officer or one of the boys' friends — sees them and begins walking slowly in their direction, and with each step the ache in their heart intensifies, the pressure inside it building. Then they realize there's no one else around now, and whoever it is walking towards them won't look in their eyes. That's the moment — right then — they know, and it's the moment their hearts break. 'Your son is dead', but the mothers don't hear the words. They don't hear anything the same now. Their world has different sounds: laughter, excitement, joy, replaced by silent sounds of tears, anguish, pain and despair. I knew those sounds. I know the sound of a mother's heart breaking. I'd been hearing them break for over thirty years.

Three lives gone, three families' lives ruined. I may have chosen not to think about it, but the ripple effect continues on into the future. And what if I'd chosen to join a different regiment? What if? Had one of a hundred thousand 'what ifs' happened then no one would have jumped into that trench, or it would have been a soldier who had, at that moment at least, some ties to humanity.

There was some talk at the time, but Captain Robertson quashed it. The talk became whispers and rumours until it seemed no one knew what was true and what was imagined. I transferred to the PT Corps and was honourably discharged five years later. My police career well underway a further six years later when they had the official inquiry into the killing of prisoners in the Falklands. My name didn't come up, and my military record remained untarnished. The words of the *Daily Telegraph* editor carried as far as the *Los Angeles Times*: 'There must be some time limit beyond which it is against the public interest to pursue alleged crimes committed in war. Today, when so few adults have known war at first hand, there is a growing tendency to suppose that the moral absolutes of peacetime civilian life can be transferred to the battlefield.'

The editor only had it partially right. 'Moral absolutes of peacetime' — an illusion. There is no peacetime. There are enemies everywhere.

I wiped the blood from my mobile and called Audrey.

She answered at the third ring, 'Thank you for calling, Inspector, we are still—.'

'Audrey, I need you to record this call. Can you put me on speaker and have someone record it on their tablet or mobile?'

'Yes, I think so, hold on.'

About a minute passed before she came back on and said, 'Right; I have it on speaker, and it's being recorded.'

'Okay, this is very important. I want you to phone this number in thirty minutes and get hold of Karen Dawes or Superintendent Carol Wilson and play this message to them. But the timing is crucial, Audrey.'

'Thirty minutes. Not before,' she said.

I then gave her the number to call, my location, and my report, missing out Mireille and missing out what I knew about the Gatekeeper project and really missing out just about everything except that the target had been the team working at South Queensferry, and they'd find those responsible here; and that in addition to all the other murders they had also tortured and killed Amanda Jeffries and killed Stephen Dowas. As an afterthought I apologized to the Superintendent for losing my temper again.

I pressed the end button, noticing how badly my hand was shaking. Despite the heat in the air I was cold. With my belt loose the blood was flowing unabated. Thirty minutes would be more than enough time. It had to end here. If it didn't I'd be taken and tortured and would eventually give out information on my contact in Glasgow and the same thing would befall him ... and then they'd have Mireille.

They say your life flashes in front of you before you die. That may be the case for some, but all I could see was a mass of mistakes; things I should have done and things I wouldn't get to do. Then there was Rebecca; she was my last love, but one that remained pure and unspoiled. And there was Major Robertson's daughter. How many professional killers would be chasing her tomorrow, though? Still, dawn was breaking, she should have a full day's head start; she would make it. She had to.

Even with my back on the wall I no longer had the strength to sit upright. I slid down on my right side until my shoulder was on the floor and made an attempt to curl up in a ball. With my head on the floor I lay in silence and watched the red stream slowly flow towards the facing wall. I'd be going into hypovolemic shock soon. I was freezing. I felt my eyelids closing.

The last time I was this cold was forty years ago. I was on leave, and had spent the night in a snow hole near Voss in Norway. It was too cold to sleep and I was up early. It had been snowing through the night and fresh snow had covered all the footprints. I stood in one spot and looked around. I was in a flat clearing about forty-feet wide, surrounded by white walls of virgin snow and above them the clearest blue sky. The sun was out, but I couldn't see it. Two colours, that's all there was — white and blue — not a bird or cloud in the sky, not a mark on the snow, and not a sound. I was alone in something pure, something perfect.

PART TWO

Mireille

TWENTY-SEVEN MONTHS LATER

Friday 1.00 A.M.

A full moon lit the solitary farmhouse. Aside from the sound of crickets there was a peaceful quiet, typical of this region of Spain. Two hours' drive away, in Barcelona, the streets and nightclubs were just coming to life. Raw energy fused with testosterone and oestrogen. Alcohol flowed and dealers got rich standing on street corners. To the young in Barcelona, watching the moon was overrated; the night needed a cocktail of narcotics to make it really come alive.

Kyle Winters, lying on his stomach in between two trees, looking though the scope of his 50-calibre rifle, felt more alive than those out on the streets in Barcelona. The other four men surrounding the farmhouse felt the same way. There was one thing that the best drugs could not manufacture: closeness to death; a death dealt out by something so terrible that it triggered a trap door in the unconscious. If you fell through that door your body and mind started to betray you.

'Tell me about when you were in prison.'

Winters looked across at the man who'd spoken. It was a good sign, he decided. His spotter's hands hadn't stopped shaking but at least he was talking.

Three hours earlier:

They were chasing the sunset. The noise was immense inside the body of the helicopter. The man in the navy suit shouted as he read off the details of the job.

'Target is twenty-one-year-old female. Five ten. 165 pounds. Shoulder-length blonde hair according to university matriculation card.' A photograph was passed around. 'We don't have anything more, other than her location — an old farmhouse in Andorra. You will be dropped at this point,' he said, stabbing the map with a chunky finger, 'twenty-three miles from her location, where a jeep will be waiting.' His finger drew a short line on the map. 'Proceed to this point, where you will leave the vehicle and make the final three miles on foot. This is a high-priority target wanted for questioning. You are advised — under no circumstances — to engage at close quarters until she's been incapacitated.'

With that, the speaker nodded to Sullion then made his way to the cockpit.

Jack Sullion looked over at the tall, freckled Irishman. 'So, it's a disabling shot, Sean. Knee: either one. Use your deer rifle. We want her in one piece. The rest of us will provide cover and engage if the target becomes a threat.'

Sean O'Connor stood up. 'This makes no sense, boss. A twenty-year-old student?' He held up the photo and pointing to her face, said, 'She looks like that French actress.'

His spotter, Chris Hughes, stood alongside him and spat the words out: 'We've been taken off a job that we've been working on all week, for what? This is bullshit! Who is this girl?'

Pollock joined in. 'What is going on, and who's the suit? Who's he working for?'

Everyone was speaking over each other. Winters remained silent. He had worked under Sullion's command on enough jobs to know something was coming ... and he wasn't going to like it.

The noise inside the cabin was so loud it almost drowned out the noise of the engine and whirring blades. Finally, Sullion lost his patience and bellowed, 'The girl is wanted for questioning over the Hot Moon killings.'

Anyone at the top of their game, especially in the military, had an inbuilt confidence, a sense of indestructibility. Yet as soon as the words were uttered, those huge egos fell silent. Every contractor who had worked in Europe knew about the Hot Moon killings in Edinburgh. They all knew that a five-man team of ex-special forces had been wiped out — supposedly by one female.

There was a lack of eye contact as O'Connor and his spotter sat down. Even the blades of the helicopter seemed muffled. Barely one word was spoken until they reached the drop-off point.

Winters studied the building 500 metres in front of him. The moon lit the entire area. He completed a full sweep before glancing over at his spotter, Jason Pollock, and said, 'I thought I told you about that.'

'We all knew you'd been off the circuit for a few years, but no one had the guts to ask you. What was it?'

The former inmate and SAS sergeant shook his head slowly. 'A fight that went too far.'

'How long?'

'Supposed to be two years but everyone I knew thought that was me away for good. When I got there I thought I'd never get out.'

'Why?'

''Cos I was surrounded by gangsters, wannabe gangsters and drug dealers. It's a different world. You live a different life, constantly watching your back. You trust no one. Bottom line: you've no friends in prison; you're on your own. And you've got to watch everything you do and say. You can't be seen to be weak. They're like a pack of hyenas. If they see weakness they'll jump on it and use it to their advantage. After a couple of months in there I was beginning to lose my grip on things ... life itself.'

'Prison life?'

'No, *my* life; where I was going. All that is respected is force. I was surrounded by violence every day. There was always the constant threat of violence. It got to the stage where I just needed to batter someone.'

'A display of force?'

'To relieve tension ... a release. It's very hard to keep violence under control with all that hate in your face the whole time. But I knew, once I started, there'd be no stopping. It would get to the point where I'd end up killing someone else. I could see it happening. I could have ended up being sent to a mental hospital. I suppose that was my greatest fear. Then I got a new cell mate. This guy was down for six years. Thing was, we came from the same town, we both knew the same people. It didn't make us friends but we watched out for each other. He was massive, a powerlifter, strong man stuff. And he was a hard bastard. Everyone in the block knew that if they messed with one of us, they would have to deal with the other as well.'

'And that made the difference? That's how you got through it?'

'In part, but that's not the reason I'm telling you about him. He had all these scars on his face: nose totally busted, jaw had been reset. He was in his late twenties and he had false teeth. I thought he'd either been in a car wreck or had taken a hell of a beating from a gang. One night, after lights-out, I asked him about it. Turned out the beating was from one man; the cop who put him away. The things he said 'bout him. He hated that guy. But the whole thing made absolutely no sense.'

'How do you mean?'

''Cos he was frightened of him. He didn't want to admit it, but you could tell. And here's the thing, the cop had used only his fists. You would have had to have seen this guy's face to understand. It didn't seem possible that one man could inflict that kind of damage without a weapon, even just to get the better of him. There was no way what he was telling me about this cop could be true. Then he told me his name ... and everything made perfect sense.' Winters paused for a couple of seconds. 'Boyle.'

Pollock stared at him. '*The* Boyle? The police detective who was found with that five-man team?'

'Yep. That girl in there, she wasn't working alone, and all the stuff she's supposed to be responsible for was probably the work of Boyle. You must have heard of him.'

'Only that he was found with the other bodies. One bullet wound. So the stories in the press were all about keeping his name clean?'

'Torture and executions took place in that house. They weren't going to drag a dead cop's name through the mud unless they had to. He used to be 3 PARA. I heard a lot of stories 'bout him. Put two of our men down.'

'Since when did SAS get into brawls?'

'He didn't give them much choice. Hell, I don't even know if there was a reason. It was just Boyle's way. He was a brutal son of a bitch. He put them down hard; both of them were unconscious. He knelt down beside them and, one after the other, lifted their right hands and snapped their trigger fingers.'

'What!'

'Broke the bones, snapped the tendons.'

Winters looked at the man again. The hands that had been shaking were now steady. The dark mood had lifted in the realization that the girl in the cottage was more myth than monster.

Winter's story about his former cellmate was accurate, but he knew he had stretched the truth when it came to the breaking of fingers. The idea had come from hearing that one of the SAS troopers had broken his knuckles on Boyle's forehead.

The story he wanted to tell his spotter would really have put him at ease, but he was unable to because it had taken place in the Falklands. Then Boyle's age would have been out in the open. Winters tried to convince himself that a man around sixty could still cut the mustard, but it wasn't working. He felt that the former sergeant in 3 PARA would have been little more than a spectator at that house in Edinburgh. What really scared him was the rumour that the girl in the farmhouse opposite had killed Boyle as well as the five-man team.

Winters had no intention of waiting for the Irishman to take the first shot. He had made up his mind as soon as they heard who the target was. It was payback time. Three of the men killed in that house had been former SAS and he had known all of them. He'd go for her legs. She might survive if they got a tourniquet on her quick enough, but it was unlikely. They had a lot of ground to cover and a 50-calibre round would most likely tear her leg clean off.

*

O'Connor felt uncomfortable with the deer rifle tucked into his shoulder. He was used to relaxing when he was out hunting. This was not the way things should be.

'D'ya reckon she's in there?' Hughes whispered.

'I don't reckon anything. Everything about this is wrong. A knee shot from 500 metres? You don't kneecap someone to question them. She'll be taken for interrogation, then killed. We don't even have extradition with Spain. If we get discovered by the locals we're in deep shite.' O'Connor continued to focus his attention on the front of the farmhouse. 'I ever mention my buddy, Adam Fleming?'

'The big fella?'

'Yeah. You know he was one of the Hot Moon team?'

'What? You didn't tell me that.'

'First thing I heard about it was his wife calling me to let me know his funeral was at the end of the week. She got upset on the phone; asked if I could come to see her. So next day we're sitting across the kitchen table and she tells me it's a closed casket. She hadn't been given a reason.

'I went to the morgue and from there to the local hospital. The pathologist I was after was off sick, but there was a medical orderly who had attended the post-mortem. I caught him on his own in the lift. Aside from the 9-mil to the head, Adam's jaw had been broken in three places, cheekbone split open to the bone. He also had severe bruising around his thorax.

'The guy was really nervous. I felt he wasn't telling me everything, so I leaned on him a little. Turned out Adam's knees were shattered so badly that, had he survived, both legs would have had to have been amputated. But the orderly was still holding back. By this time I'd jammed the lift door, so we weren't going anywhere and I leaned on him a bit more. Came out that the doctors involved in the post-mortem had asked for colleagues to attend to examine the legs. 'Bout an hour later specialists started showing up, and examined the x-rays, the knees and the bruising around the back of the knees and feet. Their opinion was inconclusive: the report read that the damage to the knees had been most likely made by driving the lower leg and upper leg in opposite directions ... simultaneously. Yet the force required to bring about this level of damage was beyond the capability of two men, let alone one.'

'What are we dealing with here?'

O'Connor remained silent.

Ten minutes passed. 'How powerful is that yoke?' Hughes asked suddenly, glancing at the deer rifle.

'That's right, you've never seen this, takes a .243 Winchester round. A 90 grain round will take down a deer clean through, but it's a wee bit light compared to this.' O'Connor's right hand moved to the 50mm rifle resting by his leg.

Hughes said, 'I've got a bad feeling about this girl. I'd feel a lot better if you used the long gun.'

'You do know this was for the last job. It's specifically for penetrating armour. Do you have any notion of an idea what it will do to a human being?'

'Who says she's human?'

O'Connor laid the deer rifle to the side and hauled the Steyr HS 50 up to the firing position, placing the butt in the soft part of his shoulder.

He took out a 50mm round, brought it to his mouth and touched it to his lips. Then, with the movement he'd carried out countless times at the ranges, he placed the round in the chamber and slowly slid the bolt forward.

*

Sullion was lying in the textbook position: legs splayed, his front as flat as he could get it, his breathing smooth. This was his favourite position and he loved being able to take it from the high ground. The wide shelf on the hill lying to the east of both of his teams afforded him that luxury. He had his FNAR on its bipod and he was tucked in behind it. Through the scope he focused on the Irish contingent of O'Connor and Hughes, and then the area around Winters and Pollock. Then back to the farmhouse.

It was a good team, the best he'd ever had, and he drew confidence from it. The mission, the target, the way the mission had been handled was all wrong. The team he was working with was the only good thing about it.

In the conference room at the heliport he had listened with incredulity when the orders were passed down to him by a suit. 'It is crucial that this woman is taken alive.'

'If intel is saying she's alone, why don't you order a forced entry raid?'

'It has to be done tonight and we can't raise a sufficient number of men in time. Besides, from the information we've been given, they would most likely fail. We don't want to leave the bodies of our men in a country with whom our diplomatic ties are, shall we say, tenuous. We have to be in and out fast. It's simple: one shot; disable the target; call it in using the codes. The target, and your team, will be airborne within ten minutes.'

One shot. Sullion didn't know which of his team would shoot first, but on learning the target's identity and knowing Winters as he did, he would be odds-on favourite.

Through his scope, Sullion checked the locations of his two shooters again: all clear.

He looked at his watch, but before the time registered, his body was driven hard into the ground. The direct impact was on the small of his back but he felt it all over. He gasped as his lungs emptied of air. Even before his mind processed that someone had landed knees first on him, his survival instinct had kicked in and the fingers of his right hand wound around the tree stump in front of him. At the same time a pair of hands clasped around his forehead and pulled his head backwards. Sullion, calling on all his strength wrenched the left side of his body across in a twisting movement. He'd used this move before: it relieved pressure on the back and would throw his assailant to one side. Then he would finish them.

And it might have worked, except that the moment before he had attained the necessary leverage, the third and fourth cervical vertebrae at the top of his back separated, severing his spinal cord.

*

'D'ya hear that?' Hughes whispered.

O'Connor's attention stayed fixed on the cottage. 'What?'

'Dunno, probably nothing.'

'Eyes on the cottage. You missed the lights coming on.'

'Where?'

'They're off now. Only on for a couple of seconds.' He brought his canteen to the side of his mouth, 'Probably got up for a glass of water.'

'Could have been on a timer.'

'Doubt anyone for fifty miles knows what a timer is. Who's

going to break in round here?' he asked as he scanned the wilderness.

*

The other team had seen the light go on and off. They ceased providing cover for O'Connor after that and began taking short shifts targeting the cottage.

On his shift Pollock listened to Winters as his story unfolded.

'When I got out things were ... well, shit. You can't switch off from the threat of violence just 'cos you're out of prison. You're conditioned to a level of awareness, to being on edge. Just being around people created conflict: one side of me wanting to relax, but the self-preservation side always dominated. It was too exhausting. I'd lost my confidence. I'd lost the ability to trust anyone. Then I started meeting Charlotte.'

'Charlotte?'

'She was the main reason I managed to do my time. Didn't really know her that well, but when I went in she starting visiting me. Man, she was hot stuff. I couldn't understand it, but there she was, once a week, regular as clockwork. When I got out she made it clear she wanted more. I pushed her away.'

'I don't get it.'

'When all that you have is yourself you develop a way of coping. You have to. That girl was everything I ever wanted, but the moment it turned physical I would have become totally dependent on her. She had everything in her life sorted out, I had nothing. I was far too vulnerable to get myself involved.'

'But after a year inside—.'

'I wanted her something terrible, but I needed my

confidence back. Instead of having that desire work against me, I used it. I pushed her away in order to fight for her. I would get back to working. Then, with a bit of cash behind me, and the foundations of a life, I would contact her. I know what you're thinking, but the way I was then, any relationship was doomed to failure. This way, she kept me focused, she kept me driven. Desire can be a powerful motivator.'

Winters scanned the cottage and surrounding area. 'The theory was sound, and it did work ... for four months. For four months I was driven, but I felt so bad about it that it started to become counterproductive. I had no choice then. I had to tell her.'

'That you were using her as a weapon? I doubt there's many women who would like hearing that. What happened?'

'Said she understood, and not to hold anything back from her again ... and to hurry up.'

'She actually said that ... really? Whoa ... so you're together then? It all worked out?'

'We moved in together, and it was all going great up until five months ago. Sunday morning she left for a week's work in Brussels. I went to the gym, and got caught up in a squatting session with three of the boys. It was one of those days when you feel indestructible and can do anything. I did a Death Set.'

Pollock stared at the cottage and sighed inwardly. 'Death Set'. Two words, and with them the realization of how this story was going to end.

*

O'Connor had a passage that occasionally went through his mind while waiting to kill someone. That it was a lot to take away. A life: the hours and care and love that went into bringing up a baby, a child, a teenager. All the worry, all the time spent preparing meals, buying and mending clothes, all the teaching. So much time, so much effort went into raising a child. It was a lot to rub out; to erase the caring of parents, teachers and friends, who had given so much to bring a child to adulthood. You erased the past when you took that life, and you erased all possible futures.

But tonight he was thinking of the funeral of his dead friend and the family he had left behind. Allison was a nurse and O'Connor had always been attracted to her. Her son, Brandon, was the best behaved seven-year-old he had ever met — with one exception, when he was allowed to play with his water rifle. Then he became both mischievous and cunning, selecting ambush points and patiently waiting to catch visitors off guard. Brandon took after his father and would, in all probability, follow his footsteps into the army and the SAS.

As O'Connor turned to look at Hughes, a fine jet of fluid hit his face. He smiled, thinking he was back at Allison's. The fine jet became a geyser, then he saw the fountain of blood rushing from Hughes's neck, a grotesque look on his face as he slumped forward, and from his side, a figure in black moved towards him. His 9mm pistol forgotten, O'Connor instinctively swung the heavy rifle round in an arc, but the figure was already on him.

*

In his prime, Pollock had considered trying the sixteen-rep deep squat Death Set. But after eight reps at his maximum weight, his legs were jelly. It would be madness to carry on. On a good day he might manage one forced rep. The thought of immediately going through a further seven was absurd. He didn't want to think of the screaming and abuse he would take from the three obligatory spotters to force him on, or the vomiting or blacking out that often occurred at the end ... or the number of deaths that had been reported over the years. Up until now he'd only known one man who had the necessary combination of insanity and bottle: Willie Kennaway. Any adventure, especially if it involved danger, Willie was always the first in line. Pollock had seen him perform a Death Set in the local gym. By the seventh forced rep Willie was done. Everyone knew it, his legs had nothing left in them. But he still refused to have the heavy barbell taken off his back. His legs were trembling and about to go into spasm when Scott Donaldson, who had been watching the proceedings stepped in. He stood directly in front of Willie, looked him in the eyes then slapped him across the face. Slapping was an accepted method of triggering the release of adrenaline and frequently used during forced reps, though seldom on the face. And the last person in the world you wanted to slap you was Scott Donaldson.

Scott was a stone-mason with forearms like sides of beef. Unbeaten at arm wrestling, he made a small fortune challenging the biggest and loudest men in bars. The sheer weight of a slap from him was bad enough, but the palms of Scott's hands were thick with callouses. The sound of his right hand connecting with Willie's face was mistaken by many in the gym complex as a clap of thunder. At the squat rack no one moved, then suddenly Willie burst into life, firing like a piston, straight down, straight up. He dropped the barbell off his shoulders on to the rack pins and stormed out of the gym. He was found unconscious half-way down the corridor. Twenty minutes later he was back to his normal self, with the exception of the bruise that was beginning to dominate the left side of his face. He went shopping before dropping in to his GP's surgery to have his bloods taken for a drug trial. An hour after he arrived home, the drug trial people phoned him, panicking, asking him if he was okay. Turned out his blood levels showed massive trauma. His white cell count was so high they thought he'd been in a car accident and had internal injuries. Pollock knew the problem for Winters wouldn't have been the increase in his white cell count, but his testosterone levels going off the chart. They would have been so high they would have been dismissed as rogue results.

'When we left the gym we went for a drink and something to eat.' Winters continued, 'The beers were flowing and all the time I'm getting this feeling that something was wrong, yet I felt so good physically — adrenaline was pumping — and I was on a high. All the signals were there and I ignored them. I knew the body is flooded with testosterone after a Death Set. I knew this was my first drink in three years. I thought I was still in control, but then we started on shots. I should have got up and left then, but I was so confident I thought I could handle it. I'd just done a Death Set, I thought I could handle anything. By the time the girl at the next table starts hitting on me it was too late, I was too far gone.'

'Shit man, Charlotte ... after all that effort.'

'Every step of that day I got the feeling something was wrong, but I shut it all out. And the same thing has happened tonight. I started feeling it when Sullion told us who the target was. It's been near constant since then.'

Pollock wasn't listening. He was seeing Charlotte stepping off her flight in Brussels and picking up the call telling her the job had been cancelled. Then her looking up at the

Departures board to find out when the next flight back was ...

'So I've been thinking 'bout it,' Winters said, unaware he was talking to himself, 'why this bad feeling? Sullion was told at the last minute 'cos they're so desperate to get Robertson. This is a job for two teams not one. We should be getting cover, but where would they go? What other points of cover are there? There's the two groups of trees where we are, and that one small ridge, and Sullion is on it. Yet we passed other empty farmhouses on the way here and they had no cover. The logical building to go to would be the one without cover. Robertson would see anyone coming from a mile away. Maybe, just maybe, we are exactly where she wants us to be.'

Winters knew that Sullion would be Robertson's first target and imagined her moving in behind him. There had been no noise, she would have used a knife. From there she would have climbed down, then crawling across the ground she would gradually move towards the Irish boys. He watched as O'Conner told Hughes a story to calm him, perhaps describing his hunting trips, asking him to join him on the next one the moment they'd finished this job; all the time unaware that Robertson was moving silently through the undergrowth, getting ever closer.

Pollock imagined Charlotte's flight arriving, landing at Heathrow, then walking to the car park. It would be dark now, her high heels clicking on the concrete. She slipped into the driver's seat of her MX-5 ... smiling as she passed the sign telling her she was twenty miles from home, the car's headlights lighting her way. Pulling up and parking a house back, she wanted to surprise the man lying in bed ... switching on the interior light, applying a fresh layer of lipstick, pursing her lips ... taking her heels off ... walking in silence up the path to the front door.

Inside the bedroom, Pollock was watching his friend slowly beginning to sober up; sensing the woman lying on his right, his arm draped over her naked back. With his desire satiated he lay in silence, listening to the sounds of her breathing, trying to block out the ever-increasing feeling that he'd done something incredibly stupid. Then, hearing a strange sound and sensing someone coming into the room. No, he tells himself he's imagining that, then deep breathing coming from his left. Someone is there, right next to him, so close that he could feel her breath on his cheek. That's odd, Pollock thought, I can feel something hot on my cheek—.

Winters was imagining Robertson moving again, leaving behind her the two unmoving bodies of the Irishmen, wiping the blade of her knife against her trousers. She had taken them easily; they had been looking in the wrong direction ... just like them.

'Cover your six!' Winters whispered as he twisted around catching a glance in Pollock's direction to make sure he'd heard. But the glance was enough; he knew straight away that his friend was dead. Winter's hand dropped to the Glock at his side but it was like a bad dream ... and he was moving in slow motion.

*

'Where *are* they?'
The man sitting at a nearby table looked over.

144

Realizing she was thinking out loud, Helen Gleason bit her bottom lip and looked down at the remnants of coffee left in her cup. Avoiding the man nearest her she studied the rest of the people, mainly couples, seated in her local café. They looked happy; their conversations infused with laughter and broad smiles. It was another world and she wished she was part of it, that carefree attitude that accompanied not just the young, but everyone in the room.

But of course, their world was vastly different from hers. They had not just sent five men to their deaths.

You don't know that for sure! Gleason's naturally optimistic nature, which tried to tell her that something out of the ordinary could have happened, was quashed by logic and intuition within seconds. The team had been due to check in four hours ago. She knew they were dead. And it was down to her. She should have warned them; they had no idea what they were going up against.

With one movement she downed her coffee. Outside the wind sent a chill through her. Tightening her coat belt she began the 200-metre walk back to the department building.

After going through two levels of security, up five floors in the lift and along two lengthy corridors, she walked into the Ops Room.

It was five past four on Friday afternoon. Gleason, like most of her team, had been working for over thirty-two hours. The sense of fatigue was accentuated by the reluctant acceptance that the mission had failed.

She clapped her hands. 'Okay, guys, it's time to go home and get some sleep.'

Her team looked around, then most powered down their monitors and stood up. Liman approached her and said quietly, 'You still need a six-man crew. I'll organize it. There are enough of us who want to stay on anyway.'

'Thanks, Tom, it's appreciated. We have the night crew coming in at midnight. We'll all leave then, no later.'

Liman smiled and returned to his desk. The Ops Room had almost emptied before he sat down.

*

The sniper opened his eyes and looked around. He was in a farm building of some sort. He was strung up, probably from a beam. His wrists had been tied together, his shoulders taking his weight. As his head cleared, the pain began to come fast. He closed his eyes to focus on his injuries.

He felt his wrists burning, then the pressure on his shoulders. Then he felt his lower back. And that was just the beginning. It seemed the pain was coming from everywhere.

He went back to the start of training. Pain, they had told him, was all about perception. You see pain for what it is — a warning signal — then you tell yourself that there is nothing to fear from it, and that all it's doing is making you stronger. That's how you handle pain. It doesn't matter what it is, or how long it will last. Pain is nothing more than an opportunity to build confidence. Embrace the pain — it is your friend.

That approach used to work for him. But Winters had always been able to localize the pain and, in so doing, had been able to exert control over it. But today it was impossible for him to even identify an area of his body that was not experiencing acute pain. Today, his approach to pain had, for the first time, failed.

Yet, he was sure he would be okay. He merely had to do what many of the battle-hardened soldiers did in wartime. They recognized that fear of death was going to make them

146

function less effectively. Instead of holding onto hope that they would survive, they surrendered hope and accepted that they were already dead. This acceptance, paradoxically, increased their chances of survival, allowing them to function without fear.

That was all he had to do, accept he was already dead. Then he would have no need for warning signals, and the messages travelling to his brain which triggered them, would be switched off.

Considering his current situation it should have been easy. Yet he couldn't get his mind around it. The pain wasn't letting him focus. It was tearing at him, pounding him, reaching dark places inside him. And it was relentless. And, worst of all, with each passing second, it was increasing.

All those years of training, all those years of controlling pain in the gym, and it had come to this.

He bowed his head and a deep animal growl came involuntarily from his lips. The growl slowly increased in volume. By the time it reached its loudest it had become a scream. Kyle Stuart Winters screamed out against the unspeakable horrors that were being performed on his body. He screamed out in despair at the mistakes he had made, at Charlotte and the life he might have lived with her. But, worse was his scream against the pain that continued to rage through him. He felt he could not suffer it another second, that it had to stop. Nothing this terrible could continue.

*

The sound of Mozart 21, from *Elvira Madigan,* softly embraced the living room of Gleason's flat. She stood at the bay window and looked out on to the night lights of Surrey.

147

As tired as she was, she couldn't sleep. The thought of what had happened to the five men wouldn't leave her. After all, as she kept reminding herself, she was the one who had sent them on this capture mission.

She went to her handbag, withdrew a piece of paper and read the words:

When will it stop raining?
When can we go downstairs?
When can I go outside?
When the man in the moon stops crying my child.
Why does he cry?
He cries because you can't play outside,
Because you can't run through his shadow,
Or see him dance with trees in the wind,
He cries for you,
Because you'll never see
The way he lit up the world at night.
But if he stops crying ... I would see him again?
He can't stop crying.
Like you?
Just like me, but his sorrow is greater,
He cries for you and every child,
Who will never run through his shadow,
Or see him dance with trees in the wind.

A simple poem, a child's questions about global warming. A distress call from the future, and reading it always raised the same question: was the group that was being hunted by Special Forces teams across the globe, not a group at all, but one person? One girl? Mireille Robertson?

It was too surreal, yet there were too many things that pointed to Mireille. The piece of paper Helen held in her hand that she'd found at the girl's home in Inverness, along with the books on global warming — far too many to be simple curiosity, this was more obsession. The timing: the killings of industrialists began two months after she'd been programmed with Hunter-Killer 9. The program itself — specifically designed to combat terrorism with greater terror. Helen had read the medical reports on the industrialists; they'd all suffered a violent and painful death. There was no one in the newly formed Extinction Rebellion, Greenpeace, or any of the organizations associated with saving the planet getting involved in violence, let alone doing something so ruthless. But Mireille, she'd been programmed to do things far worse.

All Helen's instincts screamed out to her that Mireille was top of the world's most wanted list. Dead or alive.

There was, however, one piece of the puzzle that didn't fit. What was she doing in Andorra? This region was mostly farmland. There was no connection whatsoever to global warming. It made no sense.

Her being alive, didn't make sense either. Two years earlier, not long after the murders in Edinburgh, Helen had sought the opinion of Arthur, the dear old psychologist who came up with answers to seemingly unanswerable questions. Arthur would sit in his room, surrounded by ancient books, and ponder until he found a solution. He would have been replaced years ago, but he was much loved by the younger staff so Human Resources had decided to keep him on for the morale of all, it seemed.

'Hello Helen,' Arthur stood up as she walked in to his room. He was probably the only man in the entire building who held on to the rapidly dying tradition of standing when a woman entered the room. But Helen also knew it gave him the excuse to walk to the large photograph on the wall, where he would look at it and say with pride, 'Have you seen my new car? Isn't she a beauty? All electric, charges up in two shakes of a lamb's tail.'

'I've heard that. It looks good,' Helen played along. 'I love the colour.'

'Are you still driving that diesel?'

'Yes, still have it.'

'You do know Helen, that you're in denial of global warming.'

She nodded in resignation to what was coming — Arthur's denial speech.

The psychologist began, 'Denial is a coping mechanism; it allows us to shut out things that we ordinarily would struggle with. Its existence allows us to function on a daily basis.'

Helen had heard these words a few months ago, but this speech was something that had to be suffered. An audience with Arthur came at a price ...

'When something happens, which is so traumatic that it might drive someone to suicide or insanity, we go into shock and the shock is frequently followed by denial, the mind shutting out all memory of it until such time as it is ready to accept parts of it. In this type of situation denial can be a very powerful survival mechanism. As it can be when we are unwell in hospital. When it comes to fighting illness belief is so important, and those who understand this will often deny an unfavourable prognosis and hold on to the belief that they will make a full recovery. Denial is allowing them to live each day free of fear and depression, they sleep better and the body's own resources work more efficiently. It doesn't mean they will survive, but if they can persevere with this approach it should increase their chances of survival.

'But when denial is employed at the wrong time it can be terribly dangerous. Often people go into denial of the symptoms before they see a doctor, convincing themselves that the difficulties they're experiencing will go away in time. In not starting treatment they allow disease to spread unchecked through their body.

'With global warming, denial allows us to sleep well and carry on our normal life, but in doing so, we continue doing things that will accelerate the warming as opposed to stopping it. Just like the people who are in denial of serious illness, we need to start on the right course of treatment. And the right course is to get rid of your diesel or petrol-fuelled car, stop travelling abroad and, well, I imagine you know the rest ... it's a long list.'

'As it happens, I am changing my car at the end of this year. I will be giving serious consideration to trading-in against a new electric car.'

'Oh well, at least you're thinking about it. But, while you're doing that also think on this: the main indicator of the level of denial of global warming is not the continued use of petrol and diesel-fuelled vehicles, or flights to holiday destinations, but the lack of concern by millions of parents about the future their children face.'

The psychologist allowed that to sink in for a few seconds before nodding, the signal that his lecture, and the game, had concluded. Arthur returned to sit behind his desk, Helen sat opposite him.

'Now, how can I help?' Arthur said.

'Mireille Robertson.'

'Well, I should have known. The dust has barely settled from that debacle.' Arthur opened a desk drawer, extracted a file and read from it. 'Mireille Robertson: born just outside Inverness, 20 November 1996. Scottish father, French mother, raised by her paternal grandfather; a career soldier, who had joined up at the age of fifteen at the start of the Second World War;' Arthur looked from the file to Helen, and added, 'a man who probably taught her everything he knew about the art of combat. And, from his military record, he knew a lot more than most. Here's where it gets interesting though.' He turned back to read from the file. 'Instead of choosing a career in the military, Robertson decided to study Literature at Inverness College, part of the University of the Highlands and Islands.'

Arthur closed the file. 'Now, what do you think would make her do that?'

'It doesn't make sense.' Helen replied. 'Unless she was rebelling against the discipline.'

'I think that was it exactly,' Arthur said. 'The first week of basic training in the army is pure hell, everyone screaming at you, rushed off your feet from dawn 'til dusk. This girl has probably been through thirteen years of it. Then she turns eighteen and realizes she can do what she wants. She bursts out of the locker, declaring to her grandfather that she's been a secret Jane Austen reader, burns her fatigues and combats, buys a pair of jeans and a sweatshirt and she's off to Uni.

'A year passes, then one day she's out running and happens upon a kidnapping, and without breaking stride, she kills the two kidnappers. That didn't just happen by itself. You don't stop training for a year and do that. She never stopped training. She couldn't stop, it's all she knew. She'd been brought up for combat — her body would reject the inactivity. Then what happens? A few hours later the woman she rescued, Amanda Jeffries, decides to subject her to Hunter-Killer 9. Jeffries' motive, I imagine, was self-preservation; she had almost been kidnapped, and she suspected that all her co-workers had been kidnapped, or worse. She'd witnessed Robertson's capabilities, and with the testing of HK9 being withheld from the team at South Queensferry, Jeffries thought that all she was doing was giving the girl an upgrade. It made sense, but ultimately made no difference to Jeffries — having the best protector in the world won't help if they're not around when you need them.

'So what are we left with?' Arthur stretched his arms wide, placing his hands on his desk almost two metres apart.

'On one hand, we have a nineteen-year-old who has been trained from the age of five for combat. On the other, we have the counter-terrorist program HK9, specifically designed to create a ruthless, merciless killer. Bring the two together ... ' Arthur slid his hands into the middle of the table; as they met, he mimicked an explosion, as if a huge bomb had gone off, his hands arcing in circles showing the flying debris and smoke.

'And the fall-out? Eleven men dead, but not just killed, torn apart. A five-man team of Special Forces, and a gang of six drug dealers. One of them so big it took half a dozen police and ambulancemen the better part of an hour to carry him down eight flights of stairs. This man died from multiple organ failure. The post-mortem report read that he had injuries consistent with having his mid-section beaten with a sledgehammer.

'Then, after that, nothing. No killings, no sightings, no more Robertson. The girl's dead Helen. If she weren't, there *would be bodies stacking up all over the place. And hers? It's likely she went off in to a remote forest and died. Or she went swimming in the North Sea, went as far as she could until hypothermia set in.*

'You know all too well, that no one subjected to HK9 survived longer than a month. No one. She's dead, and it's unlikely her body will ever be found.'

Helen switched off the stereo and picked up her own copy of the file. She would have to pay Arthur another visit and break the news to him.

She read over the intelligence report once more. Was it from an established source, or had it been passed down second-hand? Had sufficient checks been carried out to confirm its authenticity? She knew she had missed something and had spent most of the night looking for it; as if in finding it, she could erase the loss of five men.

She remained indoors for the rest of the weekend. On the occasions she did sleep, she woke in a state of panic every couple of hours. At first, she phoned in to check if there had been any news. By Sunday night she had given up on phoning and slept straight through until six. By the time she'd had a shower, dressed, and driven the seven miles to the Department it was 08.40.

11

Monday 8.55 A.M.

The section head, John Bannen, called out to Gleason as she walked past the open door of his office. He told her that four bodies had been found — and to report in thirty minutes to the conference room. Gleason went to her office and started preparing. She was glad she was being kept busy; she had no time to dwell on the news. Instead, she considered that, for over two years, the Department had had good reason to assume Mireille Robertson was dead. Gleason had been given the unenviable task of confirming that. A few days ago, the seemingly mundane job, had become top priority.

In the conference room Gleason went through her report with Alice Whitby '... the nearest team we had available was on a joint operation with French Special Forces 200 miles away. The IC of Delta Victor Five was informed at Nice Airport, and the team was then flown by helicopter to the target area in Andorra. Rogers briefed them en route. After landing, they travelled the next twenty miles to the target by jeep and the final three miles on foot. Rogers timed them leaving on foot at midnight, and assumed they had taken up positions around the cottage sometime between 0020 and 0040 hrs. They were due to call in at 1200 hrs. They were all former SAS and had worked together on a number of occasions with a 100 percent success rate. They were our best men. I don't understand what happened.'

Whitby said, 'I think it's fairly obvious, Helen. They were set up. *You* were set up. I expect the information was leaked deliberately. How did we source that information again?' Before Gleason could reply, Whitby changed direction. 'No, forget it. The question is, why the set-up?'

Gleason looked down at the open files in front of her. 'I don't know. We received news of a sighting of a woman fitting Robertson's description in the Andorra region. Our contact secured a photograph, from which we made a positive ID. On Thursday, he received information as to where she was staying that night.'

'You've never heard of *baiting*, Helen?'

'I had no reason to expect it. What could she want? Weapons, ammunition?'

Whitby said, 'I think there's only one reason for this: she wants information.'

'She wouldn't get that from the team. They knew nothing.'

'They'd been working for us for how long?' Whitby asked, looking at the report.

'As individuals, between two and eight years.'

'They knew something then. It's a wonder she didn't get Rogers as well.'

'He didn't remain at the pick-up point,' Gleason said. 'He's not a field op. He left the team with instructions to call in an airlift. We had two Super Pumas on stand-by.'

'Where is he now?'

'He's using his contacts over there to try and keep this quiet. He also has to confirm the identity of the four bodies, organize their recovery, and search for the fifth.'

'You're assuming the entire team is dead then?'

'There were no survivors from the house in Edinburgh. We also know Robertson was involved in the deaths of six men in a flat a few miles away. There were no survivors there either. An aspect of HK9 that dominated with a number of the test subjects, was extreme violence.'

'We don't need reminding of the number of handlers we lost.' Whitby said, as she looked at the two photographs of the target and shook her head.

'We know HK9—.'

Whitby interrupted. 'Yes, as you said. What we don't know is *where* she is.'

Gleason listed the numerous measures that had been taken to ensure all the stations, airports and docks were monitored by agents twenty-four hours a day. A team had also been assigned to go through CCTV footage. In summing up she said, 'We have to assume she's obtained a forged passport or is travelling under someone else's.'

'Who are we talking about?' Bannen said, as he closed the door behind him and sat down facing Gleason.

'Robertson.' Gleason said flatly.

'Don't tell me she was the target.'

'Yes, John, she was the target.' Whitby said.

'Really, we're still on about her? Tell me, Helen, why do you think this girl is still alive? Everyone on that test sample either went nuts and had to be eliminated immediately after programming or, over the next few weeks, committed suicide. Yet you're saying that this girl survived and, over two years later, has sufficient control to be able to wipe out an entire team of former SAS. Oh, of course, what am I thinking? It all makes perfect sense!'

'She has qualities the other test subjects didn't have.' Gleason said.

'We know all about her military upbringing.' Bannen said.

'There are other personality traits—.'

'As in?'

'The ability to adapt to dangerous situations.'

'Every single soldier goes through that kind of training.'

'Exactly, they go through that kind of training as soldiers, as adults. Robertson's training started when she was a child. A soldier has to determine the factors involved before making a conscious decision. There's a delay, and a period where emotions often cloud what's important. Robertson doesn't have to consider other factors: it's instinctive, she's already adapted.'

'Okay, how would she adapt to a program as flawed as HK9 obviously was?' Bannen said.

'That's what I want to find out. If we know that we might be able to finally use the Hunter-Killer program, all those deaths might be for something.'

Bannen shook his head slowly. 'You know, Helen, your obsession with this has cost us our best team.'

Whitby cut in, 'We are not going over this again — we are not doing it! Officially, Mireille Robertson died two years ago, and we will need more proof before we can say different. I understand your desire to get something out of this project, Helen. But for now, we need to focus on the immediate future. What are we going to do about the team to dispatch to Hong Kong? Any suggestions?'

Gleason said, 'Romeo Seven is now our best, and our only team now. We could bring another team in, but I think, for this job, we should use our own men. They'll need to be fully briefed—.'

Bannen said, 'That shouldn't take too long, just tell them there is a group going around slaughtering industrialists whose track record towards reducing emissions is a tad disappointing. Romeo is to go over there, identify and eliminate that group, and then out for a few beers ... no, hold on, they would still have to be alive to do that.'

'That's enough, John. We're all upset; Delta Five was special, but we have to move on. Now, the media are still in the dark on this. However, we know that top industrialists around the world are being murdered. Intelligence reports indicate that one small group with the objective of reversing global warming is responsible. Romeo's job is to work with the other teams that have been brought in, and the numerous law enforcement and government agencies on the ground, to facilitate the apprehension of the group.'

Bannen looked at the file in front of him and said, 'Reports indicate? Is there any evidence to support these reports, because if there isn't we don't know anything for certain, like who they are or what they want?'

Helen said, 'I imagine this group sees the industrialists as men who are aware that they are damaging the environment yet refuse to take measures to reduce that damage. Men whose only concern is to make money.'

'Well, that information doesn't really help, does it?' Bannen continued, 'What's the group's motive? Are they trying to create a deterrent, or are they just a bunch of sick, sadistic bastards using any excuse, in this case global warming, to satisfy a blood lust?'

'If you'd been listening, you would be aware of the point they're trying to make.'

Whitby cut in, 'Okay, Helen, you brief Romeo Seven, and make sure they know everything.'

Bannen shook his head in disbelief, 'She just lost our best team, and you're letting her brief another?'

Whitby ignored him and brought the meeting to a close.

*

After Gleason had left the room, Alice Whitby and John Bannen stood alongside each other at the window.

Bannen said, 'The fact that Robertson's still alive indicates that she's exerting a level of control over the program. I don't like it. I don't understand how she could have survived past the first fortnight, but now it's over two years. She could have spoken to anyone.'

'You need to keep your emotions in check. Assuming Robertson is still alive, what reason would she have to speak to anyone? The program that she was given centres on infiltration and killing. She operates alone. Helen could be right: she might have been after weapons. Perhaps she's on a killing spree and can't stop herself. If so, it won't be long before she strikes again, but this time we make sure it's the right team on the ground. A team that thrives on things being simple, and are far more effective with a shoot-to-kill order.'

'I agree, but what about Helen?' Bannen said. 'She's committed to bringing Robertson in alive.'

Whitby sighed. 'It is more than curiosity with her. She's been close to this for too long. She needs to know how the girl has managed to stay alive. She still believes HK 9 can be used.'

'She knows too much, Alice.'

Whitby turned towards her colleague. 'Yes. She has become a liability.'

'Do you want me to deal with her?'

160

'No. I have a contact who will know the best men to use for a job like this. Leave her to me,' Whitby said, as she crossed the room to the map of Europe on the wall. 'The question is, where is Robertson going to strike next?'

'We have men at the borders.'

'How long's it been since we lost contact with the team?'

'Almost seventy-two hours.'

'Three days. She could be anywhere by now.'

12

3.00 P.M.

With the force of the wind, the three decks of the ferry were deserted. Only a girl dressed in black remained. Leaning over the rail, she looked down at the black hull and the dark sea that thrashed angrily against it. She had, as far back as she could remember, loved the sea, and in particular, the feeling of the wind beating against her face. But today she felt nothing.

Whenever she travelled, her thoughts turned to her grandfather, but especially on this journey. The two of them had taken this ferry almost every summer. How she had looked forward to her breaks of freedom. The island of South Uist was her time: no school, no training, just freedom to wander the hills and walk across the beaches, sometimes with her grandfather, sometimes on her own and sometimes, when her childhood friend Cathal was around, sitting astride his shoulders.

She loved the islands and the people in them, and especially this journey, as it was always accompanied with at least one story about the family. The first stories were often about her mother, as her grandfather wanted to ensure she was motivated to continue speaking French. But, by the time Mireille had reached her teens she was bilingual, and Grandpapa began telling her stories about other members of the family, especially her grandmother.

It was a bright sunny day when Grandpapa, who was standing near the front of the ferry, said, 'Oban 1947.' It was the way he started all his stories, as if he were reading from a diary of his memories, and the location and year were at the top of each page.

'Your grandma was the second of four children. Her elder sister had left to train as a nurse, a luxury only afforded one child, so your grandma had to work and sent money home. She was fourteen when she left for Oban to take up her job as a scullery maid in a big hotel; a foreign land with streets and cars and noise, and only a smattering of her mother tongue. On her first morning, she stood at the sink with more dirty dishes before her than she had ever seen in her life. As she scrubbed and pottered, she lifted her head and from the window saw the ferry sail into the bay. Though lots of ferries converge on Oban, to your grandma this could only be a boat from South Uist, and her heart leapt as she imagined some familiar face with news from home, and busied herself, lost in the excitement. In no time, she lifted her head again and saw a ferry sail out of the bay. Her heart broke: the ferry was going home and she was not. Tears streamed down her face and she sobbed with the heartache of Cianalas, her tears landing amongst the suds of the washing-up in the huge sink in front of her.'

The yearning to feel closer to her grandma was so strong that Mireille woke early the following morning, and, after leaving a scribbled note on the kitchen table, travelled to Oban, and went to that same hotel to find that sink. Refurbishment in the sixties meant that the layout was different, but she had stood in silent homage to that heartbroken girl and wept her own silent tears, missing her.

But the days of missing loved ones were over for Mireille. The events of the summer of 2016 had seen to that. The change in her was tumultuous, and it had all begun the moment she ran into that car park and saw them try to take Amanda Jeffries. For a few days afterwards she had wondered what would have happened if things had gone differently; if she had taken a different route, or stayed with Jeffries that evening. But those thoughts left her, replaced by dark reflections that she still struggled to deal with. The past that had held such emotion was becoming merely a series of memories of events and places that had little meaning, unless they were of strategical significance.

As South Lochboisdale appeared on the port side, the girl reminded herself that speed would be essential. She strode purposefully past the other disembarking passengers. But even with the hood of her sweatshirt covering most of her face, there were still a few who tried to engage her in conversation. She ignored them, covering ground quickly, the weight of the backpack borne easily across her shoulders.

As soon as her feet touched tarmac she began jogging, steadily increasing her pace until she was running. She had no time to waste and eight miles of ground to cover before reaching her destination.

It was late afternoon when she caught sight of the cottage. It had gone through a transformation in the last few years, and was now a far cry from the 'castle' that she and Cathal had fought for as children. Sonas was one of the oldest cottages in the Outer Hebrides.

The clouds had cleared, the wind had settled, and Mireille stripped off her sweatshirt. Her black tank top accentuated the depth of the tan on her shoulders and arms. As she approached she recognized her friend working on the thatched roof. Even though he had his back towards her, there could be no mistaking him. Cathal had the broadest back she'd seen on any man.

'It'll be years before its ready. I'll be working on it every summer,' he had told her before leaving early for the summer break. But that was over two years ago. He would be surprised to see her, and more surprised when told the reason she was here.

Cathal worked his way to the side of the roof and jumped down in front of her.

'Mireille! I almost didn't recognize you.'

They hugged. He said, 'You'll have come from the ferry then. I was just getting a drink. You want one?'

'Thanks.'

They sat against the side wall, catching the warmth of the sun. Cathal turned to her and smiled. 'Well? Where have you been for the past two years?'

'Europe mostly.'

'You just took off and told no one.'

'I had to get away.'

'We all thought you'd gone back to the States.'

The girl shook her head, then tilted it towards the wall. 'It looks good. You have much to do?'

'A few days. First rental not due for a month, so I can take it easy now. How long you gonna be here for?'

'A week or two.'

'You have a place to stay?'

'Not yet.'

'You're welcome to stay here. The folks wanted me to, but there're away on a cruise so I have the run of the house.

Besides, it gives me an excuse to drive Dad's Merc. Bar a little more work on the roof, it's finished. The interior is all set up for guests ... how long has it been since you ate?'

The girl shrugged.

'Give me a few minutes — I could do with something myself.'

With Cathal in the kitchen, the girl stood up and, turning to the wall, ran the fingertips of her right hand gently over the stone directly above the window. When she felt her fingers dip, she took her hand away and studied the stone. The deep indentation was still there ...

Lying on her back in the long grass Mireille blew on her fingers to warm them. She tucked them under her armpits and searched the night sky for the North Star. She found it almost immediately, from which she confirmed she was on the correct course. After checking the time from the luminous dials on her watch, and how long she'd been crawling, she worked out the enemy stronghold should be 20 metres away. It would be another hour before sunrise but the sky would start lightening inside the next 15 minutes. She turned back on to her stomach and began crawling again. As much as she wanted to, there wasn't time to rest and look at the stars. The first attack position had been agreed the previous day as ten metres. Any further back and they risked the grenades missing the windows. With the number of men manning the fortress, if the grenades didn't reduce their number, success of the mission would be unlikely. And that would present another set of problems. She was well aware that if attackers weren't killed straight away they would be taken prisoner and tortured. She knew what to do. Whether the grenades found their target was irrelevant. She was going in, no matter what.

The day before, when they had marked their approaches on the map, she had informed Cathal that the fate of the entire country depended on the success of this mission. And that with the enemy fortress being so heavily guarded, it was likely to be a mission neither of them would return from. The boy hadn't blinked; she knew he would be at her side when they stormed the fortress. The girl loved the idea of it; her eyes always lit up whenever Grandpapa told her about the ancient warriors and how certain creeds sought out death in battle, the Spartans calling it a beautiful death. The attack force of two would be victorious, or they would fall side-by-side, and die a beautiful death.

Mireille was in position, right beside the point where the long grass had been cut away. She peered out from behind it, the outline of the target just barely visible. She couldn't see any guards on patrol. There would be some though, unless her friend had already dispatched them. She held her breath and heard the faint call of a red-necked phalarope... it was Cathal. The rare breed of bird was a frequent visitor to the Outer Hebrides, but never in the winter. She would reply with the same call, then they would both count down from ten, at which point they would throw the grenades through the same window gap, ideally ending up in opposite corners.

That was the plan, and the girl made the bird call. Ten seconds later the two grenades were thrown, and would have ended up in opposite corners of the room, except Cathal had overthrown and instead of finding the gap his stone grenade hit the lintel above the window.

The two of them counted down the seconds to the explosions that they played out in their imaginations. Then they rushed forwards, the boy charging the front door, the girl slipping through the window. Inside, the fighting was fierce and hand-to-hand. Within thirty seconds it was over — the fortress had been taken.

The smoke of battle had been swept away by the fresh breeze coming off the ocean. With the tip of the sun breaking the horizon, the two children stood outside their new HQ alongside a makeshift flagpole. The boy stood to attention and sang *An Eala Bhàn*, whilst the girl slowly raised the Saltire. No matter how many battles they fought at Sonas, the flag raising was always deeply emotional for both of them. There was more to it than simply declaring that the fortress had been taken. *An Eala Bhàn* had been written by a Cameron Highlander from Uist at the battle of the Somme. *Dòmhnall Ruadh Chorùna* was lying wounded when he'd written the song to his sweetheart with the battle still raging. Both Mireille and Cathal had a great-grandfather who had also been in the Cameron Highlanders, and had fought at the Somme. The children had decided that all three were friends and their two great-grandfathers had run forward into a hail of bullets and carried the wounded Dòmhnall to safety. The song being written later that day. In the minds of both children, the song was a result of the bravery of their ancestors and the unbreakable friendship of the three men. The children also believed that after the war Dòmhnall, a stone-mason, had been employed to work on Sonas. And although the cottage had not been lived in for many years and was now badly in need of repair, the fact that most of it was still standing was testimony to his skill. It may have been the fantasy of the two children that *An Eala Bhàn* and Sonas, or as Cathal referred to it, Mireille's castle, were embodied in such a tale of bravery and friendship. Yet, the tale was by no means inconceivable. That the foundations for it were based on fact was all the *children needed — to them, it had happened exactly as they imagined.*

By the time Mireille's Gaelic was good enough for her to sing An Eala Bhàn the days of her childhood, and the pretend battles she fought alongside Cathal had passed. But her rendition of the song was much loved by her grandfather, and she sang it to him often.

The two friends talked for the rest of the afternoon and into the evening, the girl steering the conversation away from what she'd been doing in Europe. With the warmth of the sun fading, Cathal took his tools down from the roof and prepared to leave. They stood by the door of the black Mercedes ML 300.

'You're different,' he said.

'I changed my hair.'

'I don't mean that.'

The girl nodded slowly and bowed her head. 'Cathal, I need your help. I don't want anyone to know I'm on the island.'

Her friend shrugged his shoulders. 'Okay. No one will know. Aside from me no one comes down here anyway.'

'You still into virtual reality?'

'More than ever. It's the future. People don't seem to realize that yet.'

'I was hoping you were. If you can find time, I would really like you to plan — maybe design — a virtual reality program to help people fight cancer.'

'Are you okay? Are you sick?'

'No.'

'Just like that? Just out of the blue?'

'You ever hear the story about a boy who had an inoperable tumour in his brain? He was going to die, but no one told him so he fought it. He imagined that the tumour was Apache Indians and the cavalry had been sent to kill them. Every day, without fail, he had this battle going on in his mind. One day his mum asked him how the cavalry were doing. He replied the battle was over; there were no Indians left. His parents took him for a scan and the doctors were baffled to find the tumour had gone.'

'My father heard about that boy when he was young. You know, that story has been going around for so many years I don't think anyone knows if it's true or not.'

The girl turned and looked towards the setting sun. For almost a minute there was nothing, except the sound of seagulls in the distance and the warm breeze brushing the long grass. When Mireille finally spoke, her voice was soft, almost as if she was talking to herself, 'You know, huge sums are spent on the military: training and preparing them for the horrors that await them in the remote chance they are taken prisoner. They are trained to use their minds to fight, yet for millions who face the horrors of cancer on a daily basis, there is no training, no preparation, no funding. There are millions out there desperate for a weapon to fight with.'

Cathal stared at his friend, confused and a little concerned with the route this conversation was taking. It was so unlike the girl he knew.

She turned to look at him, 'I saw the weapon. It was a virtual reality program. You say VR is the future: it is, and I know that there is a program out there that can be used to combat cancer. I don't know how it will work, but I've seen your work, and if there's one person who can come up with something, it's you.'

Cathal looked towards the setting sun and ran his fingers through his hair. He needed time to think the day through. He didn't understand; this was a subject she'd never raised before. Where had this shift in direction come from? She had been so involved with literature at uni, but now this. Something wasn't right.

As for the actual task itself, maybe, possibly, he could come up with something — if he could find a start point. How long would it take though? And would he be able to design something good enough for her? Mireille always set such high goals.

'Give me a few days.' he said.

*

Cathal didn't remember any of his drive home, parking up, or walking around the side of the house. His conscious mind finally switched on as he sat astride the stone wall at the foot of the garden. He looked to the west and the last embers of red that clung to the horizon.

He began to replay conversations from earlier. What was wrong? They'd talked for hours and she hadn't smiled once. Was he to pretend everything was alright and develop a VR program to combat cancer? Where was she coming from? Where had this originated?

He felt drained thinking about it. He had no idea what had happened to his friend, and no start point for how to combat cancer.

He went inside and began planning what to do tomorrow. He needed to bring in reinforcements.

Floraidh. She would find what he was looking for … whatever it was.

171

13

Tuesday 8.00 A.M.

Helen Gleason studied the board in her office and the two blown-up photographs in the centre: one from the literature student's matriculation card as a nineteen-year-old, and the other taken two years later in Andorra.

Mireille Robertson: she felt she knew this girl now almost as well as she knew her own daughter. But these last killings — what was she after? Gleason turned and looked out of her office window at the thick clouds that were gathering in the east.

She often felt she should have left this job after the murders in Edinburgh. At forty-four she was still young; she could have moved on. But a decision had been made, and now she had to make the best of it.

She called out in response to the knock on her door.

Liman walked in, closing the door gently behind him. 'We've more information on the four bodies.'

'Go on.'

'They were found in a wooded area twenty miles north of the farmhouse. Bodies were stripped, no sign of clothing or weapons. I don't get it. Why strip the bodies?'

Helen pursed her lips. 'It was an illegal operation in Spain. Robertson's father and grandfather were career soldiers. It's possible she was simply being patriotic. With no clue to identity it would be difficult to link this to anything, let alone a covert operation by another country. Do we know who's missing?'

'Kyle Winters.'

'Okay. Get back to Rogers, make sure the locals haven't found him, then check with hospitals, then morgues, then get back to me.'

After Liman left, Helen turned again to the window. The dark clouds had suddenly multiplied in number. They seemed to fill the sky. Kyle was on her mind. With his criminal record she should have selected someone else. But should the offence that had resulted in his discharge from the army have branded him a criminal? He hadn't started that fight. All he'd done was hit the man who had — too hard, and once too often. More importantly, Kyle was the best marksman they had. He had been the right man for the team. She wished she hadn't picked him though, he'd been through enough. Her ex-husband had trained with him at his gym. As a rule, Richard didn't voice admiration of others, Kyle was the exception. What had he gone through at the hands of the girl? A shiver ran the length of Helen's spine.

Half-an-hour later she was in the Ops Room. Liman handed her a thin file. 'Someone fitting Winters' description was found naked in a disused abattoir, as yet he's unidentified, but I think it's safe to assume it's our guy. In intensive care in hospital in Lleida initially, but is currently being moved to a special pain unit in Barcelona. The report makes clear that he was tortured. Andorra has plenty of good hospitals, but none of them have dealt with anything like this.'

'Who do we have in Barcelona?'

Liman nodded to the man on his right. Almost immediately faces and personnel summaries began appearing on the main screen. One after another the faces were dismissed by Helen. Then suddenly she saw what she was looking for.

'Her.'

Liman, who'd been checking a printout, said 'Sorry. She's fluent in English, but she's admin staff. Sofia Santiago, PA to the section head.'

'I don't care if she cleans floors. Get her on the phone and I'll brief her. Our man has been through hell. He needs to see a face like hers.'

*

Two hours later, Santiago was being driven to the hospital. She went over what had been said to her by the woman in London. The man she was going to see must be someone special — it seemed they were more interested in making sure he was looked after than obtaining information from him — and that was unusual.

She had a good idea why she was being chosen over trained agents. It wasn't the first time she'd been used for her looks, yet she knew deep down she was the best person for this particular job. It wasn't on her records, but she had nursed her father at home for years. Discharged from the army after a training accident had left him badly burned, she knew about the mentality of men in the military ... and about pain. This task was an opportunity, and she wasn't going to waste it.

In her fitted white blouse, linen indigo skirt and high heels, she was not ideally dressed for hospital, but she was confident in her ability to provide the care and compassion that London deemed so important here. She was also confident that if the man she was going to see had the information they were looking for, she would gently draw it from him.

174

*

Winters' room in the hospital was on the ground floor and was dominated by an enormous window on his right side. Someone had opened the curtains and, through the glass, he could see the girl approaching. Even though she was in full camouflage, and crept low between the bushes, he could see her. Because he'd been trained to see her, and that was the reason the others couldn't see her. She was taking her time preparing her rifle. Then, as soon as she was ready, she'd open fire and it would be all over. He had to do something, and he had to do it quickly. He couldn't walk, but convinced himself he could make it to the floor. He would be safe there, flat behind the bed, out of her line of sight. He could stay there until it became dark. He could live out another day.

It was a good plan, Kyle thought, and when the room was briefly empty of people he wriggled towards the edge of the bed. After wrenching the bed sheets away, he launched himself downwards, but didn't make it. He found himself horizontally suspended a foot off the floor. Somehow someone had caught him. At which point, the fight for his life began. He knew everything depended on making it to the floor and he was close — a foot; twelve inches from safety. He heard raised voices in a language he didn't understand. He sensed they were trying to help him, but they weren't trained to see the enemy. They didn't know she was outside. They were naive to what was about to happen. If he let them put him back in bed, when the glass window shattered, and the bullets tore through his head and body, they would realize their mistake ... but then it would be too late. They would know in future, but that wouldn't help him. He would be dead.

There were hands all over him, voices calling out to him. The pulling was gentle but somewhere in his mind he sensed it would only be a matter of time before they lifted him back to the bed. He felt the surge of adrenaline, a fury now in his actions, a last bid to stay alive, his arms and legs flailing in anger. His right arm swung wildly and hit the cool metal of the bed leg. His fingers folded around it.

*

Santiago, having followed directions to the Pain Unit, stepped into a washroom before entering. She adjusted her skirt, ran her fingers through her hair, looked at her reflection in the mirror and nodded. She may still look like she worked in an office, but in a hospital she could be anyone.

When she walked into the unit she was instantly aware of the noise coming from one of the single rooms. The man on reception was busy on the phone so she headed for the room.

*

'You must use your feet, like this ...' The physical training instructor demonstrated the correct way of climbing a rope. It was the second week of basic infantry training, and Kyle stood watching with the other young men in the squad. 'You have to use your feet correctly; your legs will take your bodyweight. Now let's see you using the right technique.' Kyle was the fifth man to climb the rope. The first three had, with a bit of forceful instruction, wrapped their feet around the rope correctly, the fourth just tried to haul himself up using the strength of his arms alone. He didn't make it very far before lactic acid built up, to the point where he could go no further.

Kyle understood the torrent of abuse the instructor doled out to the recruit, but he didn't like the smile on his face as he did it.

'Right, Winters, show this idiot how it's done.'

Kyle, very deliberately let his legs dangle freely, and climbed the length of the rope; then climbed down, again using only his hands.

'Let's see you do that again.' The instructor said quietly and watched as the recruit repeated the climb.

'And again.'

On the fourth time Kyle started to feel the strain on his biceps, but not on his hands. He'd worked with his hands since he was eight and he had the strength that working all day, every day, for years, gives.

*

A male nurse ran past Santiago and into the room where the noise originated. When the door opened, she could make out the one-way verbal traffic.

'LET GO! YOU HAVE TO LET GO!'

She stood in the doorway and looked on in amazement. Three drip stands up-ended, tubes everywhere, and four nurses holding a man in his mid-forties two feet off the floor, unable to get him back in to bed.

A nurse turned to her and explained that he had been fine all night.

Santiago's eyes narrowed. The years of frustration at being held back by her looks, building inside her, each month, each week, each day, finally finding their voice — 'KEEP THE CURTAINS CLOSED! He's seeing danger outside!' She stormed to the window and yanked the curtains shut. Without

177

waiting for the nurses to react, she marched towards Winters and dropped to her knees beside him. She looked him in the eye, and with her right hand began stroking the sweat-soaked hair back from his forehead. She leaned forward and whispered in his ear in perfect English.

'Kyle, it's all right. You're safe now. *You are safe.* I am here to protect you.'

At first Winters could neither see nor hear Santiago. He was on the rope and was climbing down for the fifteenth time.

'No one can see you, Kyle. Everything is all right now.' Santiago continued trying to engage the former soldier in eye contact. She failed to succeed but, in less than five minutes, he had surrendered his grip and allowed the nurses to put him back in bed. Sofia stood to one side as she let the two remaining nurses reconnect the drips.

Sofia Santiago had played the role of a senior doctor and saw it through, dismissing the nurses. Alone with the patient, she continued to whisper in his ear that everything was okay, he was safe, knowing all the time that everything was not okay.

*

The only library on the Isle of Uist was in Benbecula, in Lionacleit School. It was there that Floraidh was working over the summer while she studied for her MBA.

Cathal hadn't known her that well, but everything changed on the day of her graduation three years earlier.

After the ceremony, the entire class, along with partners and parents, gathered in the luxury hotel on the edge of Inverness city centre. Floraidh was there with her mum, Alana. Cathal was downstairs working in the cellar, until a distressed Polish

178

barmaid burst through the door and asked that he come up to the bar. The scene that awaited him was not a good one. It seemed Alana had accidentally spilt the drink of one of the men standing behind her, but instead of accepting the woman's apology and offer to buy him another, the man, and his friend, began to insult her. With no one prepared to challenge them, their insults became more cutting ... and louder, reaching the point where almost the entire bar was watching.

Within a few seconds of the cellarman arriving, both men were outside, one lying flat out on his front while the other, standing on unsteady legs, was bleeding profusely from his mouth.

Cathal went back in to the bar. The first person he saw was the bar manager who was shaking his head in disapproval. He avoided making eye contact and said quietly, 'You didn't have to hit anyone.' The lack of eye contact was not lost on the cellarman: the manager was pre-warning him that, before the end of his shift, he would be told his services were no longer required.

Losing his job, as he was to discover in the next few seconds, was nothing compared to what he saw in the face of Floraidh. The look she gave him, a cross between horror and revulsion, shook him to his core. He headed straight for the cellar, changed into his jeans and sweatshirt, and walked through the underground corridors, leaving by the rear entrance. He couldn't face going in to that bar again. He couldn't face Floraidh again.

Walking quickly, he slowed only when he'd created distance between himself and the hotel. It was then that he began to think of Mireille, and all the mornings they had spent on the beach training. It all began during her second summer

179

on the island. She was six and he'd just turned seven, and she used him to practise the moves her grandfather had taught her. From the beginning Cathal had loved every session. It didn't matter that each move ended with him being slammed head first in to the sand. As a child it didn't hurt, but by the age of fifteen the girl had become proficient at using his bodyweight against him; now each throw jarred his limbs and took the breath out of him. It wasn't all one-sided though, after she'd practised her moves, she would spend the same amount of time teaching him combat moves. As children it began with body strikes; by the time they were teenagers she was teaching him specialised jujitsu moves. Then, after all those summers, came the time for him to put her teaching in to action, and what did he do? The cellarman didn't know exactly what he'd done wrong — only that he had, and in a big way.

He was ashamed and confused when he spoke to Mireille about it that evening. He started to describe what had happened but she stopped him, explaining that she had heard all about it already.

Then he told her about the look on Floraidh's face. His friend shook her head knowingly, 'She was in shock, that's all. Most people aren't used to seeing that level of violence. No one in that bar was ready for it.'

'I don't understand why I didn't take it outside? I could have done it — taken them into the corner of the car park, then there would have been no witnesses. I could have dealt with them there.'

The girl shook her head and sighed, 'Cathal, you don't think like most people. You absorb data and sometimes you use logic, but more often, you intuitively know what needs to be done. I've seen you work on computer programs — all the top brains, the specialists at IBM and Apple and the other major computer companies are nowhere near the league you're in. And earlier today your brain worked in the same way; you knew what to do, and you did it.'

Her friend looked even more confused. She laid her hands on his shoulders, looked into his eyes, and said, 'You saw a mother being humiliated in front of her daughter, and that's something that would have stayed with both of them for the rest of their lives. That great mind of yours made the decision to erase that humiliation. But to do that, whatever you did, had to be done in front of everyone. You could have hurt them ten times worse outside and it would have achieved absolutely nothing. What did you do? You first action was to eliminate the threat, which you achieved by hitting the biggest one in the mouth. The shock impact of that punch took all the fight out of him — he flew out of the door. The second one you lifted off his feet and slammed into the wall; that winded him and finished him. Then, just before you manhandled him outside, you slammed his head in to the edge of the door, and as you crossed the doorway you swept his legs from under him, then dragged him outside on his stomach, as you would drag a heavy rubbish bag. Why? Your goal wasn't to throw them out, it wasn't to hurt, your goal was to humiliate. Floraidh and Alana were back to enjoying the day because what they'd felt earlier had been completely erased. How could they be upset by those men, when they were cut off mid-sentence? And, like that,' the girl snapped her fingers. 'You turned them into things — things you wipe the floor with, because that's exactly what you did with them. And when everyone saw it, the two of them became inconsequential. And you didn't just save Floraidh and her mum from being humiliated; you empowered them. They

*had seen a fellow Islander come to their aid, a man who would
protect them and crush anyone who dared to try and spoil
their day.'*

'But the look on her face—.'

*'Shock. Wait until you see her when she's not in shock.
That's something to look forward to.'*

*Of course, Mireille was right. When Alana and Floraidh
finally caught up with him on the Island they went to him with
open arms and embraced him as if he was their long-lost son
and brother.*

After a similar hug, Cathal felt a pang of guilt as he stood
opposite a smiling Floraidh in the library — guilt at knowing
the lengths she would go in order to help him. He played the
importance down, asking if she knew how patients fought
cancer, suggesting visualization as a possible route.

He had to answer the same questions he had asked
Mireille, but after convincing the temporary librarian that no
one she knew was sick, she said, 'It's not my field, but I know
a few people ... leave it with me for a day or two.'

He walked back to the Merc with Floraidh's promise that
she would drop something through his letterbox before the
end of the week.

Until that drop-off, he would see what he could find out
online ... and wonder where the girl had gone: the one who
had seen what he had missed, and appeared to know him
better than he knew himself.

*

Arthur Anderson walked over to the photo on the wall, 'Have you seen my new car, Helen? All electric—.'

'She's alive.'

Arthur didn't move, his eyes still fixed on the photograph in front of him. 'I wasn't aware there was evidence that confirmed the target in Spain was Robertson.' He said.

'How about a dead SAS team?'

'You're certain it's her?'

'I'm certain.'

Reluctantly the psychologist returned to his desk. 'Okay, for the moment, let's assume it is her, where are the bodies?'

'The bodies?'

'If it is Robertson, then where are the bodies of her targets? She would have to have a target — a constant supply of targets. She eliminates one, she moves onto the next, and so on. There would be scores of bodies littering the path behind her — unless she's been digging a lot of graves. If she doesn't have a target, she'll malfunction.'

'She's not a machine.'

'We have to consider the possibility that she might be functioning as one. The problem is that Robertson is the combination of two extremes. Her military upbringing and HK9. I don't think there is any question that she will see everything in the context of war. Where we see people who will assist us, she sees allies; we see people who might be obstructive, she sees targets to be eliminated.

'I suppose there is always the possibility she is planning something big. Robertson is an unknown entity. If she is alive, she's a loose cannon, and I don't like the fact that you've been given the task of confirming she's dead, and if she's not dead, tracking her down. Perhaps it's as well that Jeffries never lived to see what she'd created.'

'But what's her goal? Where does it all lead, and where are her targets coming from?'

'Helen, these are exactly the questions we don't have answers to. Think back, when you searched her home in Inverness, was there anything that stood out, or seemed out of place?'

'I don't remember anything' Helen lied, shaking her head as the image of the books on climate change appeared in the girl's bedroom. Part of her wanted to tell Arthur that she was almost certain Mireille was responsible for the murders of the industrialists. She was certain he would keep the information to himself, but she knew the only way to keep a secret is to tell no one. Besides, Arthur did not need to know.

Helen continued, 'Assuming that she is alive. How could she overcome the destructive side of HK9 – she's programmed to kill, how would she balance that against ... the conflict would be constant.'

The old man looked at her, shook his head, and sighed. 'Okay,' he said in resignation, 'This report is unofficial and there are big chunks of it missing, but seven years ago, a test took place somewhere near Broken Hill in New South Wales, a test that bore almost no similarity to the Hunter-Killer project, with the exception of the outcome, which was almost identical to the outcome of HK9. Within 72 hours of starting, all but one of the twenty test subjects was dead, most of them by their own hand. The sole survivor appeared to have reverted back to his childhood, and had immersed himself in something akin to a fairy tale.

'From what little information I have on the survivor, I am guessing this is a truer form of the Don Quixote Syndrome. You do know the story of Don Quixote?'

Helen shook her head. She had read the book at school,

but she couldn't help herself, she wanted to hear Arthur's take on it. The old man summarized. 'The Spanish nobleman who, having read too many stories about chivalry, set out to right the injustices in the world. But he was seeing a world that wasn't real. He had unwittingly chosen a form of insanity to avoid despair. The surviving test subject was, I believe, suffering from this syndrome and, in shutting out reality, he also shut out the need to kill himself.

'Of course, we all shut out the world to some extent; but apparently with this chap it was extreme, and there was no warning. One day he acted normally, the next it was clear that he had effectively reverted to his childhood. From what I can gather, he's still alive and has not changed since then: he lives in a fairy-tale world, every hour of every day.'

Arthur paused for a moment before adding, 'However, it's feasible that someone more in tune with their thoughts could make the choice to temporarily escape in to the world of their childhood, and then try to control the on-off switch, moving between their fantasy world and reality.

'Doing that would not always be possible though, and if we are talking about HK9, specifically Robertson, the need to kill herself would still exist — it wouldn't be suppressed as such, more side-stepped for periods of time. But if she managed to do it, then it would no longer be a version of the Don Quixote Syndrome, but the strategy of whichever fairy tale, or character within it, that she had chosen to escape into.'

As Helen was leaving, Arthur stood up and said quietly, 'Do not forget Robertson is programmed to kill anyone she deems an enemy. Any of your men come face-to-face with her, and she picks up on the slightest suggestion of threat, then their life expectancy will be measured in seconds.'

The co-ordinator of the Hunter-Killer project walked back to her office fully aware that Arthur's words were directed towards her, rather than military contractors.

14

Wednesday

'*Grandpapa! Grandpapa! C'est jolie!*' The little girl shrieked with delight as she ran across the white sand towards the expanse of the ocean.

'*Oui, Mireille, c'est beau. C'est magnifique.*'

The old man smiled as his granddaughter reached the water and waded in before diving headlong into the white surf.

She was five and it was her first visit to the island, and the first time she had been given the freedom to swim in the sea. The little girl swam out for a bit, then turned to her left and began swimming the length of the beach. She changed style every minute: breaststroke, to crawl, to backstroke. As if she'd found a new toy; her head frequently turned and, with a broad grin, she waved excitedly at her grandfather.

The novelty hadn't worn off on their next visit the following summer, but in the summers after that Mireille learnt to appreciate the beauty of the machair; in particular, the white sandy beaches, dunes and the fields of wildflowers that ran alongside them. The girl loved walking along the machair with her grandfather. Over the years, she would listen to stories about his visits to the island when he was young, and of meeting her grandmother here; about the visit, for their marriage and honeymoon, of her mother and father. After being told the story about her grandmother going to Oban, on each holiday, Mireille would find herself being drawn towards the old cottage her grandma had lived in. Although *unoccupied for decades and in a state of disrepair, she was still able to daydream that she, like her grandma, had been raised in that cottage and, before going to Oban, had toiled the croft it sat on.*

She was also drawn to the ocean. At sunrise she ran up and down the sand dunes, weaving her way along the length of the beach. On the way back she ran through the shallow water, returning to the rented cottage to find the backs of her legs covered in wet sand. After breakfast she would return to the beach where she would train with Cathal — the high point of her day. At sunset, if her friend wasn't around, she would walk along the beach on her own, often imagining she was treading in her grandma's footsteps.

On the days when the rain lashed down, she would stand at the window, longing to get out there and run through it. But her grandfather insisted she stayed in and played chess. It took her years to realize that he wasn't teaching her how to play well, but how to be patient, and how to plan.

Since reading about Boyle's death, Mireille had found it increasingly difficult to remain patient. Initially she didn't think she could hold herself together — until she developed a plan. The plan always gave her something to do, some action to take and, having that direction, allowed her to get through each day. But now she was waiting for Cathal. Until he got back to her with a virtual reality program, her engine had stalled, and she sat, like a car broken down on the fast lane of a motorway, waiting for the inevitable crash.

'*Je déteste attendre.*' Mireille said out loud as she knelt down and ran her fingers through the sand, as if she was trying to salvage some part of her that had been taken. But, the plan was all that remained. How much longer could she hold out, though? Her grandfather may have taught her about planning and patience, but he hadn't prepared her for anything like this. She consoled herself in the knowledge that he hadn't taught her about interrogation either. It had been an area he had always avoided during his life in the army. 'There will be plenty of others willing to extract information,' he told her. 'Leave it to them.' There were no others, but it didn't matter. She had known what had to be done. The Machine subjected 100 points of the body to extreme pain simultaneously.

And the Machine had broken Westley.

She looked again at the beach of her childhood, the wind swirling the sand across the dunes. Everything was different. Now she needed Cathal, and not just because he was the only person she could trust. He also had something she felt she no longer possessed. In holding to the plan so tightly, she seemed to have lost the ability to be objective about anything that didn't involve some form of physical action.

The voices had been loud through the night. Pounding. Demanding. To silence them she had run to this beach while the island still slept. But she had been here for too long; she shouldn't be trying to find herself in past memories. She would run back to North Glendale via Ben Kenneth. It was a hard run — at least, it used to be. When she returned to the cottage she would sit outside and read until the sky darkened. She would find something to do every day. She would keep herself occupied until her friend's return.

*

Helen pressed the end button on her phone. She had just been told by the head of the satellite monitoring department that someone was on his way over to see her. She wasn't optimistic; it would probably be some anomaly that they wanted to check out.

When the satellite monitoring specialist, Alex Moody, finally arrived in Gleason's office he had a female colleague, Lisa Forrest, in tow.

'I've been informed that you have something you want to report, and that I will find it of interest.' Helen added quietly, 'I hope it's worthy of your journey over here.'

The young man spoke first but not before repeatedly looking over at his companion. 'May I?' he slid his laptop in front of the manager, and pointed to the moving figure on it. 'What you're seeing is satellite footage, recorded this morning, of something moving very fast up a steep hill in the Outer Hebrides.'

'And?'

'The hill, Ben Kenneth, is incredibly steep, and the side of the hill that this figure is on ... well, you would have to swim to get to the base of it. Besides, it's impossible to run up it.'

'Impossible? Do you possess expert knowled—.'

'I do,' the girl said. 'Ben Kenneth holds a race every year for hill runners; the first Sunday in August. With the exception of 2016, when it was cancelled due to bad weather, my brother has competed for the last ten years. Before moving down South, I used to run the course with him. The runners take a different route from the one you're seeing on screen. It's a hard run, but to traverse this particular side, at this speed ... it's not possible.'

Finally we get to it. The decisiveness of the speaker sparked Helen's interest.

'Perhaps it was a trials bike?'

'It's too steep for any kind of vehicle. It would flip over.' Forrest said.

'Tail wind?'

'On this side of the hill, there was a head wind this morning.'

Moody chipped in. 'The ferries are all cancelled today because of the wind.'

'A wild animal? A large dog?'

'No.'

'Well, it has to be something, so what can it be? What do you think?'

The two of them looked at each other and the girl said, 'Unless Usain Bolt has migrated to South Uist, and acquired the ability—.'

'Where?'

'South Uist. It's the second largest—.'

'I remember, thank you. I now understand why you've been sent over. Ms Forrest, do you have experience with drone surveillance?'

She hesitated, looked at her colleague, and said, 'We both have.'

'Good. Then, you will both work from the Operations Room here. I want a photograph of this runner ASAP.'

'We don't have the authority to request a Reaper drone.'

'Use my name. Any problems, get back to me. One other thing, have you spoken to anyone else about this?'

'No. We were told to report to you immediately.'

'Let's keep it that way. As soon as you have anything, day or night — and speak to no one else.'

After they had left her office, Helen shook her head and smiled. She had only wanted Forrest, but she'd seen the way they'd looked at each other. Young love. Splitting them up might distract the girl, and Helen needed a photograph of that runner.

She walked over to her board and checked the details again. South Uist. The wedding of Mireille's parents had taken place in the township of Bornish. The island was also the birthplace of her grandmother. Of course, an island like South Uist had so few exit points, it would be seen as a death trap for someone on the run — and the last place you'd expect them to go — making it the perfect place.

Perhaps things were finally moving forwards. She had to be oprimistic, despite her inability to take anything positive from her conversation with Arthur.

She returned to her desk and picked up her phone, which on vibrate was making its way across her desk. It was Santiago, with an update on Kyle's progress.

'He's been subjected to prolonged extreme pain,' Santiago began. 'There are no clues to who's responsible, but they knew what they were doing. He was in a stress position, which placed pressure on his shoulders and lower back. Needles were inserted into the most sensitive areas of the body: the genitalia, feet, hands, face, scalp. In most cases, the needles made contact with the surface of the bone, or pierced tendons and ligaments.'

'How many needles, roughly?'

'Precisely: ninety-seven. If you add the three pressure points, you get an ugly round number. He was dehydrated when admitted. Currently his physical condition is stable. The real damage is psychological, and it's severe.'

'Permanent?'

'The doctor thinks it's possible he may recover. He shows a strong survival instinct.'

'Why am I getting the impression from your tone that you disagree?'

'I've seen this before. When the pain reaches a certain level, most will black out and that's what saves them. It's the mentally stronger who remain conscious. Ironically, they suffer for their strength. The mind is not designed to handle prolonged pain of this nature. Eventually it shuts down, and it doesn't come back.'

Long after the call ended, Helen kept going over it, even though she was aware it was destructive. She needed to become more involved in work, anything to stop her thinking of Kyle.

15

Wednesday 9.05 P.M. — Thursday morning

With no word from Floraidh, and no progress made with his own search, Cathal had spent the entire evening walking. From the harbour he walked across one beach, then another...

He hadn't intended to visit the cottage, but somehow found himself a few hundred metres away from it. He sat on the rough grass, crossed his legs, and watched the sun slowly set over Sonas.

The long grass in the field on his right swirled in the wind, a few restless seagulls argued overhead, suddenly diving for cover as a white-tailed sea eagle glided past. Cathal was oblivious, he was hearing other sounds: the wind cracking off Mireille's t-shirt, her laughter as they looked up at the darkening sky, then at each other in Bishops Road, the bolt of lightning serving as a starting gun for their three hundred metre race to the shelter of the cinema, as the downpour started. He listed the memories, going through them one at a time, searching ... Barra: the day after it had been hit by a bad storm. They had gone over on the ferry to help repair and rebuild. Whilst the others went to local crofts near the port, they had walked the length of the island to the most remote croft, spending the rest of the day driving uprooted fence posts back into the ground. The look on Mireille's face as she lifted a sledgehammer for the first time, and the distinct sound it made as it hit the sweet spot at the top of the post. The look of pleasure when she tasted the lentil broth the crofter's wife had made for them. That night, lying in the bed across from him, the words of the story she began to recite, suddenly ending as she fell asleep at the beginning of the third paragraph.

Then, the storm on Uist the following year, then the glorious summer the year after – he went through them all: all the memories, all the meetings at the ferry, all the days they'd spent together exploring the island, then at uni in Inverness; all the way up to Monday.

Why hadn't he knocked on the cottage door when he'd arrived, and asked her to explain?

He looked down and rubbed his eyes with the heels of his hands.

How much she'd changed, her shoulder length blonde hair replaced by a dark brown pixie cut. She was leaner; her tan deeper than ever. He didn't have to ask to know she'd stepped up her training. He saw the physical change as soon as he'd jumped down from the roof. But he knew, with the hug, that the real change was below the surface. Normally, Mireille would wrap her arms around him and not let go for at least five seconds. She hugged like a child – as if, at that moment, he was the only thing that existed in her world. But, on Monday it had been the briefest of contact.

Emotions: they were always on show, she never tried to hide them. It was the part of her that attracted him most. She used to be as transparent as glass, but now he could no longer see her.

'What happened to you, Mireille?' He whispered, looking directly at the cottage.

*

When he returned home, Cathal opened the front door to find a large envelope had been dropped through the letterbox. Resisting the need to tear it open, he sat down, took a deep breath, and carefully opened it.

His shoulders slumped. One magazine. Only one — and it was old. He held up a well-worn copy of a Sunday magazine from almost two decades ago. Yet the words on the cover leapt out at him. *'Your body is a medicine chest. Your Mind Can Heal'.* He quickly read the five-page piece, made himself a mug of coffee, then read it again. He walked outside to distance himself, put it into perspective. Floraidh. How long had she searched to find this article? It covered everything. It went into depth on the placebo effect: the beneficial effect produced by the patient's belief in the treatment, rather than the treatment itself. The article gave numerous extreme examples where placebos — typically sugar tablets or dummy pills — had brought about incredible results. The entire article gave the impression that there was this massive inner power that medical science simply didn't understand. It asked if the future of medicine lay in deceiving the patient. However, deception was only the key to unlocking belief in a desired outcome. Belief was the all-important factor. But it was how the article finished that had the most impact: '*gaining a deeper insight into self-healing properties of human beings could well become the holy grail of medicine in the coming century.'*

The journalist who wrote the article appeared to be saying that if we can work out a way to make people believe, they will then have access to a pharmacy full of drugs — designer medicine, but without the side-effects — or the costs.

In respect to cancer, Cathal realized his goal was straightforward: find a way for people to believe they are going to recover.

And virtual reality would be the way to make people believe, but he needed to go further back and remind himself of the basics: how it worked, why it worked, why were we deceived by immersion in an alternative reality, and why were films in IMAX able to trick us so easily?

He saw a number of reasons why immersion in a desired reality worked, but the key, he knew, was the visual cortex — the part of the brain responsible for processing images.

Then he remembered reading about the psychologist Jeanne Achterberg.

By examining and rating her patients' visualizations, Achterberg was able to predict, with 93 percent accuracy, who would recover and who would get worse or die. The recovery group were those who had a greater ability to visualize vividly, convincingly and regularly. They could, in effect, redirect the mind, and they did so through repetition. If the images are real enough, and seen often enough, they will deceive the visual cortex.

He was back to visualizing, precisely where Mireille had left him. The only difference was that now he knew why it would work, but he still had to find the route to develop a virtual reality program. What would they visualize? Seeing themselves free of cancer in the future? Seeing the doctors telling them there was no sign of cancer? That sort of thing wouldn't work with VR.

He went through it from the beginning. Mireille had asked him to design a VR program to fight cancer. Why? What had happened in the last year? Where had she been, and what was she involved in? She wanted her presence on the Island to stay secret. These were clues, but to what?

Nothing made sense. The only thing that did was the ability of VR to deceive the visual cortex. Visualizing had been the way, but VR was the future; repetition would still be required but VR possessed the potential to deceive the visual cortex far quicker. So VR would be the key to belief, and belief was a way of fighting cancer. And he was right back to Mireille's start point again.

He went down every avenue, but eventually powered down his laptop, slumped on his bed and fell instantly asleep, fully clothed.

The second Cathal woke he said quietly, 'It has to be a game.'

In the shower he went over everything, his mind speeding up as the water hit him. *It's not seeing the future, it's fighting in the present. It's seeing the cancer being hurt, then being destroyed.*

It was the same as the story about the boy seeing the Cavalry wipe out the Apaches. But VR was all about authenticity. There would be no army of enemy soldiers to represent cancer, but the tumours themselves. But what would he use to weaken, then destroy, them with?

Killer cells. Of course! Killer cells were the body's natural defence against cancer. Use a VR game to increase the production of killer cells ... no, not just the production, the direction of these cells.

There was something, he could feel it ... he'd read the blog only a few months ago: films that would make great remakes with the benefit of CGI. He'd seen the film on DVD when he was younger.

He ran down the stairs into the living room and over to the rows of shelves. A few seconds later he was out the back door and in the middle of the garden, the DVD in his hand. He held the film up to the sky in the same way Scott Brown, the Celtic captain, had held up the Scottish Cup a few months earlier, and roared, 'YES!'

'Aye, that's a rare body you have on you, Cathal. Will you be joining me for a cuppa, then?'

He looked over at his next-door neighbour, the voluptuous Morven Henderson, who was in the middle of hanging out

199

her washing. He couldn't quite remember when they'd started playing the flirting game, but today she was grinning as if— he looked down, and saw he was still dripping wet from the shower ... and completely naked. Ordinarily, he would have run back inside, but this morning all that mattered was that he had found something that would meet Mireille's expectations, and he felt the power of that surge though him. He turned to face his neighbour and smiled.

'Well, I would, Morven, but you know you're far too much woman for me.'

His neighbour laughed, 'Aye, I have to admit, I thought that myself until about twenty seconds ago. But now I think we'll get on just fine.'

Cathal smiled broadly and turned to leave.

'Still seeing that Eilidh Macpherson, I'll bet. You know, you're wasted on that young girl.'

Cathal suddenly realized that he hadn't thought of Eilidh once since Mireille appeared. He stepped back in the house, Morven calling out to him as he closed the door, 'No need to get dressed on my part—.'

In his bedroom, he pulled on a pair of jeans and threw on a T-shirt. He would take the rest of the day to plan the game in detail, then over to Sonas in the morning.

16

Friday 11.20 A.M.

Cathal parked up by the cottage. He went inside and called out to his friend, but the place was empty. After loading the film into the DVD player in the living room, he grabbed a can of Coke from the fridge, a bag of nuts from the cupboard and sat down on the sofa. The short journey in the car was long enough to plan what he was going to say, but his mind was still racing. He studied the DVD case then picked up a magazine from the table and uncovered a lilac and purple hardback book. He did not recognize the cover but the title was unmistakable. This was Mireille's favourite book, but it was not the version she had told him about. Her first UK edition of *The Princess Bride* was her most treasured possession. It had been a present to her father from her grandfather, and carried an inscription on the inside cover. The book Cathal held in his hands was almost forty years newer, and was a French translation. It did not have the red print when the author spoke directly to the reader. Mireille had described every aspect of the book to him and, though he had never read it, he had seen the film and they'd discussed the story at length.

Her views on the book were surprising. Everyone who knew the story knew the main characters were Westley and Buttercup. Everyone, that is, except Mireille, who saw their story as being a minor subplot. To her, the entire book revolved around the Spaniard, Inigo Montoya, and his quest for revenge on the six-fingered man who had killed his father.

Mireille's eyes would light up when she talked about Inigo: 'Can you imagine the kind of drive he has, the single-mindedness, to dedicate himself every day for ten years to learn the sword, then to do nothing other than search for the six-fingered man?'

The one thing they were in agreement on was that if you took out the humour and the miracle, it became not just a tragedy, but a horror story with Westley being tortured to death, Buttercup committing suicide and Inigo—.

Cathal heard the cottage door opening. 'In here,' he said.

His friend stood at the living room door, her face glistening, her wet hair swept back from her face. 'Good swim?' he asked.

She nodded. 'I was going to change into some dry clothes. Are you in a rush?'

'Take your time.'

A few minutes later Mireille appeared wearing a black tank top and black combat pants. She sat down opposite Cathal on the armchair.

He placed the can beside the empty wrapper and said quietly, 'I've found something.'

The girl said, 'I hoped you might.'

'Okay, I take it you know about Jeanne Achterberg and the visual cortex.'

'The outline; I don't know the detail,' Mireille said.

'The story about the boy and the tumour ... he was using a visualization technique. The Apache represented the tumour, and the Cavalry were the body's natural defences against cancer. The boy kept visualizing to the point where his visual cortex was deceived and he started to believe. Re-directing the mind in this way can take weeks, even months, but virtual reality deceives our minds far quicker. We become totally immersed in this alternative world — we believe what we see, and we react to it physically. If you've seen a film in IMAX you'll have experienced it.'

'I have. But virtual reality isn't IMAX.'

'IMAX has recently moved into the virtual-reality side. The two are so closely related, it was always going to happen. Now, I want you to watch a film.'

'In virtual reality?'

'No, a film made in the sixties.'

The film transpired to be *The Fantastic Voyage*. A few minutes in, Mireille, having read the cover of the DVD, pressed the stop button. 'You haven't developed a program have you? This is a game about a miniaturised submarine travelling through the bloodstream until it reaches the site of the tumour.'

Cathal nodded.

'And then it ... what, shoots it?'

'You need to think in terms of an alternative reality. You've either been miniaturised and you're inside a miniscule submarine, or you have cameras inside it and you're operating it remotely from a control room. Yes, the sub is travelling through your bloodstream. This is about authenticity — everything about it has to seem real — you have to locate the tumour, move the submarine into firing position, open the torpedo doors, range the target then fire the torpedoes, each one penetrating the walls of the tumour before releasing its payload.'

'Which is?'

'Killer cells.'

'So it's an attack sub ... a hunter-killer?'

Cathal nodded, 'You are on the bridge, or in control of the bridge. You have a main screen on which you'll see what's in front of the sub, but other screens will be available that show different things, one being your location in an overview of the body. On that screen you will also see the general location of the tumour but you will have to travel for a number of minutes, and overcome certain obstacles, before you reach it. This is part of the game — you have to hunt the cancerous areas down. The quality of what you're seeing and your ability to interact with it is crucial, so that, whilst you're playing the game you really believe what's taking place in this alternative world. Belief is the goal. Belief is everything. The game could be made even more authentic by having the equivalent of stethoscopes attached to certain areas of your body, so that you would hear your heartbeat and other internal sounds along with the sounds from the submarine, like the torpedoes being fired. You could also program in the actual scan results, so the real life tumours are exactly where they appear on the screen.'

Mireille stood up and walked over to the window, 'If this game helps us believe our bodies are combating cancer, why isn't it out there already?'

'It doesn't just help us believe; it deceives the visual cortex. Normally belief is a complex act involving numerous factors. With cancer, it would be affected by levels of pain and discomfort, scan results, environment, feelings of self-belief, self-worth, the attitude of people around us. But a game of this nature, if it's good enough, can eclipse those. If you play the game often enough you *will* believe what you see, and that might worry a lot of people.

'You said it when we spoke on Monday: the current system expects us to lie back and do nothing. Virtual reality is one thing when used in a theme park on a ghost train program to scare the shit out of thrill-seekers, or teaching training methods to surgeons and everything in between, but when it's going to allow patients to get involved in combating cancer to such a high degree, it becomes a very different story. The pharmaceutical industry, private healthcare sector, and a lot of health organizations will always oppose any threat to revenue: it's standard business practice, and they have the money to hire the top lawyers to resist it.'

'Even though the NHS is in financial crisis?'

'Care in the UK will go the same route as it has in the US. It will, over time, be privatized. It's already happening. The winners will be private healthcare and medical insurance companies. It will be patients that suffer.'

Mireille began pacing up and down the room. 'A game like this might stop that from happening for the people who are prepared to take the risk of believing. And this is not alternative medicine – it's not a substitute for traditional health care; it's complementary, right?'

'Absolutely. It wouldn't change the medical treatment; that would continue as normal. Whilst the game might have zero effect on the production of killer cells, it will allow us to believe, and belief can only enhance the treatment given by doctors.'

'It also allows patients to engage in the fight. Currently they are shut out from that. Having the ability to fight will change everything for them, and–.'

'What?'

Mireille had stopped pacing and was staring at the floor.

Cathal waited for his friend to add something, but after a few seconds of silence he said, 'You know, the manufacturers advertise these games along the lines that you *step into another reality and live the adventure*. But something like this would be the ultimate combat game, because the enemy is real and it's inside you. This game allows you to use your mind, and, potentially, all the internal processes that the mind can trigger, to work with medication to attack and destroy that enemy. You can't get more real than that. The fact that it is a game, it is an enjoyable experience, means that patients want to play. Repeatedly visualizing the same thing is extremely difficult, but playing an enjoyable game by-passes that difficulty.

'Then there is the control issue. When you engage in the fight you retake a level of control and perceive pain and discomfort differently. The person who actively fights is not a victim; someone who is prevented from fighting, generally is.'

Mireille was still staring at the floor, but she was hearing George Boyle and his prediction about what would happen with Gatekeeper 17. She'd become so focused on her plan that she had forgotten his warning. The game her friend was describing did not use subliminal images, nor did it have the coding used in Gatekeeper 17, yet it wasn't so far away from producing similar results. He had, once again, lived up to her expectations.

Cathal continued, 'I have a friend in Glasgow who works on the development of virtual reality programs. His fiancée is a lawyer. We can trust both of them. I have to go to Glasgow on Wednesday anyway, so I can go and see them and discuss the legalities. Why don't you come with me?'

'I've made a mistake. This is too dangerous for you to be involved in.'

'How? Pharmaceutical companies can be very subtle and devious, but they are no different from many businesses out there. They have to be to survive. We're simply talking about a legal battle. Come with me to Glasgow.'

The girl shook her head. 'They won't risk a legal battle. This is all about money, and there's too much of it involved.

They won't allow the unknown potential of the mind to be directed in this way against illness. They have to maintain the monopoly. There is a dark alliance among the pharmaceutical industry, the private health-care industry and a lot of medical organizations, and they'll do whatever is necessary to protect one another. *Whatever* is necessary.'

'Whatever is necessary? Dark alliance? Really?'

'They will stop it outside the courts. They will find a way to sabotage—.'

'Suppose they don't. Suppose the game doesn't even need regulatory approval.'

'Then they will have a well-known company put a game on the market that creates harm to the player and ruins its reputation, or they will simply bribe the big companies involved in virtual reality to make sure they don't ever enter this market. They may have done it already, and that could be a reason the game's not out there now. If smaller VR companies get financial backing then a lot of people are going to start disappearing.'

'I'm talking about legal action; you're talking about mass murder. What happened to you, Mireille?'

They were both standing now. The girl stepped towards her friend and, placing her left hand on his chest, pushed him up against the wall. 'You are not listening to me. You are underestimating the amount of money involved. Don't! I know what they are capable of. I have seen it.'

Cathal blinked as the hairs on the back of his neck stood up. He struggled to understand what had just happened. Suddenly the conversation was forgotten, as was everything else except for an overpowering need to get outside.

'I take your point, but I have to go now.'

She withdrew her hand, took a step back and said softly, 'If you are still going to Glasgow on Wednesday then it would be good if you could take me in the back of the Merc. I had enough problems avoiding people on the ferry on the way here, and I need to go to London.'

Mireille watched the car disappear into the distance, then turned to look at the cottage, then the hills to the west of it. Behind the hills there was a rock face on the edge of the ocean. Considering what had just happened, and with the wind building, it seemed the right place to be.

*

Helen Gleason stared into space as she stood at her office window. She had just taken a call informing her that Kyle's condition had worsened. Despite what Santiago had said, she still hoped he might recover. It was human nature to hold on to hope — even though she knew it was only a fine thread, she clung to it.

She turned to see Forrest standing across from her. 'I didn't expect to see you without your colleague.'

'Alex was covering the drone through the night. I didn't want to wake him.'

'You work well as a team. Well, I'm hoping you've found something.'

'Unless I'm mistaken, *this* … is your runner.' Forrest pulled an A4 photo from a folder and slid it across the desk.

Helen studied the photograph, 'When was this taken?'

'Twenty minutes ago. The time and coordinates are at the foot of the page. I had the drone follow her for as long as possible. It was running out of flight time.'

'We don't have a start or final location?'

'No, only her running ... unnaturally fast.'

'You have more photographs?'

'Yes. You want me to leave the file?'

'Please. Well done. I'll organize your transfer to my team.'

'Thank you. I have a question: are you transferring Alex as well?'

'Of course, Lisa.'

'I have another question.'

'You want to know who the runner is.'

'Well ... yes.'

'Let's get the transfers sorted out first.'

The girl nodded, smiled and left.

Helen turned to her board and pinned up the picture alongside the other two.

'Got you,' she whispered.

She knew she had enough now to get a raid organized and Mireille captured. She would be sure to use sufficient men this time. But raising enough of the right men for this kind of job might take a while.

She made some initial phone calls to set things in motion. The calls went well, and within two hours she received confirmation that, by Monday, the military contractors she had chosen would be on the island. They would attempt the capture on Monday night, Tuesday morning.

After what had happened in Andorra, she had no choice but to notify Bannen and Whitby. To her surprise, they were delighted this was moving ahead so quickly and confirmed that, as soon as they had the target secure, Helen would be the first to question her.

After Helen left Bannen's office, Whitby turned to him. 'This has gone quicker than we anticipated.'

'It's perfect, Alice,' Bannen replied. 'Let me make a call.'

209

Using a secure line, he got straight through to Bruce Commons.

'Bruce, John Bannen here. I have a job you might be interested in. Mireille Robertson ... we know where she is.'

The phone went silent for a few seconds. 'We are very interested. She's a priority target for us after what she did in Edinburgh.'

'The Department's interest in Robertson has changed, Bruce. In the past we've been looking to question her — that no longer applies. In fact, we don't want anyone questioning her.'

'Go on.'

'The one difficult area is timing, We have a positive ID of her in South Uist less than an hour ago, in the Lochboisdale area. We want the task completed this weekend, do you think you can manage that?'

'We will mobilize immediately. We have five, four-man teams on short notice call out. All of them are very keen to be involved in any operation where the target is Robertson. The task will be completed within your timescale.'

After Bannen hung up the phone, he looked at Whitby. 'Okay, that's the girl taken care of. What about Helen? She won't be happy when she comes in on Monday.'

Alice smiled. 'That's been in place for a few days. Ms Gleason won't be in on Monday.'

*

Mireille sat on the narrow ledge and looked down at the waves breaking on the rocks below her.

Five years earlier, late in the evening, with a full-blown storm raging, she had managed to convince Cathal to come here with her for what she had described as a confidence-building exercise.

The sun was nearing the horizon but you wouldn't have known it — the sky full of dark, angry clouds that cast a giant shadow over the entire island. The rain beat down hard, the wind tearing at both their soaked t-shirts. Mireille turned to Cathal and shouted, 'Almost there. At the edge you put me on your shoulders and we stand there for a minute.'

Her friend held his arms out wide. 'Are you mad? It's far too dangerous!'

'It has to be dangerous, otherwise it wouldn't build confidence. They do stuff like this in the army all the time.'

'Who told you that?'

'Grandpapa.'

'Your grandfather would beat me with an iron bar if he found out we were even up here in this storm. We need to go back. This will get us killed.'

'I'm going to the edge.'

'You're going to the edge of a ledge that is barely four feet wide! This is madness, Mireille, and I'll have no part in it. I'm going back.' Without waiting for an answer, the boy turned and began his descent.

The girl watched him leave the bluff. She felt a pang of regret. Although she realized doing this alone should give her even more confidence, it would mean little without her friend at her side. But, she had come this far; she had to see it through. She leaned forward as the wind gusted. When she reached the edge she realized she was now being caught by a crosswind from which the cliff had sheltered her. She planted her right leg, bending it at the knee, steadied herself and began counting down from sixty.

211

As she looked out at the raging sea she felt more alone than ever before, because she suddenly saw that Cathal had been right — this was going to get her killed, and it was now too late to do anything about it.

Mireille had never seen a wave like the one bearing down on her. She stood unmoving, mesmerized by the sheer size and dark perfection of it. She didn't brace for the impact, there was little point, and as her body relaxed she felt herself being picked up and spun mid-air by a large pair of hands. Hands that she knew could only belong to one person.

As the wave hit, and the world exploded, and her eardrums seemed to burst, she pressed her head into her friend's chest, instinctively driving forwards with her legs to counter the natural force that tried to hurl both of them into the rock face.

By the time the water had receded off the bluff, she was still gasping for breath. Cathal was still standing next to her, his hands still pressed into the rock either side of her head, his arms still forming a shield around her face. More importantly, his arms, having maintained enough pressure on the rock, had provided a fixed point of stability.

Seeing that he had turned her fully 180 degrees in towards his chest, Mireille arched her neck backwards to look at him. She had never seen him like this, and she cupped her hand to his cheek, as if she could somehow turn the clock back and take away all the pain that she saw in his eyes. He had come back to protect her, and the giant wave — the wave that should have killed her — had broken its back against him.

Mireille followed him in silence on the descent to the beach. She looked at his broad back and the remnants of the t-shirt that had been torn apart by the wave. She knew he would never speak of this night. He would pretend it hadn't happened, as would she. But it didn't stop the tears from *rolling down her cheeks the entire descent. As they walked across the beach the storm lessened in intensity and, though the waves still crashed in, the rain had stopped and the light from the setting sun, hidden until now by the storm clouds, lit up the horizon in an orange hue.*

The girl began to wonder if her friend would ever speak to her again, but he slowed his pace and, as she caught up to him, their hands touched and their fingers interlinked. They walked the rest of the way back like that, their hands in silent embrace.

At the path to the rented cottage where Mireille was staying, there was no good-bye hug, no words. Cathal merely turned away and began walking in the direction of his home.

Lying in bed that night, the girl could not sleep. She was not thinking about the enormity of the wave, but what she'd seen in the light of the dying sun the moment her friend had turned to walk home. The remains of the white t-shirt contrasting sharply to the blackness of his skin; she had never seen bruising like that before. She wept in silence until the curtains in her room lightened with the coming of dawn, at which point sleep finally took hold.

It transpired that she did not see Cathal again for the rest of that holiday until the day of her departure. She stood at the pier on her own, her grandfather having gone to speak to someone, when she felt her friend's hand gently rest on her shoulder. She knew it was him instantly and she turned and looked into his dark brown eyes and searched for the pain, but it was gone, and they hugged each other for minutes until she heard Grandpapa say, 'Hello Cathal. I hate to break this up, Mireille, but the ferry's going to leave without us if I don't.'

With a last look at his face, the girl and her grandfather

213

boarded the ferry. Mireille stood at the handrail and watched her protector stand at the pier until he'd disappeared into the distance. She turned away only when she couldn't see the island anymore, realizing that not one word had passed between them since the wave hit. But they had never really needed words to communicate what they felt. That night, on the mainland, she walked outside and, looking up at the stars, vowed that she would never knowingly put Cathal in danger again.

Now, sitting on the cliff edge, the girl looked out at the ocean once more. She felt that this time she may have broken the friendship that, after the night of the storm, she had thought unbreakable. But a vow was a vow and, while everything else in life was breakable, a vow was not.

She needed to get off the island, and to London, as soon as she could.

17

10.00 P.M.

Cathal woke to the sound of his mobile. He dug into his pocket, accidently hitting the answer button. He heard the sound of chanting, mixed with the music from the jukebox, a bar full of people and Eilidh's voice shouting above all of it. The Borrodale! He had told her he'd be there at nine.

'Cathal, where are you?'

'Shit! I've just woken up.'

'What? We're all waiting for you.'

Davey's voice, unmistakeable as he shouted, 'Like hell we are! You take the night off big man, give me a chance to—.'

He could picture Eilidh ripping the phone out of Davey's grasp. It was her voice he heard next, 'Well, are you coming? Are you gonna save me from a fate worse than death?'

'I'll be there in ten minutes.'

'The clock is ticking.'

Cathal leapt off the bed and changed into a fresh pair of jeans and a t-shirt, brushed his teeth and ran down the stairs, slamming the front door behind him. He turned and opened it and grabbed his Tomcat leather jacket from the back of it. The wind had picked up. He zipped the jacket to the top and broke into a jog. Saturday night in the Borrodale was always a mini adventure, anything could happen, and he had caught the atmosphere from the brief phone call. He wanted to be there in the thick of it. Five minutes later, he was in the car park and ran up the steps to the back door. The door swung open just as he moved to push it. Eilidh's eyes lit up as she almost collided with him. Before he could say anything her arms were wrapped around his waist and her lips were up against his, her tongue probing, the taste of Glayva sweet and warming; the familiar smell of her perfume, intoxicating. He could feel her breasts against his chest and her thighs pushing against him.

'Did I make it in time?' He whispered in her ear, as he hugged her.

'Twenty-three seconds to spare.'

As they walked into the bar, the noise hit his senses. There was a cheer from a group of about ten at the far end. 'Cathal! Cathal!' The chanting started, then stopped as he reached them. Most of them were hammered already. Thirty minutes and three double vodkas later, he was fast catching up on them.

He became engaged in a conversation with three of his friends. The language used would have baffled an outsider. One would say something in Gaelic, and the response would be in English; another would join in, their sentences a mixture of both languages.

Cathal saw his childhood friend Niall engrossed in a game of pool. The odds were usually high when Niall played, and he was potting the last yellow, setting himself up on the black. Niall slammed it into the side pocket, taking the game. Cathal downed his vodka and walked towards him, but collided with Ruairidh the big mechanic who, on exiting the toilets, was still buttoning his flies.

Ruairidh bounced backwards, his feet caught together and he went straight down, his ample rump hitting the floor with a loud thump that shook the entire bar and brought laughter to everyone in it. Two of his friends helped him to his feet, all three of them laughing out loud. 'Ach, it's yourself, Cathal. If there's a man not to bump into in a bar it's you, you big bastard. It's like hitting a fuckin' rock!' Ruairidh shouted, as he wrapped his arm as far as it could go across Cathal's back and hugged him, kissing him on the cheek.

One of the many wearing a Celtic top put Tina Turner's 'Simply the Best' on the jukebox. With Celtic having thundered to a second successive domestic treble, they had achieved something unprecedented in Scottish football. Confidence was so high, many fans believed they would secure a third treble, and the song triggered the entire room to join in the chorus. The back bar of the Borrodale in Daliburgh in the Isle of South Uist had slipped into a higher gear, and almost everyone was on a high. And Cathal, with Eilidh's arm around his waist, was slap bang in the middle of it.

Except he was no longer there.

He hadn't moved when Ruairidh had walked into him. It happened almost every night he was in the bar: someone would bounce off him. But the impact had taken him back to Sonas. The memory of what had occurred there flew across the hills and beaches and took his breath. He had been in a daze when he left the cottage and, as soon as he arrived home and lay down on his bed, he was asleep. Now he finally woke up to what had taken place.

With the bar jumping, Cathal was alone in a world of silence. Voices calling to him didn't penetrate the walls of his fortress and, within that fortress, questions appeared from nowhere.

What had happened to her? Mireille's power was in her legs, but all she'd used were her left hand and shoulder to push him up against the wall. Where had that strength come from? It wasn't natural, yet her face showed no signs of the steroid abuse he'd first seen in a gym in Inverness.

Besides, you couldn't get that kind of power from training, no matter how much gear you were on. And there was the warning; words that hit him with more force now. Could she be right? It would be standard business tactics for the pharmaceutical industry to pay the top virtual reality companies to stay away from health care. That could well be the reason such a game was not out there already.

He tried to imagine the amount of money involved, recalling pictures he'd seen of drug houses after they'd been raided by the police. The cash, stacked neatly in bundles on top of each other, went from floor to ceiling, filling entire rooms. He tried to imagine that every single minute, that amount of money was being spent on pharmaceutical drugs. No, not every minute, every second. No, every hundredth of a second. His head began to spin, different voices were talking to him; he heard Eilidh's voice in the distance calling him. He burst through the bar door and, turning right, threw the outer door open and stepped outside into the cool night air. He took in big gulps of it as he tried to quieten the voices that rang out to him. He walked across the car park and turned right on to the quiet road that led to the church, then stopped when he reached the small loch. He looked at the water, the wind rippling the surface. He knelt down and fell over onto his side. He rolled onto his back and looked up at the stars, as if that would clear his head and somehow bring respite from the questions that bombarded it.

How much she'd changed ... and yet hadn't changed. When she arrived on Monday she was wearing black, and every time he'd seen her since then — black top, black leggings or combats, black trainers. She had once spent an entire summer wearing black but how long ago was that? Nine, ten years? He was too tired to work it out.

He lay for hours, the bar long closed, when he finally stood up. His legs were numb but at least he had placed his thoughts in a crude prioritization. As he limped home, he listed the most relevant points. It didn't matter if his friend was right, or wrong, about her warning. It didn't matter that she had changed, or the extent of the change. The girl he knew was full of smiles and laughter, but he hadn't seen her smile once since she'd been back. Something had happened, and the girl he knew had gone, but that did not negate the possibility that she would return. Though Eilidh was fun to be with and the sex was great, that was all it was. He loved Mireille, he always had, and he could not, and would not, accept that the girl he knew had gone forever.

She needed to go to London. He didn't know the reason, but he knew she would have one. She always had a reason. She also wanted to get the VR game moving forwards. He looked at his watch: 04.20. With the muscles in his legs beginning to work again, he lumbered the last few metres home. In the kitchen he was about to put a large spoon of coffee in a mug, but instead put it back in the jar and went to the top shelf. He needed to be on top form today and that required something considerably stronger than Nescafé.

After running up the stairs he stripped off his damp clothes and jumped into a hot shower. He dressed quickly in blue jeans and combat boots. He threw a few clothes and toiletries into a sports bag, placed his laptop in the side compartment, donned a clean navy sweatshirt and ran down the stairs into the kitchen. He poured half a mug of the freshly brewed Sons of Amazon coffee, added cold water and gulped it down. He grabbed a steak pie from the fridge, and, scooping up his jacket on the way out of the door, swung it closed in a single movement. He was in the car and halfway to North Glendale and the cottage, on autopilot.

18

Saturday 5.15 A.M.

She was flying. The wind was at her back and she was unstoppable. She was running so fast now she couldn't hear the sound of her bare feet touching the wooden floor of the bridge.

At least, she thought it was a bridge. It was odd that she couldn't hear any sound coming from her feet hitting it. *I should hear sound. Am I running on a bridge? It had looked like a bridge when I approached it. I should check it's there. I need to know what I'm running on, don't I?*

No, just keep running.

But don't I have to know?

No, you have to keep running.

So she ran. Then, after a while she looked into the distance, but what she had seen earlier was no longer there. There was nothing there. She tried to feel what was beneath the soles of her feet, but she felt nothing.

Keep running.

Where am I? What am I running on?

It doesn't matter. Nothing matters except the run.

I have to check, to make sure ...

You don't have to do anything. Nothing matters here, just the run.

But I need to know. I need to make sense of this.

No, you only think you do. But it's not true, nothing is true: there is only the run, nothing else.

But what is the run if I can't see where I'm going ... if I can't see what I'm running on? I need to see what I'm running on.
Why do you need to know anything?
I don't know why, I just have to. I have to look now.

Mireille woke with a start, and sat up in bed to the sound of a vehicle approaching.

Opening the front door, she found herself looking at Cathal standing at the side of the Merc. 'We go this morning,' he said.

Thirty minutes later, the car sat in the queue waiting to drive on to the ferry. The girl lay in the back hidden under the screen. Even without it, the windows were so dark that anyone looking in would have struggled to see her.

*

Helen was working from home and finalized the Monday night raid over the phone before nine. After briefing the senior man she finished dressing, slipping on beige chinos and a brown silk blouse. She glanced at her watch. She was going to be late.

An hour later she beamed with pride as she listened to her daughter describe her latest adventures.

At the same time as the two women sat in a restaurant in London, the ferry pulled into Mallaig.

Cathal had been restless during the crossing. The strong coffee had fully kicked in and his mind wouldn't rest. The priorities were being dealt with so the underlying questions had resurfaced. He couldn't stop thinking about Mireille sleeping in the back of the car and why she had to go to London now. The virtual reality game was clearly important to her, so why London? And why not Glasgow to see his friends who could really get the project moving? Would she go back to the island, or to university in Inverness? Virtual reality games in health care ... was she right to say they would never be made? Was she in danger?

The ferry neared the port and Cathal returned to the car. As he opened the driver's door he looked over at the back screen. He slid into the driver's seat and quietly closed the door. He sat in silence for ten minutes, his body relaxed, his brain in overdrive. The ramp finally went down and the queue of vehicles slowly drove off the ferry. Minutes passed. He knew disembarking was slow, but he couldn't remember it taking this long before. There were men walking the length of the vehicles in front of him, talking to the drivers, noting registration numbers. Cathal let his window down and called over one of the port staff.

'What goes, Hamish?'

'Some kind o' transport census, for the ferry company, I s'pose. They wanna know how many folks are in each vehicle.'

'Did you know about this?'

'Naw, they pulled up twenty minutes ago. Oh, 'ere you go.'

With that, Hamish stood back to let the official step up to the Merc.

The man looked the length of the car, and, not seeing through the tinted windows, pushed his head in next to the driver and scanned the back.

'What the hell are you doing?' Cathal said.

'Travelling with anyone today, sir?'

Cathal could feel anger rising up in him. He looked down the line. There were about four of them. He wanted to open the door into this man's face, throw him to the ground and confront the rest of them. 'You got eyes in your heid. You see

223

anyone else?'

'And where are you going today, sir?'

'Inverness.'

'Thank you.'

In his wing mirror Cathal watched the man walk to the vehicle behind him. This was no census. In his first year at uni he had trained at a city gym with a soldier. The soldier had always avoided telling him the unit he was in. He had a very particular way of walking, his demeanour and body language a reflection of extreme confidence. The man now looking into the vehicle at the back of him moved in exactly the same way.

Cathal gently pulled the Merc on to the main road to Fort William and Glasgow. He didn't want to acknowledge the possibility that the men at Mallaig might have been looking for his passenger. Why? What had she become involved in? She had told him yesterday that she knew what *they* were capable of, and she'd clearly meant murder. But who were *they*?

A part of him wanted to stop and get her to explain the whole thing to him. If she didn't, he could drop her off and return to the port. But what would he do? Take one of the men aside and beat the truth out of him? No, he wouldn't do that because if Mireille didn't want him to know, there would be a reason. But a lot of questions had resurfaced, and they weren't going away.

Parked in the drop-off point at Central Station, they stood alongside the car. He told her what happened at Mallaig. It turned out she had been awake and had heard everything.

'Let me go with you, Mireille. I can help.'

'I need to do this alone,' she said. 'If you want to help, then forget all about the virtual reality game.'

He nodded slowly in resignation. His friend was involved

224

in a world that he didn't understand. He'd known since yesterday at the cottage, when she'd pushed him up against the wall. He had no choice but to accept that the days when he could protect her were over, and that she might put herself in danger protecting him.

He wanted to say something though, to tell her how he felt. He'd stayed silent for too many years. Before he could, she said, 'I was careful. I didn't leave a trail when I came to the island, so I don't understand how they would know, but I'll find out in London. Until I return, I want you to wait here for me, don't go—.'

'I'll be here,' he said, then looked closely at the girl standing in front of him. She held a large brown envelope in her left hand and was wearing black leggings and a tight fitting long sleeved black top. 'You can't go just wearing that.'

'I need to travel light.'

Cathal unzipped his leather jacket and handed it to his friend.

She shook her head, 'Not your Tomcat, you love that jacket.'

'You've always liked it, Mireille. You said it would give you room to move, and it is black. Besides, there are people I love a lot more than this jacket.'

And then it happened. Everything changed in the next few seconds.

He watched her turn and walk towards the ticket office. He kept watch until she disappeared amongst the crowds of travellers.

Sitting in the Merc, he took one last glance at the train station and then pulled out in to Hope Street. He would be at Seb's flat in twenty minutes, and the work would begin. He would be going against Mireille's wishes, but he had to do something. If he didn't, he'd drive himself mad fretting about her. As he sat in traffic he wondered how long he would have to wait in Glasgow before she returned.

It didn't matter. He would wait. He would work. He would develop the game.

19

Richmond, Surrey

There is a grass square near the centre of Richmond; a perfect grass square surrounded by Georgian town houses. Mireille had been fascinated by it as a child on her previous visit. It had been winter and she had sat with her grandfather and looked up at the almost constant passing of flashing lights in the sky. 'What are they?' she had asked, as she pointed upwards.

'Aeroplanes, like the one we came here on.'

'But there are so many of them.'

'That's London, sweetheart. They do everything faster here.'

'They're pretty.'

Mireille stood on the same spot, reliving the memory, before banishing it to the vaults at the back of her mind. She pulled the zip on Cathal's Tomcat up to the collar.

Ten minutes later she had identified the target property, accessed the rear, scaled the brick wall, and gained entry through a large window. She was aware of noise coming from behind the curtains, but assumed it was coming from the flat's occupant: her target, Helen Gleason. She stepped in to the room, letting the curtain fall behind her. She had entered the main living room, the focal point, every room in the flat leading off it.

Dawson, a man in his late twenties, saw her immediately. 'Who the fuck are you?' he said in amazement.

A giant shadow appeared on Mireille's right side. A man of similar dimensions followed, 'It's the daughter. She must have been hidin' somewhere.'

Dawson glanced over at Adams, then returned his attention to the girl, 'Are you sure she's alone?' he said, as he began darting from room to room sticking his head in each one.

'Why don't you ask her?'

After glancing behind the curtains, Dawson returned to his original position. 'No point. Look at her, she's frozen with fear.'

Adams looked her up and down. 'Check those fuckin' legs out.'

Dawson's confidence, which had momentarily been shaken by Mireille's sudden appearance, had returned after finding no one else in the flat. The girl's body language couldn't hide the fact that she was alone. He had total confidence in Adams. He had seen his power on numerous occasions. They were in control, and Dawson loved being in control of young women. As much as he tried he couldn't keep the excitement out of his voice.

'I'll get a better look of those legs when I get those pants off her.'

'I'm having that jacket,' Adams said.

A third man, in his late forties, stood in the doorway of the bedroom, his face defined by the scars over his eyes and broken nose. He wore a navy boiler suit and a woollen commando hat. He hooked his thumb over his shoulder. 'Get her in 'ere.'

Adams tossed a roll of gaffa tape to Dawson, knowing he would move in and tape the girl's mouth as soon as she was on the ground. He stepped towards her. He would use the same move as always. When something proved effective, you

228

didn't try anything else. As soon as he was within reach, he would grab the girl's hair from the top of her head, and, bending his knees, simultaneously whip his arm down. The move jarred into action the huge muscles on his thighs, shoulder, arm and back. The whole thing took less than a second, and in that time the girl went from standing upright, to being winded, on her knees, her face against the floor. The shock took any possible resistance out of her. By the end of that second, no matter who she was, or whatever she'd achieved in life, she would be, from that point onwards, a victim.

Ordinarily, Mireille would have seen the move coming. But when she saw the third man appear, she began thinking of Inigo, and the question he asked his friend Fezzik: how many men could he defeat in combat at once?

For a second Mireille couldn't remember Fezzik's answer, her confusion a result of the difference in number between book and film and, whilst she was deep in thought, Adams' huge hand had hold of her hair, his knees were bending, and the whiplash of his arm, descending with the force of a pile driver, had begun.

The girl was too late to stop the move.

Lost in that second.

20

10.45 P.M.

Helen turned the key, opened the front door, and walked into her flat. It was darker than normal but the thought didn't register on her consciousness as her attention was on her handbag, more specially, on finding her ringing mobile. She quickly walked into the centre of the room, located and pulled her iPhone out of the bag, and hit the answer button. It was Santiago and she was speaking at twice her normal speed.

After Helen asked her three times to slow down and start again, Santiago's words eventually began to make sense. Helen was then able to form a picture of what had taken place over the last fifteen minutes. Kyle's heart had stopped. The crash team arrived and after a number of attempts managed to start his heart again. But, it seemed his heart was not the only thing that responded to the defibrillator — he had regained full consciousness — and he wanted to speak to her.

'How is he? What about permanent damage? Is he coherent? Is he making sense?' Helen asked.

'I don't know. He kept saying the same thing, insisting I contact someone from your department. When I told him you were my contact he said he needed to speak to you urgently.'

The clicking of heels that had accompanied the entire phone conversation suddenly stopped. 'We're here. I am going into his room,' Santiago said quietly.

Helen held her breath as the line fell silent.

'Ms Gleason?'

Although his family had moved to England when he was nine, the former soldier's accent from the east coast of Scotland was unmistakable. Though weak, Helen recognized the deep husky voice immediately.

'Yes, Kyle, it's so good to hear you—.'

'A few years ago your husband had engine trouble. I fixed it, but my hands were covered in oil. I am sorry, she knows. She knows where—.'

Helen was already halfway to the front door. 'It's okay, Kyle, I'll call you back,' the almost forgotten memory of her husband telling her he'd had to call one of the boys from the gym to pick him up as he couldn't get his car started, but the car had been fixed. Richard hadn't told her Kyle had been in the flat to wash his hands after working on the engine. Why would he?

Helen had her key in her hand, almost at the door now, her mind racing, picking up on the things she'd missed; the dampness in the carpet at the door, the darkness of the flat ... the key entering the lock, her bodyweight shifting ready for the run down the corridor to the lift ... thinking the fire stairs might be better, they were closer, but before she could move, she sensed someone step behind her.

'Tell me about Gatekeeper 17.'

Helen sighed, her head bowed in resignation. She had always feared this moment would come, ever since her last conversation with Arthur. Her one hope of survival was in the truth: 'Don't you want to know about Hunter-Killer 9?'

'Why should I?'

'Amanda Jeffries didn't tell you everything.' Helen said, as she turned to face the girl.

'Gatekeeper 17— tell me about it.'

'It was the breakthrough, the only program that had the coding and allowed direct access to the unconscious.'

'I know about that.'

'Did you know that while it was being developed, Hunter-Killer 9 was being tested?'

'Amanda told me about Gatekeeper 9 but not—.'

'There was no Gatekeeper 9. Amanda misled you. Officially it was known as the Hunter-Killer project. It was a military program from the onset. She didn't tell you that, did she?'

'No.' Mireille turned on a sidelight and told Helen to sit down. 'I'm assuming your department works for the government?'

Helen studied the girl standing five feet away. Her university matriculation photograph had been stuck in the centre of the main wall in her office for the last two years. None of the three photos she had, caught Mireille's physical presence — the taut muscle that lay underneath the tight black top and leggings, the sense of raw power almost mesmerizing. Then, remembering the question, she said, 'It's not that simple. Officially, the government knows nothing of our existence. You understand plausible deniability?'

Mireille nodded. 'You said Amanda knew it was a military program.'

'They all knew. The purpose of the Hunter-Killer project was to create the perfect soldier for today's wars. We know the dangers of using existing training and tactics to combat a new enemy. The French lost their country in weeks in 1940 because they had thrown all their resources into the Maginot line, expecting a repeat of the trench warfare that defined the First World War. In general, NATO countries have not adapted to the war on terrorism. We face an invisible enemy that walks amongst us and employs everyday vehicles as weapons of destruction; an enemy that will think nothing of using civilians as shields to protect their fighters. While they use brutal and ruthless tactics, we rely on sophisticated intelligence gathering and sharing information with our allies. It's too reactive and defensive. We need to adapt to this new kind of warfare, so our department was tasked with finding a more proactive and aggressive way of combating terrorism.

'The Hunter-Killer program was designed specifically to create, with a few weeks' training, a mentally and physically enhanced soldier who would be able to infiltrate the senior echelons of the enemy, wait for the opportunity and then kill as many as possible — if necessary, without weapons — and with little or no regard for personal safety. Our troops would use intellect initially, then resort to a base level — losing all sense of humanity, they would become merciless cold-bloodied killers.'

'Terrorize the terrorists,' Mireille whispered under her breath.

'It was a theoretical ideal, a program that had been planned but was never expected to be implemented. But with the rise in power of IS, the Hunter-Killer program was given a green light. After the Paris attacks in January 2015, the program received additional funding. Following the coordinated attacks in the same city ten months later, the timescale was brought forwards, and testing commenced with HK9 in January 2016.

'It was a disaster that never got beyond the initial testing stage. There were ten test subjects and, on the first day, two attacked and killed their handlers and a number of the monitoring team before being shot dead by security. We isolated the rest, but were unable to stop three killing themselves within the first week. By the end of the second week, all of the five left alive were diagnosed as clinically insane. Even in a special hospital, and on suicide watch, they all managed to kill themselves within the month.

'The team in South Queensferry was not informed of this, only that HK9 was deemed to create too many inner conflicts to be effective. It was agreed with Thompson that the mind was too complex and fragile to have high-intellect functioning alongside brutal killer imperatives. Even though it existed in real life, the balancing act of achieving this state via a virtual reality program was probably impossible.

'Thompson and his team decided to go to the root of the problem. They felt that, in order to control the mind of the soldier, they needed to have total control of the unconscious, and they continued work on this basis. A few weeks later they made the breakthrough. They stated they had eliminated internal conflicts, because they had, by accident, uncovered a coding that allowed direct access to the unconscious.

'We all knew that, in having the ability to tap the power of the unconscious at will, Thompson and his team had achieved something extraordinary. Amanda put forward a proposal that would temporarily shift the direction of the program they were working on, from creating a weapon against terrorism, to creating a weapon against cancer and other life-threatening illnesses. The team began work on what they stated would be a one-off program: Gatekeeper 17, the number denoting the year they would go public and commence clinical trials. The mistake they made was in going through the chain of command. It was clear to those in charge that the temporary shift proposed by Amanda would end up being permanent. When news of the deaths surrounding HK9, and the termination of the Hunter-Killer project reached their employers there would be repercussions. The two in charge decided they had to come up with a way to save their careers. I am certain they leaked information about Gatekeeper 17 to the pharmaceutical and private healthcare industries.

'It was a sell-out, a total betrayal of those involved, and resulted in the murders that took place in Edinburgh two years ago. With the exception of our master copy of HK9, all traces of the project were destroyed. I think you know most of the rest. A former SAS major was set up for the murders of Thompson, his team at South Queensferry, and the other doctors in Edinburgh. Shortly before DI Boyle died, witnesses have stated that he made it clear on a recorded message that the SAS Major wasn't involved, but the recording was never found. The head of the organization where the recording was made, Audrey Hall, was killed in a hit-and-run the day after the murders. Major Dowas, and the team of contractors he supposedly employed, ended up taking the blame for all the murders which, I imagine, was what was originally planned. Boyle's intervention proved pointless in the end. As far as the public were concerned, Boyle was responsible for cracking the case, along with the deaths of the team of military contractors in a shoot-out.

'We knew of your involvement, and that you'd been programmed with HK9, because the team of contractors relayed that information to their employers hours before you hit them. The information was passed on to us, but you were deliberately omitted from all our reports. We expected you to be found dead within the week anyway. The following month our department was granted an undisclosed sum from an anonymous source. Bannen and Whitby both received bonuses.'

'How much money was involved?'

'I wouldn't even like to hazard a guess.'

'So you believe this Bannen and Whitby are to blame for the betrayal?'

'I am sure of it. I wanted to make it public, but it was so far-fetched, who would have believed it?' Helen paused then said, looking directly at Mireille. 'I also wanted to stay alive. I *still* want to stay alive, if that's possible.'

'Whitby and Bannen, who are they?'

'Alice Whitby, head of operations, and John Bannen, my section head.'

'Who else was involved?'

'From our side, I think it was just them.'

'You say you're certain that the pharmaceutical and private healthcare industries are behind the murders, that they would have been the ones who employed the contractors. Do you have any proof?'

'No, but it makes sense that they financed the whole thing, made the grant, organized the set-up and the murders. They have the motive and the money, and they weren't interested in HK9. That's why the information about you was passed on to us.'

'I want names. I want to know the people who brought in and paid for the contractors.'

'If anyone knows, it'll be Bannen and Whitby.'

'That makes it easier. I want to see them anyway. Where are they now?'

'I don't know, they will be in Monday for sure. We have teams preparing to travel to South Uist that morning to capture you.'

Mireille stared at the carpet, coming to terms with confirmation that the men at Mallaig had been looking for her.

She said quietly, 'They are there now.'

'That's not possible. They are travelling to the ports tomorrow night for Monday's sailings.'

'Then there is another team involved. They were at Mallaig this morning, checking all the vehicles coming off the ferry. They were looking for me.'

Helen shook her head. She should have been told about this. A few seconds passed in silence then she said, 'If you're right, then Bannen and Whitby must have organized their own team to go in early. They'll want to remove anything that could be linked to them. It'll be an assassination team on the island, which will mean both of them will probably be at the department. I'll find out.'

Helen was about to call Liman, but opted to call Lisa Forrest. After the call was over, she placed her mobile on the table and said, 'They *are* still at the department. All team members were stood down an hour ago. My contact overheard a conversation about a strike force moving at one in the morning. My guess is it will be monitored by drone.'

The woman stared at the girl and drew a deep breath, 'Mireille, everything I've told you is true, but I don't understand why you would even listen to me, let alone believe me.'

'I know you're telling the truth.'

'How can you?'

'It doesn't matter,' Mireille said as she stood up, slipped on Cathal's Tomcat, and zipped it up halfway. 'Let's go.'

'Where?'

'The Ops Room. You have a car?'

'A friend's, mine is in for servicing.'

'Good, I might have to use it for a day or two.' Mireille turned towards the front door.

'Wait. We can't just walk in. There's security to pass.'

'And?'

'I can sign you in, but you can't wear that on your head; you look like a cat burglar.'

'I'll need to wear something.'

'Give me a minute.' Helen made her way towards the bedroom.

'Don't go in there.'

When someone asked Helen *not* to do something, she had a tendency to do it. She switched the light on as she opened the door, froze for a second and then vomited. Mireille pulled her gently out of the room, closed the door and steered her across the living room in to the nearest chair.

Mireille sat next to her and said quietly, 'That's why I knew you were telling the truth. When I arrived they were already here, and they were sent to kill you.'

Helen rubbed her eyes. 'How could you know that?'

'One of them told me. Those men were used for this particular type of job: to make it look as if you'd walked in on a burglary. They were to rape you first. They thought I was your daughter and they intended to rape and kill me.'

A silence followed as the girl allowed that to sink in. It achieved the result she wanted: nothing quite like a mother thinking her child was in that kind of danger to bring out the protective instinct, and the cold purposefulness that went with it.

Helen stood and walked straight into her bedroom, and came back with a moleskin flat cap.

'It was my ex-husband's favourite. I hid it when he came to collect his things.'

Mireille walked into the bathroom and took off the commando hat that covered the wound. The bleeding had stopped but a large patch of her scalp was red raw ...

As he wrenched his arm downwards Adams thought the move was going as it should. There was, as usual, some natural resistance, but momentum always worked for him — the longer the move went on, the greater the downward force. But just at the point where maximum force should have been attained, the resistance was gone; there was nothing. His arm swung at far greater speed than it should have. He was thrown off balance and crashed to the floor. He stared at the clump of hair he held in his right hand, unable to grasp that it had been the girl's core strength, particularly the strength in her legs and neck, that had kept her standing. All three men stared at the girl, stunned by her apparent indifference. She looked at the ground and said one word: 'Huit.'

The second in which Mireille had been lost ended with the answer to Inigo's question. Ignoring the blood running down her face she moved towards the nearest man, who was trying to get to his feet. Dropping to one knee and with a narrow fist, made with the second and third knuckles, the girl drove a straight right to the centre of his throat.

As he watched his friend slump to the carpet, fear shook Dawson into action. He turned and ran towards the front door. He reached it before remembering he'd locked it, but it didn't matter because he'd remembered something else — how effective Harrison was with a knife. He chided himself for being so stupid as to panic, and was in the process of turning around when he heard the scream. It was high-pitched, and it was a scream of pain and terror. Dawson had heard a lot of screams, but none half as terrible as that one, because this was no girl's scream. It was Harrison ... and he was screaming out Dawson's name. Instead of going back,

Dawson stood like a child at a locked door, his bladder emptying. The screaming stopped abruptly, and he heard footsteps approaching behind him. He wrenched at the door handle, frantically trying to tear the door off its hinges. His eyes closed as his senses exploded with the force of his face being slammed against the door. His nose gave way instantly, followed by his front teeth ...

When he regained consciousness, he was lying on his back on the carpet in the main bedroom. His ankles had been taped together; his hands taped together behind his back. Adams' body lay to his right, having ceased breathing the moment his windpipe had been crushed. Harrison's body lay on his left.

The girl didn't have to start working on him. Dawson gave her everything he knew. She wiped the blood from his mouth, taped over it, and disappeared into the living room.

A few seconds later she reappeared with what Dawson thought looked like Harrison's knife in her right hand. She walked to the far side of the room, took off her jacket, closed her eyes and stood in silence for a minute. Then she began ...

Dawson had seen Harrison train with the knife on a number of occasions, but this was nothing like that. Where Harrison's moves were slick and fancy these were structured and precise, and as the seconds passed the moves came faster and with more power, The girl's feet barely touched the carpet at the beginning, now her leg muscles bulged as her feet slammed down. Her hips twisted one way then another. Dawson was mesmerised, with what he thought at first was a knife ballet before realizing the girl's movements were similar to those he had seen on the screen. She wasn't holding the knife like it was a knife, she was holding it as if it was a foil, a sabre, a sword of some kind. As the seconds became minutes another thought entered his mind. He had seen these movements performed before with bare hands and feet. This was karate, a kata: a specific series of movements designed to be performed regularly, thereby allowing the movements to take place in combat without conscious thought.

After what seemed an age, the sword kata ended, and the girl stood straight. The only movement coming from the gentle rising of her chest and the rivers of sweat which ran freely down her face and neck. Dawson was confused; she was clearly a professional, and she had been waiting for them behind the curtain — which would make it a set-up, but that wouldn't work — no professional would allow anyone to grab their hair so easily. Who was she? And what was she doing here? None of it made sense. She was moving again. He watched the girl turn towards him. She was close now, he could see the beads of sweat dropping off her face, the knife glinting in her hand ...

Sunday 0.05 A.M.

The city of London was a hive of activity around midnight. The Volvo sped past numerous black cabs as it made its way towards the department building.

The early part of the journey passed with Helen describing the protocol at the security desks and the layout of the fifth floor.

When the driver felt she had adequately prepared the girl she said, 'There's something I don't understand: how you were able to stay sane. Was it partly because you always had a target? The test group hadn't had that programmed into them, it was going to come later. But you always had a target, didn't you?'

The girl sat in silence.

'Mireille, you saved me back there. Now it's my turn to save you—.'

'I wasn't aware I needed saving.'

'There are teams of assassins, special forces and former special forces, men and women from all over the world working together. They are well-informed with intel being provided from security services and government agencies, all of them with the goal of bringing you down. They know where you've been and they have teams assembling in all the places you are likely to be. The trap is closing. Right now, they're assembling in Khabarovsk, Muroran, and Hong Kong. The only piece of info they don't have is who you are, and they won't learn that from me. I may not understand your tactics, but I understand the reason behind what you're doing.'

'And, what am I doing?'

'Mireille, I was in charge of the team that searched your home.'

'And?'

' ... *He cries for you and every child, who will never run through his shadow, or see him dance with trees in the wind.*'

Mireille looked at Helen, 'You made your decision based on a doodle?'

'A poem.'

'That was hardly a poem.'

'I also found the books.'

'I read. I was studying literature.'

'There were too many books about climate change, and all together far too many coincidences. I understand you're working to create a deterrent, but you must know that everything you've done is being kept quiet, the media know nothing about any of the fifteen murders.'

A long silence followed, with Helen negotiating several roundabouts before the girl in the passenger seat said, 'Twenty-eight. It appears some of your security services and government agencies do not want to share information after all.'

'Where ... what countries?'

'You should find out on Tuesday. I had always planned to notify the press from London. I mailed the letters as soon as I arrived here.'

'Do you really think twenty-eight will be enough?'

'The research on deterrent shows that increasing the likelihood of being caught is far more effective than increasing

243

the punishment. But the research is flawed: it looks at longer prison sentences being given out, not terrible, premature deaths. Fear is the real deterrent. It's not as if I am asking them to close their businesses. I am asking that they take measures to protect the environment.'

'Asking? You're hardly asking. You were programmed to do this, but you can't keep travelling the world, hunting down men and women who care nothing about the planet and killing them. You will be caught and killed. Any deterrent you've created will then cease to exist.'

Mireille said quietly, 'They care nothing about the children.'

'The children?'

A police car pulled out on to the road in front of them. They drove behind it for two minutes before it indicated, then turned right.

Mireille broke the silence, 'You're like the rest of them, aren't you?'

'The rest of who?'

'In a far-off galaxy a teacher is asking questions of her class. "Planet 745 in sector nine of the fourth quadrant, what was the reason for the end to life?"

'A student at the back calls out, "Denial."

'"Denial of what?" the teacher asks.

'"Climate change and its implications."

'"Good. And do you know the root cause of the denial? Anyone? Okay, the human race had, over time, forgotten one of the fundamental rules to life. And it's the same rule for every life form on every planet in the universe. Survival requires a fight. The human race thought there was no need to fight climate change, fight those making money out of it, fight their own selfish habits that ultimately boosted the whole thing. They started taking life for granted. In their own words — they sowed the seed and left their children to reap the whirlwind.''

They waited at traffic lights. Helen wanted to say something, but again it was the girl who spoke.

'The priority isn't enforcing measures to reduce carbon emissions: it is bringing down the wall of denial. Once that wall is down, there will be no need to enforce anything, everyone will be onboard and doing everything they can to help. People won't drive cars that run off petrol or diesel. Houses won't be built without proper insulation. Air travel will effectively end except for essential and emergency services. Instead of going abroad on holiday, people will volunteer to plant trees, or build irrigation and drainage systems to prevent flooding. Everyone will work together to ensure survival, but the wall of denial has to come down first.'

'Okay, tell me, why do you think the world is in denial?'

'We've been told by the experts, we know the problems. Overpopulation being one of the biggest, birth rates may be falling — but not quickly enough — they need to literally plummet. Car manufacturers are still designing and building petrol and diesel driven cars, and the public are still buying them. People know the damage air travel makes to the environment, yet they still flock to the airports during the holidays. We talk about planting millions of trees, cutting carbon emissions to zero by 2050. There's far too much talk and minimal action. It seems the world has suddenly and conveniently forgotten the meaning of the verb 'accelerate', and how difficult it is to stop something when it gathers momentum. You can stop this car in a second, but an oil tanker takes twenty minutes to stop. Think size, and how infinitesimally tiny an oil tanker is, compared to the planet.

The ice caps have started melting, how long do you think it's going to take to stop that process? I don't know of any trees that grow when they are on fire, or have been swept into a river, and 2050 will be far too late, as will 2040, and 2030. By 2030 we will have passed the point of no return.'

'Alright. So there's a wall of denial, how do you breach it?'

'Jeanne Achterberg.'

'What ... who?'

'Never mind. One route is through the visual cortex, the area of the brain responsible for processing images. The visual cortex can't tell the difference between what is vividly imagined and reality. Clarity of image and repetition being the key factors.'

'You've lost me.'

'It's the repetition that's important. When I watched the film *An Inconvenient Truth* the message went right in, but then, after a few days, it started to fade. Yet, every time I saw an image that related to the original message in the film, I felt the truth of it again. I didn't need to see the film again. I didn't need the context. The image on its own was enough.'

'You do know that the vast majority of the public won't watch a film on global warming.'

'Yes, but the military and the police will, they don't have a choice. The government made sure they had the police and the military behind them before taking on the Miners' Union in 1983. Thatcher knew it was going to be a long fight, she had everything set up in preparation for it.'

'Okay, let's assume you have every member of parliament, every police officer and member of the military watch at least one film. I admit, the imagery in these films is powerful. So, those in power, and those who enforce power are on board, but for how long? A few days, weeks, and to what end? What's the point if you can't make the public watch films?'

'Not films, no. But you can get the messages through by using powerful images and repetition. Achterberg researched this. One of the most powerful images is that of an emaciated polar bear. Others of beached whales that had become confused by changes to the ocean, terrified animals on fire running out of burning forests, drowned cattle, and sheep floating in lakes where fields used to be. There are thousands of genuine images that scream out the warnings of what's happening to the planet ... vast chunks of icebergs sliding in to the ocean, dry ground cracked with the heat of the sun where lakes used to be. Let people see the then and now photos, the deterioration, the trend.'

'But where are the public going to see these images?'

'In newspapers, on billboards, on television. In every magazine, every TV channel, every cinema, every single film clip on the internet. Go in gently at first, so the public barely notices. The films need to be short anyway, just two or three seconds, short enough that there isn't time to switch off or change channel. Target those in charge of the Media. They will all have their legal responsibility spelt out to them: that they will have to incorporate a certain number of images or short films on a daily basis, spread out evenly. And, if they don't comply, they face huge fines, and if they don't pay the fines, they go to jail. No trial dates, no appeals, no delays.'

'Why don't you just lock them up in the Tower and starve them to death? What you're saying is far too extreme.'

'The government — all governments — need to be decisive. All the opposition parties need to stop their bickering, drop their agendas and unify on this, just like they do in war time.'

'But what laws are going to ... the Government will be thrown out. You're talking about Big Brother gone mad.'

'Yes, you're right, it is Big Brother, but protecting everyone in the country who is, in ignoring global warming, effectively committing suicide ... and dragging the rest of us down with them.'

The car swerved.

'You'd best watch the road,' Mireille said softly.

Helen shook her head, 'There is a twisted, almost perverse logic to what you've just said. If you're going to go that route, then you missed out prison wardens from the list of those who will have to watch the films. And, the Government preparation should probably include building a lot of new prisons, and initiating a major recruiting drive for prison wardens, police officers and the military.'

A few seconds passed in silence, before Helen added, 'And, you're forgetting something else — the billions around the world who don't have access to newspapers, billboards, television and the internet.'

'If you'd ever lived in the highlands of Scotland, you would know that there is a specially adapted lorry that drives from village to village. The lorry is a mobile cinema. In warmer climates, huge screens could be set up outside, and films shown to thousands at a time.'

'But we're back to the original stumbling block — you simply can't make people watch films on global warming.'

'Have the main film about something else entirely. Have a break in the middle where you show the country's heroes, actors, sportsmen and women, or the senior and well-respected figures from that area, talking about global warming and what the general public can do to help.'

'Fine, let's assume you are right. Why are *you* not trying to breach the wall of denial, promote your ideas instead of killing a few industrialists?'

'From everything I've seen and read, it seems that the risk of extinction is too big for the mind to handle. Yet people should be able to grasp the level of violence that will take place if the major crops fail. At the moment people don't associate global warming with extreme violence. Yet they should as the two are inexorably linked.'

'But that link will only go to you—'

'You're missing the point — what do you think I put in the letters to all those journalists?'

'So, you told them what you've just told me, okay, that makes sense.'

The girl nodded, 'Journalists look for headlines before they'll take the time to read through what you've written. The level of violence grabs their attention. They know there is a story there to start with. And in a lot of cases the journalists concerned will have children.'

Helen, remembering Arthur mentioning the children, said, 'Everyone keeps talking about the children? We all know they have the most to lose.'

'It will hit them hardest. They're not responsible for destroying the planet. They are the ones who are doing what they can to protect it. And they've finally found their voice through a girl from Sweden. And if people don't listen to her, if we, as a planet stay in denial, all the children will suffer terribly when we realize we've passed the point of no return and hell—.'

'So we're back to the breakdown of law and order?'

'Breakdown? No. Breakdown implies recovery. There will be no recovery. Law and order will end — period — and that's entirely different. When I talk about extreme violence, you're thinking of something else. You are like most of the population, naive when it comes to understanding violence.

When law and order ends the things that will take place will make what I did to the industrialists, the three men in your flat, and what those men intended doing to you and your daughter seem tame in comparison. There's a film, *Irreversible*, it has a scene in a deserted subway that a lot of people were unable to watch, so they walked out of the cinema. Their minds just wouldn't go there; it was too disturbing, too shocking. The terrible truth is, that after we pass the point of no return, the acts in this film will become commonplace. It will be bedlam; and it will be irreversible.'

'It's just a film, Mireille, the people who walked out probably knew it was deliberate shock tactics by the director, and that it would never take place in real life.'

The girl looked out of her side window. Seconds passed in silence until she said, 'When I turned fifteen, I sat down with my grandfather and told him that I was becoming jaded with the daily unarmed combat training. The skill level that he had taken me to, after ten years, would be more than enough to handle any situation that came my way. He sat across from me and nodded, and said I was old enough to make my own decision, and that he was fine with it. That took me by surprise. Anyway, the following week we're watching a French film a friend of his had recommended. Neither of us had heard of it before. Five minutes in, Grandpapa takes a phone call and explains he has to go out for a while. I'm left watching the film on my own. I had no idea at that point that the whole thing was a set-up. An hour later, I knew. Not long after the film ended, Grandpapa returns and asks me if I watched the rest of the film. I say I have, and I want to restart combat training tomorrow. The way I say it, he recognizes I know he set the whole thing up to achieve just that. I remember clearly what he said then, because he was angry, and I'd never seen him angry before. "I am sorry, sweetheart, I am sorry you had to see that. But you need to know that what happened in that film happens in the real world. Similar incidents are taking place right now, all over the world. Right now! Never forget how cruel people can be.""

'And the film ... it was *Irreversible*?' Helen asked.

The girl nodded.

A long silence followed.

Helen said, 'Hunter-Killer 9—.'

'Stop! Haven't you heard a word I've said?' Mireille looked down and shook her head. 'The point of no return is looming, and you need to acknowledge that. And when you do, when the wall of denial comes down, you'll know because you will be indifferent to anything associated with the Hunter-Killer project. Your focus will be on what you can do to save the planet and your daughter.

'You just have to look around to see what's happening in the world, and it's the opposite of what should be happening. At a time when we need unity, we are still trying to negotiate a deal to break away from Europe. We should have known that the EU would put us through the wringer. We will never get a good deal. If we did, everyone would leave. Instead, we are being used as a deterrent, a stark warning of what will happen to the next country that tries to leave. The way things are now, the government can't say that the UK has decided to postpone leaving the EU until after the climate crisis, because no one would believe that was the reason. So, the talks and negotiations are going to continue, and the thousands upon thousands of man-hours spent on this will continue to rise, and more millions will be lost, money that could have gone towards helping resolve the climate crisis.

'It's too late for the UK to set an example, but it's not for

Scotland. Back home the demand for a second independence referendum is gathering momentum. If there was no wall of denial, then the first minister of Scotland could inform the prime minister that the Scottish Government would put independence on hold and work with the UK Government to help resolve the climate crisis, but when things were turned around, and it became clear that the ice caps had stopped melting, then a second referendum would be required. The prime minister, and the leaders of all the main parties would agree in writing, and publicly declare that the Scottish Government could name the day for the referendum when that happened.'

Helen shook her head, 'Do you actually think that might happen?'

'Of course not. It is fantasy. It's a pity though, everyone knows how passionate the Scottish National Party and its members are when it comes to independence. If the world saw them giving that up for an unknown number of years and investing the time and money that would be spent on an independence campaign into halting global warming, it would put a big hole in the wall of denial. We need acts like that, symbols of recognition of the danger and the need for unity; examples for others to follow, and we need them now.'

'Knowing your family history in the British Army, I am guessing you're against independence.'

'What I want and what the population of Scotland want is irrelevant. This isn't about independence — it's about survival, nothing else. The fact that Scotland is currently pressing for another independence referendum has to be seen for what it is — an opportunity to set an example. But, it is also a chance to attain unity. Right now Scotland is a divided country, split down the middle on independence. But if the SNP postponed their pursuit of independence until after the climate crisis, they would win the referendum by a landslide. Then you would have a truly independent Scotland.'

Helen, who had been shaking her head, said, 'Why would people who have been for the union all their lives suddenly vote for independence?'

'My father and my grandfather always believed in the strength and unity of the United Kingdom, and I feel the same way, but if the SNP postponed their dream of independence and set an example of unity to the world, then they would have my vote after that – no matter what they wanted.'

'But you're an exception. You've been brought up to see the violence, the horrors, that's your world, but the rest of Scotland don't see it that way.'

'Helen, if we don't get on top of this climate crisis, people won't just see it, they'll suffer a terrible death in it. There will be no exceptions then. And there will be no Scotland, England, Wales, Ireland, or Northern Ireland, there will be seas and oceans and small sections of uninhabited wasteland – nothing else.

'We are so predictable; we continue to live in Never-Never Land where it's okay to think we can wait until the last minute before we need to take action. We have so much experience of resolving issues at the eleventh hour that, with a bit more effort, there's nothing we can't fix. But there's a thing about momentum: you don't see it until it's too late.

'Right now, we have meetings where top professors and scientists with masses of qualifications and experience, stand up and give a detailed lecture on the damage we're doing to the planet. We don't need any more detail – it's simple: we have never experienced anything on this scale before, and with such a force of momentum. We don't know how fast things are going to deteriorate. We don't know how much momentum global warming has already built. We don't know where the point of no return is. So how can we hold back from taking decisive action? If there's a fire in a block of flats you don't talk about the details of how fast the fire is burning, and measure temperatures, or discuss how much of the building can be saved – you get everyone the hell out of there as fast as you can – and put the fire out. You only begin to address the rest after you know everyone is safe. We can't evacuate the planet, and the people who are spending billions on exploring space under the premise that we can, are delusional – there isn't time! If we keep talking about this problem it will continue to gather pace, and we won't be able to stop it. What will the governments do then? Say we're sorry, but we'd never experienced anything like this before, we underestimated so many things ... if only we'd started earlier. We are so sorry, but we don't want anyone to have to face the large gangs that are now running amok across the globe, so just go to your local pharmacy where suicide tablets are being distributed.

'It won't be survival of the fittest, Helen, it will be survival of the cruellest! And even they won't survive long. When things get so bad that we realize we have to act, it will be far too late. The fight for survival isn't tomorrow, it is today, it is now. And right now we need men and women to stand up and be counted; it won't take that many – the rest will follow. There are so many opportunities that are available, yet they're not being taken. So far, I only know of only one example: a leading rock band that has stopped touring. But it is a start. The wall of denial comes down soon, and I mean soon, we unify and start acting decisively. The wall stays up too long, major crops fail, law and order ends, bedlam ensues and the spark that was the human race is extinguished forever. There's no grey area here, no middle ground. It's one or the other … and we're running out of time.'

*

As they approached the Department building, Mireille turned towards the driver, 'How did you find me?'

'By chance. One of the satellite monitoring team is a fell runner and she raised concerns.'

They parked and passed the security desks without incident. With Mireille wearing the cap and a visitor's pass on her jacket, she and Helen walked along the long corridor leading to the Ops Room.

The older woman asked, 'Having a target would have helped, but it wouldn't have been enough. Please tell me, how did you manage to stay sane all this time?'

'It's not important.'

'Too many have died already for this information. We still have the master copy of HK 9–.'

'Destroy it.'

They reached the door. The girl went to open it but Helen placed her hand firmly on top of hers. 'I must know.'

Mireille made and held eye contact. She shook her head slowly, then turned the handle and opened the door.

With the main lights off, the Ops room could have been mistaken for a movie theatre.

Helen looked at her watch, 'We're early, it won't begin for another 30 minutes. They won't be in before then. We need to lie low for a while.' She led the girl to the back of the room and the two of them sat on the floor behind rows of chairs.

The co-ordinator's mind had been running on adrenaline through the entire week. She had had some serious issues going on, tasks to perform, and since coming home, a confrontation with probably the most violent person on the entire planet. It now appeared as if she would survive her meeting with Mireille, and, as the girl was about to 'deal with' the people at her work who wanted Helen dead, other issues surfaced, but only briefly, as they too appeared to be resolved. She also now knew that the girl she suspected of killing the industrialists was indeed the killer, even though the information was, in a sense, useless, as Helen would do nothing with it — she wasn't about to betray the person who had saved her life. She rested her head against the back of a chair and let out a long breath, at the same time allowing her shoulders to relax. For the first time since the girl had been spotted in Andorra, Helen's mind was at peace.

Sitting next to her, Mireille was planning ahead, and the best way to extract the information she wanted. Time, however, was against her, so the reliable way was off the table, replaced by the quickest way, and that way involved violence. Fortunately, there were two targets, and two potential sources of information. The logic of it was simple, make an example of one, and extract the information from the other.

In contrast, like a television on stand-by, the mind of the woman sitting next to her was a blank screen. And that's how the co-ordinator wanted it to stay, exactly like the giant screen in the Ops room. But at the back of that room, sitting in the dark, in silence, her thoughts started to do the one thing she should not have allowed them to do: wander.

The screen that was her mind slowly came to life as events played out in total silence. Helen watched the girl writing letters to journalists on the ferry to the mainland, then stepping off the train at Euston, immediately looking for a post-box. Then, her dragging the unconscious bodies of the three men into Helen's own bedroom, the knife flashing in her hand as she prepared to make the first cut ... the blunt weapon grasped firmly as she brought it down hard on a man's ankle ... the long needle held lightly between her fingers as she carefully slid the point into a knee, gently pushing, searching for the cartilage to inflict the most damage and cause the greatest pain ... suddenly, the noise of the scream piercing, distressing, harrowing. But this was not a soldier's scream, or a man's, this was the scream of a boy, a boy with beautiful brown hair and a body of youth, undamaged, perfect. A body that was being systematically ruined with each needle, and a mind that was being systematically broken with each twist and turn. One more, one more heartrending scream, one more, one more, how much longer? The supply of needles looked endless—.

Suddenly the world fell silent, as if someone had hit the mute button. A warm breeze hit her face and bare shoulders, the trees forming a blanket of cherry blossom above them. Her summer dress now lifting, but not by the boy with brown hair, by her own trembling hands, letting him know that she was all his, all of her, because this was love, and right at that moment, she truly thought her first love, would be her only love. She couldn't imagine anything else coming close to this feeling. She looked in his hazel eyes, and saw the desire in them, and she rejoiced at the sight of it. After they made love, she fell asleep, but then the needles were flashing again, sliding, searching, ruining. A voice cut in, 'The mind is not designed to handle prolonged pain of this nature. Eventually it shuts down—.'

Helen spoke softly, 'What about the men from bars and nightclubs?'

The girl stared at her.

The co-ordinator continued, 'The men from almost every country in Europe who left a bar or club shortly after a girl in black wearing a baseball cap left. I managed to convince most of the investigating officers to send a copy of the CCTV footage directly to me. None of them took the time to check on similar incidents taking place in other countries. I did though. You've been busy.'

Mireille remined silent.

'Interesting how the peak of that baseball cap covered almost all of your face. These men, I checked out most of them, but I couldn't find any link to global warming.'

'Probably because there wasn't one,' the girl said softly.

'Then, why target them?'

'I didn't target them. They targeted me.'

'Why would they target you?'

'Most evenings I go out to the local bar for a beer.'

'And then you walk home?'

'Of course, what would you expect me to do?'

'So, these men, they leave after you, I assume. Then they follow you, wait until you're on a quiet path before approaching you.'

'Sometimes, but if I've been to the bar before, they know the direction I'll leave in, and they leave before me, pick a quiet spot and wait.'

'But you know what's going to happen?'

'I often have a sense of what's going down. I feel something's wrong. The times I'm positive are when they've tried to distract me, so one of them can spike my drink.'

'Do they succeed?'

'If I've been distracted, I don't drink anymore.'

'But you pretend to?'

'Yes.'

'And you still walk home.'

'Of course.'

'When they make their move, what form does it take ... do they simply rugby tackle you to the ground?'

'If there is more than one, they often try that, but when there's only one they usually start by talking, making out they're my friend, and they just so happen to be walking in my direction.'

Helen could see the scene unfolding, playing it out in her mind as the girl spoke.

'They keep talking and trying to engage me in conversation, and while this is going on they make contact physically, a brushing of the arms as they're walking alongside, the contact seemingly accidental at first. Then, it increases to their hand brushing my shoulder, touching the small of my back, sniffing my neck, telling me my perfume's lovely, complementing me, and all the time trying to engage me in conversation. And, when I don't respond to any of it, and keep walking, they assume that I am afraid, and they have control, and that they can do what they want, certain I will be too afraid to resist. It's at this point that the hand contact becomes far more than touching my shoulder or my back—.'

Helen, the film in her mind playing out to show the shocking brutal finale, said, almost in a whisper, 'And that's the point when these men suddenly realize they've been set up and they've just made the biggest mistake of their life.'

'I didn't set anybody up.' Mireille said.

'You wanted to be attacked, that's why you went out on your own. You're creating a deterrent, aren't you?'

'I go out because I want a beer. I'm alone because that's the way I live now. Are you trying to tell me that I can' t go out on my own in the evening because I'm a woman?'

'It's unusual. You'll be taken for a woman who's wanting to be picked up.'

'Men go out on their own, are all of them out because they want to be picked up?'

'Of course not, but they're viewed differently.'

'Why are they? What happened to equality? If a man can do it, then a woman should be able to do it without being labelled—.'

'Why don't you acknowledge you're making a point ... and setting a deterrent while you're at it?'

'If I'd been wanting to set a deterrent, there would have been uniformity. I would have harmed them all in exactly the same way.'

'You mean you would have either killed all of them or crippled all of them.'

'I've told you; I just went out for a drink. On occasion, I was attacked on the way home, I fended off the attack, and continued on my journey.'

'Over a two year period you were attacked around a dozen times. On average that's one attack every two months. You would have to have gone out for a drink almost every night for that to happen.'

'I didn't realize there was a law against going out for a drink every night.'

'You are saying you went out for a drink not expecting to be harassed or attacked on your way home?'

'I did nothing to warrant it — why should I expect it?'

'Then why the weapon? In every attack, massive damage was inflicted by a heavy blunt weapon, medical reports suggest something akin to a hammer was used. Some of the men were killed by a single blow to the head. The few who survived, their elbows, knees and shoulders were all shattered by blows from this weapon. You went out wanting to be attacked. You were ready. You were prepared. You wouldn't carry a weapon otherwise!'

'Why are you so angry — why the hostility? What is this anyway, an interrogation? You're calling them victims. They attacked me. Who was around to help me? No one. I was alone, and they came at me, singly, in pairs, or in threes. I have a right to defend myself. I have a right to express my anger, my rage against men who would ruin my life without giving it a second's thought. Men who would leave me broken with nightmares every night and a constant feeling of being violated. Why? Because they felt a sexual urge? Because they felt a need to express power? Because I was weaker than them? Because they could? Because they were sure they would get away with it? Yet you're siding with them ... they got exactly what they deserved. Now they'll know what it feels like to be a victim ... now they'll have the nightmares.'

A few seconds passed in silence. When Helen spoke, her voice was softer, 'I'm not siding with anyone, Mireille. I know you set those men up. If you didn't, then please answer my question — why were you carrying a weapon?'

'I carry a two-kilo stonemason's hammer in my backpack, but not to use as a weapon.' The girl was about to explain, but suddenly realized something she should have seen earlier. 'It's not those men that you're angry about ... it's one man. The man I interrogated in Andorra. The man I tortured. The sniper. You knew him. This is all about him, isn't it?'

Things had moved so quickly since the phone call, that Helen hadn't had time to react to speaking to Kyle. Almost as soon as she had closed her eyes the memories triggered by the sound of his voice had flooded into her conscious.

They both sat in silence. Helen wiped away the tear that was running down her cheek.

'Kyle Winters. Physically he was perfect, and he had the most beautiful brown hair. He was the captain of the football team, best player our school ever had. Everyone called him Win, and when he played that's what we did. Every girl in the school had a crush on him, and I think half the teachers as well. And I was the one he chose. Me. Any idea how good that makes you feel, when you're sixteen, to be envied by hundreds of other girls? Two years then the army took him, and uni took me.'

Mireille started to speak but changed her mind.

'It's not your fault', Helen said quietly, 'and I am not angry with you, I am angry with myself. I made sure he was on that team in Andorra. I should have made sure the team were properly briefed. They weren't prepared, not for you. And there should have been a back-up team. I should have waited until at least one back-up team was available, even if that meant losing you.' Wiping away any trace of tears she turned to the girl and smiled, 'So tell me, I am curious, why carry a stone hammer?'

'The one I have has a longer handle than your normal hammer. I spin it like you would spin a tennis racquet.'

'Why?'

'I became bored squeezing rocks. I'd been doing that since I was eleven, to strengthen my wrists and hands. A stone hammer produces better results far quicker. You know that Gate— the program, only improves what's already there. I have to keep training, or I get weaker.'

The pair fell silent as Whitby and Bannen entered and took their seats in the centre of the room. For five minutes the two of them engaged in conversation but fell silent when the screen finally came to life.

The screen was dimly lit, though the outline of the cottage was easy enough to make out. Mireille could tell, by the lay of the land, that the military contractors were targeting the old cottage her grandmother had been brought up in. No one had stayed there for years. To the east, four small white dots moved slowly towards the centre. From the north, another four dots appeared, moving in the same formation. The radio transmissions could be heard clearly.

As soon as the teams were in position there was nothing for almost five minutes, then two bright flashes lit up the edges of the cottage.

From the back of the room, the girl followed Helen and the two of them made their way to the door leading on to the main corridor. The two managers continued to watch the screen as numerous dots closed in, and then entered the cottage.

Three shouts of 'Clear', as the men moved through each room.

Then a moment of quiet, before, 'Cottage empty. No signs of anyone staying here.'

*

Bannen followed Whitby into her office. 'She's still on the island,' he said. 'They have cut off any possible escape route. There are twenty of them, they'll find—.'

He stopped speaking as his eyes fell on Gleason standing on his left. Whitby was the first to recover and said, 'Helen, what are you doing here? I thought it had been decided that you were going to be conducting the interrogation next week, and that you were going home for the weekend.'

'I did go home.' She walked up to the director of operations and slapped her hard across the face.

Mireille appeared from behind a high-backed executive armchair and had hold of Bannen almost immediately. Her voice was calm and deliberate as she said, 'You get one chance. One. Who hired the men who took part in the murders in Edinburgh two years ago? Tell me. Now.'

Bannen hesitated for a second, then said, 'I have absolutely no idea what you're talking about!'

The girl leant in and whispered in his ear.

Helen only caught a couple of the words spoken in French, but thinking about the literal translation, didn't see the blow that preceded Bannen hitting the floor.

Before Whitby had time to do anything, the girl turned towards her. The director of operations held her hands palm upwards and cried out, 'Stop, Stop! STOP! I will tell you everything. Just stop for a moment and listen to me.'

Mireille took a step back, while the older woman staggered on rubber legs, over to a cabinet from which she took out a bottle of Gordon's gin and a glass, ignoring the lemon and bottle of tonic that sat alongside them. After filling the glass, she drank half of it. She started speaking as soon as she sat down.

'Look,' she said firmly, her composure returning as the alcohol began its journey into her system. 'We put the information out through our channels that a program had been created that would have an impact on health. A few days later we were contacted by a financier, a money man, who put an offer in for more information.'

'Who was he representing?' Mireille said.

'We don't know who he represented. I don't think he even knew. We gave him names and the address where the research was taking place. The funds were transferred to our department a month later. But—.'

Helen said, 'You gave him Gatekeeper 17.'

'We had no choice! The change would have been catastrophic. It had to be destroyed. You must realize that.'

Mireille was now standing over her.

In her last week of her second year as an undergraduate at Cambridge University, Alice Whitby had, after a few glasses of wine, taken up the invitation to go to a freshman's room on a hot Saturday afternoon. Josh Barclay-Adams was the prize of the college having achieved the rare feat of earning a Rugby Blue in his freshman year. A lock forward, he was over a foot taller than Alice and she had eagerly accepted the invitation. Confident of her body, she had stripped first. She stood naked, hands on her hips, and watched with a playful smile as he slowly undressed in front of her. Yet, as comfortable as she was with him, there was one moment, when he took off his shirt, a split second, when Alice saw the raw power in his upper torso that she was suddenly afraid, aware for the first time in her life of just how vulnerable she was.

A moment later the passion took over, but now, as Mireille took off her jacket, Whitby felt that fear again, and this time it didn't pass. This time it was far more acute. Unlike Barclay-Adams, who had put his power on open show, the girl's was restrained, almost as if there was something underneath the tight black top that had to be concealed.

In a dark cavern of Whitby's mind, she knew precisely what was about to happen, and no amount of wishing, pleading, begging or praying was going to make a difference. As she was hauled off her chair, she looked closely at the girl whose shoulders suddenly seemed gargantuan, the veins in her neck like steel cords.

Whitby's last thoughts went back to the moment she had signed the approval letter for the testing of a program specifically designed to create the most ruthless killer imaginable — and the unmistakeable voice of her mother — 'Oh, Alice dear. You read Shelley, what were you thinking?'

22

'Helen! Helen! Lunch is on the table. We are all waiting for you.'

Lunch, already? Helen thought, as she reluctantly closed the lid of the piano. She called over to her border collie who was sleeping at the window: *'Pete, I have been summoned. You wait here and guard the piano until I return.'* The girl skipped out of the drawing room onto the landing and looked over the banister. She was yet to find out why people used the stairs when they could slide down. It made absolutely no sense walking down, when a faster and far more pleasurable journey was right in front of them. As the slide lasted but a second or two, there was no point in straddling the banister, the nine-year old always slid down *'side saddle'*. As she swivelled her waist and her feet left the ground, Pete scurried past, sprinting down the stairs.

'Oh Pete, you silly dog, we are not going out', Helen called to him as she landed on the banister. But her concentration had been momentarily broken, and the fraction of a second when she should have slowed was missed. Instead of sliding down, she slid straight over, momentum lifting her feet high in the air. She didn't remember the trip down, it was only one flight, so it was brief. But she remembered the impact. The shock of her left hand catching between the posts of the balustrade, three of her fingers snapping instantly, followed immediately by her left hip hitting the floor, hard. The nausea, the terrible shaking of her limbs that she couldn't control.

She remembered the pain — the physical pain — and the emotional pain when, after two weeks in hospital she overheard the doctors talking to her mother: 'The fractured hip will heal; in time your daughter will walk normally, but I am afraid she will never regain the full mobility or feeling in her left hand. The nerves and tendons are irreparably damaged.'

A girl's dreams of becoming a famous pianist — obliterated in a second. Although it would be her inability to play the piano again that transpired to be the greater pain. But it was the physical pain that she felt now, the same pain in her left hip, a pain that engulfed her. She couldn't think who she was, all she could remember from the past was the pain. She was vaguely aware of being gently lifted on to a stretcher, and then carried along a corridor in to a lift. Then another corridor. She tried to open her eyes to see what was going on, but failed. They felt glued shut. She didn't know who the people around her were, or the year, or where she was. She knew nothing. From the relative quiet of the corridor in to a hive of activity, people moving everywhere.

Noise, so much noise, so many voices. One voice above the others, someone in charge, barking out instructions.

'Get those bodies out of here now. You two, who is this, is she alive?'

'She's unconscious. We won't know the full extent of her injuries until we get her in to hospital.'

'Armed unit, where are you? Okay Ferguson, Mitchell, over here ... this is probably the only person left alive in the building who might be able to tell us what happened. Stick to her like glue. She goes in to theatre, you two are outside the door. You stay with her until I relieve you. No one speaks to her but me. She regains consciousness, I want to know immediately. Now get on it.'

Inwardly, Helen was panicking. What bodies? Where am I? Why would I be the only person left alive? I have questions. What are you going to do when I can't tell you what happened? I have no idea what happened. I don't even know who I am. Tell me who I am.

*

The mood was sombre when Helen's parents brought her home from hospital. The three of them sat in silence in the drawing room. The baby grand piano sat in the corner, her mother suddenly hit by the realization that this was not the best room to be in to tell her daughter she would never play again.

Helen broke the silence, along with the bonds of childhood, when she said: 'I know about the piano, and that I will never play it again. I heard the doctors talking. It's okay, I will find something else that I can do well, better than I ever would have been on the piano. Anyway, I have more time for schoolwork now, and that means a better university.'

That day was a turning point in Helen's life, her brief speech a reflection of her selflessness and love for her parents.

Decades later, she was to witness the same characteristics in her own daughter, and it was that moment, triggered by the siren being switched on as the ambulance pulled in to traffic, that broke through the blockage in her mind, allowing access to her memory banks.

*

Shortly after her daughter's sixteenth birthday, Helen received a visit from a childhood friend who worked in the same building as Richard. Carole gently broke the news about Richard's all too close relationship with his secretary. In some respects, it was a shock, but Helen had become increasingly aware of her husband's lack of interest in sex. Now she realized the disinterest was not in sex, but in sex with her.

If there was one thing Helen had strong views on, it was marriage. One betrayal of trust. One, and that was it — the marriage was over. No discussions, no excuses, no nothing. She phoned a locksmith and, while he was changing the locks, phoned Richard at work. She told him the locks had been changed and, before he had the chance to ask why, suggested he stay at his secretary's flat. Natalie was sixteen, and old enough to decide who she would stay with and who she would visit. It was all in the lawyer's hands now. She hung up and immediately phoned Natalie, left a voicemail, telling her the locks had been changed, to ring the buzzer and she would tell her about it when she was home.

Three hours later, Natalie sat in silence listening to her mother relay the information passed on by Carole, followed by the details of the telephone call with her father. The entire time the girl remained silent, and after Helen had stopped speaking, the silence continued. She had to say something, but the girl wasn't even moving, let alone speaking. Doubt seeped through Helen's conscious. After two minutes she began to accept that her daughter's next move would be to stand, walk to her bedroom, pack a bag and leave, phoning her father on her mobile as she made her way through the flat door. An emergency vehicle siren was audible in the distance. As the

270

sound grew in volume, her daughter stood up. Here it comes, Helen thought as her heart seemed to drop in her chest, Natalie walking now, but not in the direction of her bedroom. Instead, she walked to the window and looked out at the flashing blue light as an ambulance sped past, its siren at its loudest before rapidly fading into the distance. Natalie turned to her mother and, shaking her head, said 'He's not going to sell much ice cream going at that speed.'

Laughter was followed by a raid on the freezer and two tubs of Häagen-Dazs were devoured during a long girls' talk. Natalie reassuring her mum that Richard hadn't just betrayed her, he had betrayed the whole family.

Every time Helen heard a siren after that, she was reminded of her daughter's perfect delivery of the classic Eric Morecambe line. And now, lying in the ambulance, in pain, in distress, unable to open her eyes, with the siren blaring in her ears, she remembered everything.

23

Sunday 7.30 A.M.

'Good morning, Ms Gleason.'

Helen tried to reply but the first word came out of her mouth as a strained whisper. Immediately, she put her hand up to her neck, and felt a thick layer of bandages. She glanced around the room, realizing she was in hospital. She turned back to the man in the white coat and looked to him for an explanation.

'You suffered a blow to the throat. You're fortunate because, as opposed to crushing your windpipe, it has only damaged it. Your throat will heal, but you need to avoid straining it. For now, don't try to speak at all.'

He held up a crayon and a writing board. Helen took them and quickly scribbled on the board, then turned it towards the doctor: *How long will I be here?*

'You hit the ground with such force your left hip is fractured. We still have to bring in the orthopaedic surgeons on that. With falls of this nature, there is a possibility that your head hit the ground as well. I suspect you have a concussion. You need to have a CAT scan.'

Another scribble: *Why the wait?*

'Ms Gleason, you are probably not aware how long you've been here. It's seven-thirty on Sunday morning. You've been here less than six hours. There are two police officers outside the door of this room. I don't know what's been happening, that's not my job, but I do know that the police officers are provided in a protective role. I also have two police detectives who want to see you, and some very impatient men in dark suits from a government department, but they refuse to tell me which one. I would be happier if you didn't see anyone today, but I'm here to evaluate and establish if you are well enough to see them.'

The patient raised her eyebrows in anticipation.

'I think you have recently suffered a number of traumatic events. I suspect you are still in shock. What I am certain of is that you need peace and quiet and bed rest. Is there anything so pressing that you need to speak to any of the parties outside today?'

Helen shook her head.

'Is there anyone else you would like to see today?'

My daughter.

'You know her number?'

Enthusiastic nod.

'Do you want me to speak to her or would you prefer to send a text?'

The patient tapped her hand to her chest.

'I'll return for this in ten minutes,' he said, as he laid his mobile on her bedside table, 'I will inform the waiting parties to come back tomorrow.'

Smiling, Helen mouthed the words, *Thank you.*

*

When the patient woke late afternoon, she lay still for a long time and stared into space. The events that had taken place the previous evening were beginning to find some sort of order. She now realized just how fortunate she had been. The chain of events that had led to Mireille saving her could so

273

easily have been broken. She was alive purely as a stroke of luck. Or was it Fate? She thought for a long time about her place in the world and why she was still alive, but thinking about that, she eventually realized, was not achieving anything. She was going to have to speak to company agents and the police tomorrow morning, and she had to make sense of this before then. All she had to do was tell the truth: she had not committed any crime, but then she had — she had signed in a high-priority target of the company through two security desks. What would be her excuse? That Mireille threatened to kill her on the spot if she refused? It was the obvious choice and, with the medical evidence, it was clear the girl had intended to kill her and had left her for dead along with Bannen and Whitby.

Except she knew that Mireille had given her a way out. After killing Whitby, the girl had walked over to her, and instructed her to stand completely still and close her eyes. The blow that she'd then delivered was precisely where she intended. What came out of this was that, despite the ruthlessness of her actions, Mireille was very selective about her targets, which indicated that at least one part of the Hunter-Killer program was functioning effectively. What eluded Helen was the girl's motivation. What was she achieving by risking everything to kill those responsible for the murders associated with Gatekeeper 17? And why Gatekeeper 17, when HK9 had destroyed the girl she used to be? And what was it she had said in French to Bannen before killing him?

It had to be personal. Yet Mireille's father, mother and grandmother had died in a car crash when she was four. The occupants of the other car, including the drunk driver, had also died. Her grandfather had died in his sleep in his nineties.

It was all on record. On the day she had been programmed with HK9, she had interacted with two people who were killed later the same day. She had had no contact with either of them prior to that. Boyle had been in 3 PARA at the same time as her father but, in a battalion of close to 600 men, that meant nothing by itself. If there had been a connection it would have been on his military record, and they'd checked.

It had to be something else, but what? And how had the girl survived, and remained sane for over two years after being programmed with HK9?

Helen looked at the two drip-stands holding bags of fluid that stood like guards at the side of her hospital bed. She spied pink sponge sticks lying on the table next to her. She unwrapped one, dipped it in the plastic beaker of water and rolled it around the inside of her mouth. She figured she wouldn't be drinking anything until her throat had healed. It would be too painful anyway. Her hip ached though. She had never coped with pain well. Her thoughts turned to Kyle — how long had the girl tortured him, how many minutes? How many hours? She had left him for dead. It was pure chance that he'd been discovered not long after.

She wanted to see him and began to plan how that might work. Would it compromise her position in the department? Only if people found out about it. But how long would it be before she was fit enough to travel? How long would she be in hospital? She didn't want to be walking on crutches when she saw him. She wasn't even sure he'd made the connection to the girl he had dated at school. During their brief phone conversation he'd shown no indication that he recognized her voice. More importantly, would he want to see her? After what he'd been through, would he ever forgive her for sending his team in against Mireille, unprepared and without back-up?

Helen's idea of reunion with her first love, which had seemed so appealing at first, was now seen for what it was; a romantic notion of a child that had no place in the real world.

She thought again about how lucky she was. If it wasn't for the pain, she might have laughed at the absurdity of the situation. Two opposing forces had broken into her flat, one with the intention of interrogating and killing her, the other to rape and kill her. Yet here she was alive and safe. She would never be able to go back to her flat though, not having seen what the girl had done to those men. What sort of childhood had Mireille had that would allow her to be so terribly clinical in her destruction? At the tender age of fifteen her grandfather had set her up to watch a film that contained a scene in a subway that was so horrific that it made men and women in cinemas around the world stand up and walk out.

A scene that seemed to symbolize the girl's views on the industrialists most responsible for contributing to global warming. To Mireille these men were taking the entire population of the world into that subway, fully aware, yet indifferent to the horrors that awaited every man, woman and child. There would no walking out this time, the scene would play out for real, over seven billion times. If the girl did indeed see it that way, it was hardly surprising that she went around brutally murdering the guilty parties in a variety of ways.

Helen knew the situation wasn't good, but why did Mireille see something far worse than everyone else? Was it simply that she saw everything in military terms, in terms of combat? She sees the threat, and the need to respond to that threat. She sees the danger in waiting to act, in the same way Churchill saw it in the 1930s. In parliament, his speech from *The Gathering Storm* listed facts and figures detailing the extent of German rearmament "... we must act decisively. And we must act now ... if we do not, history will cast its verdict with those terrible, chilling words — too late."

Was it the similarity in upbringing that held the answer to why both of them identified the threat that so many others were either overlooking or in denial of? Churchill's upbringing was strict, most of it spent in boarding school. His training to be a soldier began around the age of fifteen.

That could be it. They were both brought up with the same military perspective. But it was too general, if it was that then the armed forces would be united on this issue, and generals, admirals, and air marshals would be raising concerns to the prime minister on a daily basis. It had to be something more specific. Suddenly, the mist cleared in Helen's mind. They were both looking for it. Churchill and Mireille. In the 1930's, following the disastrous Gallipoli Campaign and the scandal where he was found to have been paid to lobby the government on behalf of a major oil company, Churchill's political reputation was in tatters. He was constantly looking, hoping to find the spark to relight his political career and restore his reputation. When Germany's rearmament caught his attention, he looked deeper and, when he saw the full extent of the growth, he saw the danger. He saw it because he was open to the truth of it.

Looking at it objectively, Helen could see the problem with global warming: the public weren't open to the truth of it. The truth intruded too much into their day-to-day lives, their own problems. The truth was just too daunting and, as a result, the danger signs were being missed. However, post HK9, Mireille, like Churchill, was looking. She was looking for targets, and this time, open to the truth, there was no overlooking the danger signs; she saw them clearly — along with a multitude of targets. Yet it wasn't really about killing;

her goal was to stop global warming. She wanted to attract the attention of journalists so she could spell out her concerns.

Arthur was wrong. The girl was not functioning as a machine as a result of HK9. She had a higher goal, and it appeared she was using the program to strive towards achieving that goal. She was signposting a direct link between global warming and horrific violence — that the innocent children running around school playgrounds today, would, as adults, be subjected to. Would it work though? In theory people would recognize the potential for law and order to end and the pandemic of rape and violence that would follow if the major crops failed, far easier than they would recognize extinction.

In practice it would be totally dependent upon politicians and journalists. The girl had to sell it them, and they had to sell it to the public. It was a hard sell though, even with some crops failing now, and regular announcements of record temperatures, albeit not helped by the almost congratulatory attitude of weather presenters making those announcements.

With denial so widespread, it was always going to be a hard sell, no matter how you looked at it.

The patient looked out of the window at the hospital grounds. What was driving the girl? She must have undergone some sort of mental adjustment. Had she overridden the program, or had she found a way to adapt it? She had certainly done something. But what exactly ... and how had she done it?

Then there was Arthur's take on it. Mireille splitting her reality between actual reality and a fairy tale. Helen smiled at the memory of the conversation. It was a lovely theory that the old man had come up with and he may well be right — and the girl was living in a fairy tale. Ironic as she seemed to think that almost the entire population of the world was living in an entirely different fairy tale, in Never-Never Land, a place where we could ignore the warning signs of global warming and they would simply go away and everything would turn out fine. Whereas Arthur had drawn a parallel between denial of global warming and denial of serious illness, with both requiring treatment.

There was far too much denial, and it was all becoming a little too complex — who was pretending global warming wasn't a threat to survival and who wasn't. Were we all not pretending though when it came to global warming? We were, all of us, in some way. We were all living a lie.

Except the children.

Only the children could see the world for what it truly was, that the adults who were running it, were going to destroy it for them.

The big picture was too depressing, so Helen decided to stay focused on the girl and forget about the rest for now. It was feasible that she was using a fairy tale as a way of side-stepping some aspects of the program. But was she? Were there were any fairy tales where men were tortured to death and then brought back to life? Were there any where the heroine was a ruthless cold-bloodied killer?

Too many questions remained unanswered. When she'd asked Mireille how she'd taken control of HK9, the girl's response had been to tell her to destroy the program, which could be interpreted in a number of different ways. But it would seem that she hadn't gained total control, and that the need to kill herself remained. Was Arthur right about her needing targets, going from one to the next? All that killing: Delta Five, the men who attacked her on her way home, and the three in Helen's own flat, could be explained by her training — she would defend herself against those who attacked her, but that wouldn't account for her desire to kill those responsible for the deaths in Edinburgh.

It had to be Amanda Jeffries. She was the one who convinced Thompson and the rest of his team to shelve the military aspect of the Hunter-Killer project and instead work on developing Gatekeeper 17 to kill cancer. She would have told the girl all about changing the direction of the project. Of course, that had to be the reason. So, as far as Mireille was concerned the team of contractors, and whoever sent them, were responsible for not just torturing and killing Jeffries, but in destroying Gatekeeper 17, all the millions who might have been saved by the VR program. She and Boyle had wiped out the team who carried out the task on the ground, now she was bent on killing those responsible for organizing the whole thing.

All this time, the girl had had two targets. The first was about bringing down the wall of denial. The second target, however, had nothing to do with the climate crisis. It was personal. Mireille had targeted those responsible for torturing and killing Jeffries and destroying Gatekeeper 17.

Were all the killings enough though, enough to keep the destructive side of HK9 in check? It appeared they were, but what would the girl who had saved her life and wreaked destruction on those responsible for causing so much harm do now? If she had to have a target, would she simply go back to hunting down and killing industrialists? Yes, that would be what she would most likely do; besides in relation to her other target, who was left to kill that had been in some way responsible for the destruction of Gatekeeper 17? Where would she start when she didn't have any hard evidence that the pharmaceutical industry and private health care were directly involved? It could have been shareholders in these companies that had been responsible.

The patient looked at the clock on the wall. 6 p.m. Where would the girl be now? Where was she going? What was she thinking? Would she ignore the warning and already be en route to one of the three cities she'd been told to avoid? No, she would have plenty of other targets. She would probably pick one at random.

Helen heard the voice of her daughter in the corridor. Ignoring the pain from her hip, she sat up in bed, a smile breaking out on her face as she watched her little girl walk into the room.

24

6.10 P.M.

With the force of the wind the deck of the ferry was almost deserted. Only a girl dressed in black remained. Leaning over the rail she looked off into the distance, and the past.

She turned to look at her grandfather who, on her first trip on this ferry, had stood at the same spot and told her a story about her mother. Now, at seventeen, Mireille stood fully two inches taller than the old man, but she still looked to him with the same childlike anticipation for the customary story that accompanied each journey.

'Belfast, 1978. Ardoyne.'

Mireille interrupted. 'I thought my Father never spoke about the troubles in Northern Ireland.'

'He told me about this incident, and it was the exception; there's always an exception, sweetheart.'

'Always?'

'Always. And there's always a reason.' The old man paused for a moment, as if turning a page in his mind. 'It was raining heavily when the patrol left its base in Flax Street Mill, which was at the junction of Flax Street and Crumlin Road — a Protestant/Catholic interface. The patrol consisted of 3 x 4-man bricks commanded by your father, who was in the lead brick, the other two bricks satelliting left and right. There were two mobiles: Landrovers, each with a four-man crew, which

constantly circled the area covered by the patrol.

'The lead brick moved up Oakfield Street with one of the other bricks following a short distance behind. Suddenly, they came under fire from several positions. More than thirty shots were fired, during which, five members of the patrol were hit. Two were in a very bad way. There was a lot of confusion due to heavy rain, and NCOs screaming out different orders. With the third brick joining them, the entire patrol returned fire and then provided covering fire when the first mobile arrived to rescue the two worst casualties. The foot patrol then retreated out of Oakfield Street taking their other three casualties with them. The first mobile arrived back at The Mill and reported that the IRA had started setting up barricades to close off Oakfield Street at both ends. On the ground, now out of line-of-sight of the snipers, the patrol took time to attend to the three wounded. It was at this point that they realized they had lost their platoon commander.

'Your father had been badly wounded in his right leg in the opening exchange of fire. He went down alongside a parked car. The radio he carried had received a direct hit, but he yelled out orders and, along with the rest of the patrol, returned fire with his SLR. He could see the patrol beginning to retreat, but the wound to his leg made it impossible to join them. So, to avoid the unrelenting sniper fire, he dragged himself along the ground to the nearest position of cover, the narrow entrance to a row of houses. In the dark shadows he applied a tourniquet to his leg.

'Back in the Ops room, the Quick Reaction Force had been despatched to a Pig and the ambulance was leaving the Medical Reception Station. By this time, the patrol was only a few hundred yards from The Mill. Meanwhile, Boyle had run over from the gym in his training kit and was listening to the net in the Ops Room when the radio message came in that the OC of the patrol was trapped in Oakfield Street. A few seconds later, the QRF commander was back in the Ops room complaining that the RCT staff couldn't start the one remaining serviceable Pig. The other had broken down earlier in the day. Boyle had heard enough. He ran out of the Ops room and headed directly to 14 Int. He knew they had prepared a car to look like a senior IRA man's Mk II Cortina. The operators at 14 Int had sprayed it the exact colour, sunset red – a colour not ordinarily used on the Cortina. The IRA man's car was unique and everyone knew it by sight. 14 Int had done a great job of replicating it and they'd also dropped in a three-litre engine, in place of the 1600. There were two SAS troopers on site who refused to give Boyle the car. Aware that seconds were crucial, Boyle went in hard, both troopers later having to be hospitalized.

'Meanwhile, in Oakfield Street, the sniper fire was now focused on the position from where your father continued to return fire, but he was running low on ammunition. The IRA on the ground had surrounded the houses and slowly began to move in.

'At the entrance to Oakfield Street, the red Cortina was instantly recognized and Boyle made it through the barricades at speed. It didn't take him long to identify where your father was by the advancing IRA. He went off the road, and drove across pavements until he skidded to a halt, with the passenger door facing the entrance. He jumped out and ran into the building, coming out a few seconds later, dragging your father across the ground by his jacket collar, hands looking as if they had been tied behind his back. The ploy might have worked, *but one of the nearest IRA men saw that the driver of the Cortina was not who it should have been. By this time, your father was in the passenger seat, and Boyle, who had left the engine running, was halfway into the driver's seat.*

'When Boyle, having taken your father into the Medical Reception Station, returned the car to 14 Int it was shot to pieces. As soon as he stepped out of the car, he was surrounded by five SAS troopers, but an approaching major, who knew what had taken place, shouted out orders that no one was to touch him. Boyle shouldered his way through the troopers and jogged back to the MRS to see your father.'

Mireille said quietly, 'I had no idea George Boyle saved Dad's life.'

'That was the first time he saved your father's life, and the other time was also years before your father met your mother. The Oakfield Street incident was an embarrassment to 3 PARA — a platoon had lost their OC, and the QRF were unable to reach him because of failures to maintain the two armoured vehicles. The incident was embarrassing to 14 Int as they had to abandon a planned mission after losing a specially prepared car to a young lance corporal. The entire episode was hushed up.'

Mireille shook her head. 'I don't understand why you never told me this before. Why did you wait until now?'

'I wanted it to have more relevance, sweetheart. At your parents' funeral Boyle spoke to me about you. I remember his exact words because of the intensity with which he said them: "If Mireille ever needs anything, anything at all, you let me know." The other thing that I have never mentioned to you is the money. Every month since the funeral I have received money into my account from an unknown source. Even the bank couldn't tell me where it was coming from, but

I am certain it is from Boyle. In the future, if you ever need help, seek him out. He is currently a detective inspector in Edinburgh. It's not only me saying this, it's what your father would say, he knew Boyle will protect you as if you were his own.'

'But why? He's not—.'

Mireille stopped mid-sentence, realizing that, after everything her grandfather had just told her about George Boyle, the question didn't need to be asked.

The girl looked again in the direction of South Uist, her grandfather's words from four years ago still clear in her mind.

The hunt for George's killers was over. The trail had ended in Whitby's office.

She pulled the collar of Cathal's jacket up around her neck. She loved the smell of the leather and the feel of it against her skin, the closeness of him.

Ahead of her, on the island, twenty military contractors would be searching for her. If they hadn't already, at some point they would search Sonas. She had left clothes in the wardrobe, though none that would give a clue to her identity. But she'd also left the book. That it was in her mother's tongue was minor compared to the real problem: she'd written a poem for Cathal on the inside cover. She'd even signed her name. At Hope Street, she'd told him to wait for her, concerned that the men at the port had been looking for her. But when she had written the poem she had no intention of returning to Glasgow or the island. The poem was a farewell note, a love letter, written on Friday evening after she'd run back from the cliff face. Less than 48 hours, yet so much had happened since then.

Where you will find me

Don't look in the past
At old pictures
Or search through a wardrobe of my clothes
Don't scour through a library of memories
I'm not there
My love isn't there

My love is in the lightest breeze
That caresses your neck
Brushes your lips
Flickers through your hair
My love is in the wind of the wildest storm
That builds on dark seas
Into waves
That pound on your windows
The message
I never left you
You don't need to look
Just step outside
I am here

The poem that was written to say she would never return to the island, had become the reason she had to return. It would be easy enough for the contractors to find out who was working on the cottage, especially as she'd written Cathal's name on the large envelope that contained the book. If they couldn't find her, they'd start searching for him. With the resources available to them, it would only be a matter of a day or two.

She had no choice. She couldn't risk taking the fight to Glasgow. She wanted to keep them all in one place. The number of men she faced was irrelevant.

Finally, she had the mission she had always craved as a child. Then, it was a romantic ideal, a game. She smiled at the irony of it, now that she had so much to live for. She would have liked to have seen the press' reaction to her letters: how far they explored Achterberg's findings on repetitive imagery, and whether they stopped writing about extinction and instead focused on the terrible wave of violence that would sweep across the planet if the major crops fail. She would also have liked to have seen at least a version of Amanda's vision come to pass by having Cathal's outline developed then made into a VR game. A game that was a weapon. As soon as you give people a weapon and allow them to fulfil a natural need to fight an enemy intent on harming them, their entire perspective changes.

Yes, she had a lot to fight for. The start point was to put the first man down. Then she would have a weapon, and ammunition. If he was still alive, he would tell her where the others were. She also had home advantage. She knew the ground. Cathal had carried her on his shoulders across the entire island. They had noted every point of high ground, every position of cover, her friend listening intently as she passed on her grandfather's military wisdom.

But then, there was a different reality and a logic that told her these men had already taken every position of high ground on the island, and that the approach to almost every position would receive covering fire from at least one other position. And, on an island where the wind was so fierce that trees didn't grow, how many points of cover were there?

She crushed those thoughts before they could take hold. Instead, she thought of her friend, and the last time she saw him in Hope Street.

Was it when he gave her his jacket that she first suspected

the program was fading? Whether it was fading or not, didn't matter, not anymore. What did, was that the emotions she had kept hidden for years had surfaced before it was too late. Without warning, she'd wrapped her arms around Cathal and held him tightly. Then she'd lifted her hands, folded them around the back of his neck and kissed him, her lips barely brushing against his, lingering, caressing ...

Cathal. She thought of him waiting in Glasgow. She thought of their time in Barra after a storm when they were replacing fence posts, the moment she picked up a sledgehammer for the first time, the alarm in the crofter's voice on seeing her friend wrap his hands around the top of the post. 'Don't hold it like that lad! If she doesn't hit it plum centre, that hammer will skim off and break your arm.'

Cathal didn't even turn to look at the crofter, his gaze never left her, as he smiled broadly and said, 'She'll hit it.'

Mireille felt her spine tingle as it had then.

She looked forward at the island which had appeared on the horizon. From behind dark clouds the sun broke its way out and lit up the side of Ben Kenneth — the side facing the water — and one of the few places on the island that could not receive covering fire. She wouldn't wait for the ferry to dock. There was a small deck empty of passengers on the starboard side. The noise from the wind would cover the sound of her dive. By the time she had to surface she'd be half-way there, one breath and she would be. She'd wait until sundown before hitting the snipers on the summit. From there she would work her way to the site of countless battles from her childhood, Sonas.

Changes to the truth in the story

Prologue
The five-year-old girl was with her father, not her grandfather. John Benaicha did not witness the girl's run (the author being the observer). The genetically gifted Benaicha did not begin training until well into his thirties, missing his window to become a professional athlete.

Chapter 4
The incident in Lothian Road, in which Jimmy Pace was injured, took place after the Falklands conflict, rather than before it. The incident involving the German sailor, and the ship's crew, took place at the Elm bar in Leith. Aside from these minor details, all other information relating to Jimmy Pace is true.

Chapter 5
Rab's Gym (officially known as Gracemount Gym) is one of the few remaining hard-core body building and combat gyms in the country. A level of licence, albeit minimal, was taken in describing it. The gym was refitted during lockdown 2020.

Chapter 9
'... last of the boy soldiers'
The first units specifically designed for Junior Soldiers opened in 1947, taking boys from the age of 15 and retaining them until they were old enough to enter adult service. Hence, its members became known throughout the Army as 'Boy Soldiers', a term that was still being used when Boyle would have joined up 25 years later in 1972. With the school leaving age being raised to 16 later that year, Boyle would have been amongst the last of the 15-year-olds to enlist in the Colours. As a Junior Soldier, Boyle's integration into adult service would have been more gradual than depicted in the novel — it

is unlikely he would have received the 'kill the enemy' speech which was given to the author as a direct entry recruit in 1977.

Chapter 10
The incident involving Willie Kennaway took place in the mid-1980s, long before the publication of Dinosaur Training (which described the Death Set in detail). It was the blood test following a heavy squatting session by Kennaway that resulted in panic by the drug testing team. The slap from his childhood friend, Scott Donaldson did not take place. All other information about the two men is true — Scott Donaldson remaining unbeaten at arm-wrestling for almost three decades.

Chapter 12
The cottage that featured in the earlier versions of The Hunter Killer was Taigh Mairi Anndra, arguably the most well-known cottage in the Outer Hebrides: the famous Gaelic folklorist, Margaret Fay Shaw, lodging there on the occasions she resided on the island. With the rewrite and, in particular, the addition of impending violence on the site, it was decided to change it to a fictional cottage. Sonas is the same size, and is located on the same isolated part of North Glendale, as Taigh Mairi Anndra.

Chapter 14
In the scene where Helen speaks to two members of the Satellite monitoring team, a description is given, of an object moving at speed up the highest peak on the island of South Uist. To achieve images giving this level of detail and movement requires a constellation of a large number of satellites which will give high enough spatial and temporal resolution. This kind of constellation was not available in 2018 though is currently under development.

Chapter 21
This part of the novel is set late September 2018. However, in this chapter there are two occasions where reference is made to events that took place at the end of 2019: terrified animals on fire running out of burning forests is based on the images and footage of koala bears attempting to escape bush fires in Australia. It is estimated that thousands of koala bears perished in these fires. The reference to the rock band who are setting an example was inspired by the announcement by Coldplay that they had stopped touring until such time as it becomes 'environmentally beneficial.'

The section of this chapter that deals with Mireille being repeatedly attacked on her way home, was inspired by the actions of the Jewish strongman, Joseph Greenstein, who, in his later years, waged a personal campaign against muggers. At five foot four and weighing 140 pounds he was repeatedly targeted and attacked. They came at him with guns and knives, in the open, and from the shadows — the old strongman broke their arms.

Copyright acknowledgements

Prologue

Paris, B. (1997) *Gorilla Suit.* St Martin's Press

Part 1

Mailer, N. (1975) *The Fight.* Boston: Little, Brown & Co.

Goldman, W. (1974) *Marathon Man.* Delacorte Press

Jack Reacher (2012) [Film] C McQuarrie (Director) U.S.A. Paramount Pictures

White, T. J. (1969) *Rainy Night in Georgia* (Chris Young 2009)

Kubik, B.D. (1996) *Dinosaur Training: Lost Secrets of Strength and Development.* Brooks D Kubik

Spotlight (2015) [Film] T McCarthy (Director) U.S.A. Open Road Films, Sony Pictures Releasing International, Stage 6 Films

Part 2

MacDonald, D. (1916) *An Eala Bhàn*

Goldman, W. (1973) *The Princess Bride.* New York, Harcourt Brace Jovanovich

Cornwell, J. (2000, December 24). *Trick or treatment?* The Sunday Times Magazine, 23-28

295

Achterberg, J., & Lawlis, G.F. (1980). *Bridges of the Bodymind: Behavioural Approaches for Health Care,* Champaign, IL: Institute for Personality and Ability Testing.

Fantastic Voyage (1966) [Film] R Fleischer (Director) USA: Twentieth Century Fox

An Inconvenient Truth (2006) [Film] D Guggenheim (Director) USA: Paramount Classics

Irreversible (2002) [Film]. G Noé (Director) France: Mars Distribution

Spielman, E. (1979). *The Mighty Atom: The Life and Times of Joseph L. Greenstein.* New York: Viking Press.

The Gathering Storm (2002) [Film] R Loncraine (Director) UK-USA: BBC-HBO

About the Author

A H FitzSimons was born in Johnstone, near Glasgow, in 1958. He served in the British Army in the 1970s and 1980s before joining Lothian and Borders Police. He studied in Edinburgh, winning two Scottish Business Education Council Awards, including the C.A. Oakley gold medal. He began writing in 2005 following a sixteen-month stay in hospital.

Also by A H FitzSimons

Fiction
The Game
Break Lima

Non-fiction
The Fight

Milton Keynes UK
Ingram Content Group UK Ltd.
UKHW052318181223
434584UK00022B/1475

9 781838 382933